BLACK RIVER

ELISABETH GRAVES

NORTHAMPTON HOUSE PRESS

Cover design by Northampton House.

1993 edition published by Berkley Books, New York. Norwegian edition published by Fredhois Forlag, Oslo, as SVART ELV in 1999.

Updated and revised 2026 edition published by Northampton House Press, ISBN 978-1937997373.

10   9   8   7   6   5   4   3

The old Florida, always a strange, damp, dark land in spite of its much-advertised sunshine, is fading away faster every day. For assisting me in trying to preserve one small, exotic corner, this book is dedicated to the late James Allen, Linda Gail Erickson, Frank Green, Barbara Hamby, Lise Hobdy, Florence Humphrey, Lucy Marhefka, David Poyer, Naia Poyer, Valerie Rivers, and especially to Andrew Zack, who early on believed in and appreciated this story.

It is not good to answer the first time your name is called. It may be
a spirit
   and if you answer it you will die shortly.

Zora Neale Hurston, *Mules and Men*

BLACK RIVER

PROLOGUE

With the crackle of footsteps on twigs and pine straw, a pale, thin woman and a small child followed a vanishing path through the trees. The woman's eyes darted at every sound as she pushed roughly through the wild grapevine and palmetto spikes that barred the way. The little girl stumbled along, clutching her mother's hand. Shivering in thin cotton pajamas, she gazed at the night with sleepy, puzzled eyes. "Mama, I don't like it here. Where we going?"

The woman tightened her grip on the girl's hand, and said nothing.

"I don't like it, I don't like it," the child whispered to herself.

The humid night air was weighted with damp red clay and pine resin. The tangled forest around them grew thicker; the woman's look more determined, her step more certain. Just as the lush growth began to seem an impassable jungle, a gap appeared.

The woman stopped abruptly.

The child ran into her legs full force and sprawled backward on the damp ground.

The woman didn't look back. She stared straight ahead at a small whitewashed cabin set in the middle of a clearing, her body rigid, as if with great fear − or intense yearning.

Pale smoke trickled from the brick chimney that rose behind the house. The sparse grass of the front yard hosted a crowd of concrete and stone garden ornaments. A cement greyhound, one ear gone, crouched among deer, chickens, sea horses and peeling pink flamingoes, as if keeping a cold-eyed watch on the forest.

The fallen child picked herself up, sobbing.

The woman looked back with something like revulsion, then bent and swept the little girl up. She ran with her burden toward the shuttered house. Ran breathlessly past the statuary as though the stone beasts were in pursuit, clattering up the front porch steps, and stopped before the unpainted front door. One hand rose to knock, but hesitated.

A faint splash echoed through the trees. Beyond the pines surrounding the house a dark river ran deep and quick, swirling through the knotty cypress roots that studded its banks. A low, moaning cry followed the splash. "Gator," the woman whispered. She glanced down at the child in her arms and shuddered, then knocked softly on rough wood.

Only silence from within until, finally, rusty mattress springs groaned. Shuffling footsteps made a slow path to the door.

Outside, the woman pressed her ear to the splintered cypress boards, breathing quickly. The child kept silent, eyes wide and unblinking in the dark.

Inside, the footsteps stopped. There came a lengthy, wheezing cough, rusty as the bed springs. Then, "Who out there now?"

The woman looked blankly about for a moment, as though she too wondered, then shook herself and blurted out, "It's me. Louvinia." She tightened her grip on the child, who whimpered. After a moment of waiting silence, broken only by the chirping of frogs and cicadas, the door swung open slowly. A thin, elderly black woman stood in the doorway, silhouetted in the yellow glow of a kerosene lamp, wearing a faded print cotton dress with large red buttons from neck to hem. Her hair, set for the night in paper twists, was wrapped in a pale yellow cloth that accentuated the darkness of the weathered face.

Under her close scrutiny, the younger woman trembled. She dropped her gaze to the old woman's feet. They were bare, strong and calloused as cypress roots.

The elder one stepped back wordlessly, and Louvinia rushed in without meeting that gaze again. She stopped in the middle of the room, and the old woman shut the door unhurriedly.

"Auntie Swann," Louvinia gasped, "Here." She thrust the child out.

The little girl clutched handfuls of her mother's lank blond hair. "No, no," she screamed, struggling against the thin, wiry arms that reached for her. "Mama!"

"Hush, pretty baby," the old woman crooned in a sing-song voice. "You all right."

The child stopped fighting and sighed, but still stared fearfully at the dark corners, the flickering shadows cast by a crude limestone fireplace.

Her mother searched the room too, looking all around, hands clasped before her, fingers twining and untwining. "Where is it—where? I can't see. It's too dark in here!" She wheeled suddenly on the old woman. "You promised," she whispered fiercely.

Auntie Swann stroked the child's head as softly as one would a puppy. Finally she looked up. "Over there, 'neath the quilt. Just like I said." She smiled indifferently, and continued to pet the motionless child.

Louvinia rushed to the far corner where faded patchwork draped a long pine box, jerked the quilt from the coffin and knelt beside it. She bent until her long hair swept the lid. Sobbing, she pressed one pale cheek to the sanded, varnished wood.

Auntie Swann carried the child to the other side of the room, murmuring a wordless song to the little girl, whose eyelids now drooped sleepily.

The younger woman raised her head to look at them, a smear of dirt on one cheek.

The ancient placed the child in a small painted rocking chair and set a chipped blue enamel bowl on her lap. The girl, nodding in sleep now, seemed oblivious. Her head lolled on one shoulder, mouth slightly open. Her chest rose and fell evenly.

From the folds of her calico skirt, Auntie Swann pulled a small, sharp knife.

Across the room, Louvinia's right hand crept up to cover her mouth as her left continued to stroke the lid of the pine coffin. The blade glittered, and then flashed in the lantern light. She shut her eyes tightly and tensed as if expecting a scream.

The room was still silent, save for the snapping embers of the dying fire. Finally, hesitantly, Louvinia raised her head again. Now a cotton blanket was draped over the tiny chair and the slumped shape in it. Auntie Swann was shuffling across the warped floorboards toward her, carrying the blue enamel bowl.

When she shrank back, the old woman frowned. "You gettin' what you asked for, missy," she snapped. "So move aside."

Louvinia scrambled away from the box on all fours and knelt a short distance away. Her mouth trembled and her hands twisted in her lap, but she kept silent.

The elder woman raised the lid of the pine coffin, revealing the body of a young man; handsome, not long dead.

Louvinia groaned.

Auntie Swann turned to glare. "More than anything, I hates whinin'."

Louvinia was immediately quiet.

The old woman balanced the bowl on the dead man's white-shirted chest. Rummaging through one deep skirt pocket again, she pulled out a tarnished silver spoon and a small glass jar. She twisted off the lid and dipped one bony finger into its greasy, bitter-smelling contents. Then traced a pattern on the dead forehead, eyes, and lips, muttering a string of words several times over.

The younger woman leaned forward, holding her breath, straining to hear. The pale, plain face was distorted by the effort, but her frown revealed she could not make any sense of the sounds.

Finally, the old woman returned the jar to the folds of her skirt. Her hand emerged this time with a small pair of silver sewing scissors shaped like a stork. Deftly she snipped each of the half-dozen tiny sutures holding the man's lips together. With two fingers she opened his mouth, and began carefully to ladle in the contents of the enamel bowl with the silver spoon.

Louvinia closed her eyes and gagged.

Auntie Swann silenced her with a look this time, and continued. After a few moments she stopped, spoon poised in mid air, gleaming in the firelight, one dark ruby drop suspended from the tip of its bowl.

The corpse's throat made a faint, convulsive movement. The young woman leaned forward, cheeks bright with color now.

Auntie Swann let another spoonful dribble in, slowly.

The dead man's eyes opened. He stared blankly at the low-beamed ceiling.

The witch-woman nodded slowly to herself. "Well, missy. He all yours again."

Louvinia struggled to her feet, wincing, stumbling a little at a pins-and-needles prickling as the circulation returned to cramped muscles. She smiled at Auntie Swann and opened her mouth to speak.

5

"Jus' take him," the older woman barked, cutting her off. "Quick, afore he really sees. You got some little time 'til he come all the way back."

Louvinia stretched out both pale, sun-freckled arms and took hold of the man's hand. He sat up in the box stiffly, without expression, then awkwardly swung his legs over the side. She hauled him to his feet with some difficulty. He allowed her to lead him across the floor as trustingly as a sleepwalking child.

At the door the younger woman turned back. Two hectic spots of color lit her cheeks like fever. Despite the snarled, uncombed hair and sweat-soaked cotton dress, she now appeared almost pretty. "I want . . . want to thank you . . . " She fumbled at one pocket of the dress and dug out a wad of crumpled bills. "Here. From her."

Auntie Swann's hand darted out to snatch the money. She dropped it carelessly on a nearby table. "Don't you thank me. I don't want your thanks. Nor hers."

The other woman's eyes shifted for a moment to the small, covered shape across the room. "What–"

"Just git. You got plenty else to keep you busy now. Some fancy talkin', for instance, to explain what you done with his child."

Louvinia's eyes widened. "But I didn't do anything. It was you, not . . . " She lifted her chin. "I mean, she's dead now. Dead and gone. And it's not my fault. That's all I'll tell him."

Aunty Swann smiled, a grim twitch of the lips. "There's some as thinks dead is dead. An' alive is just alive. But the dead ain't always gone. And some as thinks they living – well, they ain't. Things never only what they seem, 'especially around the river."

"I don't know in the world what you're mumbling about." Louvinia gave the woman a swift glare. "You're a crazy old witch. I can't talk to you no more."

The door slammed, and the old woman stood alone. Nodding her head slowly as if listening to someone speaking. "They treat the valuable things just like paper. Vanity, all vanity," she muttered, as if in answer to a question.

Outside, the panting young woman pulled at the silent, unresisting man. Dragging him past clumps of blood-red lantana and spiked cabbage palm, away into the dark pines.

"Hurry, Jonah! Please hurry," she whispered, urging him on. And then they disappeared into the shadows of the densely wooded hammock.

***

In the sunny bedroom of a white frame house, Louvinia yawned, stretched, and turned over. A wood-bladed ceiling fan shirred a lazy breeze, cooling the rumpled sheets. Bits of grass and leaf mold clung to the damp cotton and, here and there, to the skin of the bed's two occupants.

She threw one arm possessively over the broad tanned back of the man lying beside her.

"Wasn't that nice, Jonah?"

The man turned his head on the pillow to face her. He smiled in return, tracing the curve of her face with one finger. "Where's Abby this morning?"

The woman's smile faltered. She buried her face against his shoulder.

"Louvinia." He grasped her chin gently and raised her face to his. Still smiling, he said, "Did you send her over to Mama's so we could —?"

Louvinia lowered her head and shook it slightly. "No," she whispered.

A slight frown creased his forehead. "Oh. Then where?"

She glanced up, then quickly rose from the brass bed. Slipped her arms into a bright silk kimono, and pulled the sash tight with a vicious tug. She twisted the knob of the

7

Philco on the nightstand. After a few moments Benny Goodman's swing filled the room. She swayed in time to the music.

"Remember this, Jonah?" She smiled at him but her eyes were bright and desperate. Humming, a few bars, she began to sing. " . . . a little lamb who's lost in the wood, I know I could always be good . . . "

She turned, arms extended invitingly. "Dance with me, Jonah. It's our song."

But he was staring at the far wall now, and didn't answer.

Her smile trembled. "Didn't you hear me, honey?"

"I was just trying to remember something," he said, more to himself than to her. The effort of retrieving some small elusive memory made him frown. "Something that happened . . . something . . . in town? Yes, in town. Wasn't I there to buy something yesterday?"

Louvinia shook her head, blinking back tears, but one escaped to trickle down her cheek. She brushed at it, missed. "No."

He looked up, puzzled. "But I did go," he said with growing certainty. "To buy . . . a dress. Yes, a dress! For Abby. A pink, lacy one—with a crinoline." He seemed pleased with this small, remembered detail. "For her birthday."

Louvinia's arms fell to her sides with a slap. She stared at him dully.

"A pretty dress for our baby girl. Today's her birthday, isn't it? So she should be here to open the–"

"No." Louvinia said again, more sharply. Her smile compressed to a thin, bitter line.

But Jonah continued as if she hadn't spoken. "We better go pick her up, so she can try on her new dress. When I saw it in the window of Linzey's, I knew it was for her. They wrapped it nice, with pink ribbon. Then I left, to hurry home. I crossed the street and . . . " He stopped, shaking his head." I left the store, and then went to cross, but . . . "

He looked up, clutching the sheet in frustration. "Now, why can't I remember anything after that?" He thought hard, face screwed up in a deliberately comic effort. "Help me out, darlin'. I left the store, and went to cross the street. Stepped out into the intersection, but–"

Louvinia cried out, as if in pain.

He stopped in mid-sentence, staring.

"Stop! Jonah, don't talk about it." Her whisper sounded more like a fervent prayer, the words so faint he had to strain to catch them. "Don't. Don't even think about it."

"But I can't remember!" His fist punched the pillow. A few downy feathers drifted slowly away from the bed. Then he stopped pounding, and stared at his left forearm where a long, purple-red bruise reached from wrist to elbow. His clouded eyes suddenly cleared.

"A car," he said simply. "It was a car." He looked up at his wife.

She was shaking her head again. *No. No. No.* Finally her lips formed the word, but no sound escaped.

Jonah sat up, gaze still on her face. "I remember stepping out into the street downtown. And then a car came speeding 'round the corner from Blunt's grocery. Came right at me. I saw it, but it came on too fast. I couldn't get out of the way."

Louvinia sobbed.

"It came right at me. So I turned. I turned and . . . " He got up off the bed and stood in front of his wife. "Louvinia."

She refused to lift her head and look at him.

"The car was speeding."

She nodded, barely.

"I couldn't get out of the way. So it hit me."

Another sob escaped her trembling lips.

"It hit me real hard." Strong fingers dug into her narrow shoulders, making her wince. "Hit me so hard that I was . . . I mean, I can't really be–"

She nodded again, tears streaming down her face.

"My God. But what have you done? How did you–" Horror crept over his face. "Tell me now. Where's Abby!" He shook her. "What have you done with her? What the hell have you done!"

"Her!" She spit the word out like a bad taste. "You don't see. You still don't see! I only wanted you, just you. And I couldn't stand the sight of her, with you gone. She kept asking, always asking for you! I had to do it, I just had to. Couldn't live like that, not alone with just her. Mama Abbott said that Auntie Swann–" She stopped abruptly, hand over mouth to trap the words, but they were already gone.

Jonah's face went pale. "The old conjure woman. You went to her, with Abby? Made some bargain and came back with . . . with me, like this." He shoved her away.

Louvinia struck the side of the rope bed and slid to the bare pine floor, weeping. Jonah stood over her for a moment, but he was staring again at the livid bruise on his arm.

"Oh my God. Abby," he whispered. Then turned and started for the door.

Louvinia lunged after him and grabbed at his legs. She missed and fell, crying, "Jonah! Jonah, come back. I did it for us. You have to love me now, just me!"

He ran from the house naked, oblivious, pursued by her cries. "Abby," he gasped, "Abby." He turned away from the house, toward the highway, the river, Auntie Swann.

***

Without knowing, Jonah followed the same path he'd taken a few hours before, in the dark. He traveled it much more quickly this time, not needing Louvinia to pull and lead him. A few minutes later, he came crashing out of a thick stand of camphor and ligustrum bushes that lined the narrow road by the river. Beyond those woods full of scrub pine and water oak and palmetto, toward the river, stood the house of Mattie Swann.

***

Where the road turned to bridge, a naked man leapt out onto the unpaved clay. Shouting, waving his arms, he ran directly into the path of a black Packard Clipper sedan.

Inside the car, the encyclopedia salesman from New Orleans only had time to shut his eyes before he struck the wild, pale apparition that had appeared suddenly in the road before him. Closing his eyes, he shrieked and clutched the wheel. The impact threw him forward; the thump of tires over some large object made him shudder with horror. He meant to go back and look, but somehow his arms simply wouldn't turn the wheel.

By the time he'd gone a half mile more, though, the salesman had convinced himself it had only been a deer. A big, funny-looking one, yes . . . but a deer, right enough. What else would come leaping out of the pine woods like a damn gazelle, straight in front of a speeding car? Only a big, dumb animal would do such a thing as that.

And he wasn't about to go into the nearest town and report it, no sir. He knew what these North Florida hick towns were like. Lock you up, empty your pockets, swallow the key. No, he didn't care to stop the car and go back to look. Not with all those big, mossy oaks and black pine trees, the creepy ferns on the river bluff waving like pale green arms in the breeze. Why should he, just to give the last rites to some fucking deer?

"No," he muttered to his own pale, shocked face in the rearview. "Just drive straight through to Jacksonville. No stops, and that's that."

He took another pull on the half-empty flask from his glove compartment, and settled into a nice cruising speed of sixty.

***

Jonah, flung many yards off the road by the impact, toppled over the bridge railing and sank slowly beneath the river. It didn't matter to him that the salesman from New Orleans had hurried on to Jacksonville without stopping. His eyes stared into the black water, unseeing. He didn't hear the quick, muffled splash an alligator made sliding into the water from the muddy riverbank, leaving only faint, widening ripples behind.

ONE

The part of northern Florida known as the Panhandle is not the Florida advertised by travel agents. The cities are smaller, the beaches less eye-dazzling, the roads narrower and lined with magnolias, dogwoods, and canopy oaks rather than soldierly rows of palm trees. Steaming in summer, frigid in winter, the Panhandle is neither all Florida nor all Georgia, but somehow stuck in between. Highway 90 connects most of the areas large enough to be called towns with the capital city, Tallahassee. Before Interstate 10 was built, 90 was the first choice for traveling across north Florida.

Now, most tourists prefer the bland unsurprising asphalt of Interstate 10, happy enough to bypass annoying little towns with one perpetually red stoplight and rural byways blocked by farmers bouncing along on wheezing green tractors flat-out at five miles an hour. For travelers who feel no thrill at the sight of beef cows and rotting tobacco barns, the interstate is a flat lifeline from coastal Jacksonville to Pensacola, New Orleans, and beyond.

But by late afternoon Kay Abbott was sick of the broad, endless stretch of faded asphalt. Sick of countless minivans packed with nuclear families battling over melting popsicles and crumpled Mickey Mouse hats. At last she left I-10 at Live Oak in favor of Highway 90 and slow rural scenery. According to MapQuest, the two-lane road would lead her directly to their destination. Packed snugly into the no-longer-new Volvo were Kay, her nine-year-old daughter Chloe, a great deal of luggage and cardboard boxes, and Angus, their marmalade cat. They'd left Miami at noon, hoping to arrive in Abaton by dark. The town had been her late husband's birthplace—named, he used to joke, for some influential but forgotten ancestor, and then recorded by a well-meaning but less than literate map-maker.

Their stay in Abaton would be temporary, she'd assured Chloe—who was almost as unenthused about the trip as the cat. She'd pointed out to her incredulous friends in Miami that it wasn't such a crazy move. Abaton might be a backwater village, but there was a house there for them, part of Jack's estate. If the place was too terrible to live in, then she could always sell it.

This would be her first glimpse of the property, though. During the twelve years of their marriage, Jack had always put off visiting his hometown, and she'd finally given up asking. The shock of his sudden death six months ago in an accident had lessened, though only a bit. The condolences had begun to wear thin, and she really needed to get away from Miami. A freelance illustrator of children's books, she'd taken a new assignment just before his death. After putting off working on it as long as possible, now it was time to either finish up or give up.

She didn't intend to give up. The city had its fine points, true—beautiful beaches, Art Deco architecture, reliable weather, fewer hurricanes than it used to. But more and more she felt Miami was not the best place to raise a child, especially alone—the beaches were too crowded to use, too many people were being mugged and assaulted within the shadows of those lovely old Art Deco hotels, too many drivers had pistols tucked in glove compartments, as if not only expecting but hoping for some lethal traffic encounter. To take advantage of the tropical weather it was necessary to go outside and face the occasional possibility of drug dealers shooting it out in the streets, of hookers boldly strolling Biscayne Boulevard. Miami just had too much of everything.

It'd really been Jack's town, anyhow, and her sense of belonging had eroded after his death. His business, a successful architectural firm, was still there; his partners continued to manage it. But it was already becoming clear that Jack's insurance money would not keep them forever. She needed to earn a living, and her work could be done anywhere. So now she felt not simply justified in traveling this winding back road to a town she'd never seen before; she felt practical. Without Jack's support, the future depended on her. She drove with determination, vintage Ray-Bans sliding down her short, narrow nose, curly brown hair pulled back with a tortoise shell clip. Swerving to miss lazy dogs and lumbering farm machinery, cursing discreetly when the cat's tranquilizer wore off sooner than the vet had promised.

She turned up the radio to drown Angus's escalating yowls.

Chloe finally broke a long silence. "Mom."

"Yes, little sandspur?"

Her daughter rolled green eyes so much like Jack's Kay felt a renewed ache.

"I just thought of something else," said Chloe. "I bet they don't have any sushi up here."

Kay tried not to smile. Her daughter was surveying the moss-draped trees and lush green pastures with disgust. "And I bet there's not even one Pinkberry store."

Kay's jaw muscles quivered, gave way, and she laughed out loud.

Chloe glared, pulling impatiently at a curl of auburn hair. "Just what's so funny? Those are important things."

"I know they are, Chloe." She squeezed the girl's knee. "So considering the size of your appetite, we'll probably have to fly food in from out of town."

"Ha. Ha." Chloe pushed her bangs back and squirmed impatiently. "As if." Since Gainesville she'd complained of seeing nothing but creepy, mossy old trees and one-dog towns with a single gas pump. And , as she'd said, "Not even a McDonald's!"

Now she sighed. "Well, it's awful . . . primitive . . . here."

"It's not as bad as you think, sweetie. We'll be in Tallahassee soon. We can stop and have dinner. I bet we can even scare up some frozen yogurt for dessert."

That got a smile. Food seemed to be the key. A pity it wasn't as easy to turn down the howls of the furry little demon in the cat carrier. Angus had come back to life in the last few miles. He'd been drugged and kidnapped by lunatics, and wanted every passing car to know it. Kay thought wistfully of earplugs, or even a tiny, cat-sized gag.

"I bet you'll like it up here, once we get settled in. Just think, the same house your father was born in!"

"Eew." Chloe shuddered.

"He and I both went to college in Tallahassee. That's not far from Abaton. I really want to see his hometown—" she swerved to avoid a large box turtle. "Don't you? The place belongs to us now. We have to decide what to do with it."

"We? Like, I get a vote?" Chloe's expression left no doubt as to what she thought they should do with it.

But Kay persisted. "Besides, I really have to finish this assignment. I've put it off as long as I could. When it's done, we can decide whether to go back to Miami, or . . . or what. Anyhow, a neat old house will be fun to explore, don't you think?"

Chloe rolled her eyes up at the car's head liner. "I don't see why you couldn't finish the stupid drawings at home. What's wrong with Miami? You had a studio and

16

everything. I thought it was our h-home." Her lower lip trembled.

They both fell silent then.

If I told her the real reason, she wouldn't understand, Kay thought. Even six months after Jack's death, she still couldn't bear to work in the studio he'd designed and built for her. A few days after the funeral, she'd had a nightmare. Unpleasant, yes – but no big deal. Not then. Even after waking in a cold, shivering sweat she couldn't recall much of it. Just some basic lost-in-a-strange-place details. But the next night the dream had returned. And then the next. Exhausted, sleep-deprived, she soon found it impossible to concentrate during the day. At night, she craved sleep as much as she dreaded it.

Was it guilt? Because she thought sometimes she didn't miss Jack as much as she should. They'd had what all their friends called a good marriage; perhaps because most of them were on their own second and third. After Jack's firm had doubled in size he'd been away from home frequently. When not out of town, he was always going over plans or in meetings at the office. His work had eaten into their weekends and evenings like a greedy cancer. She believed he loved them both, but in a vague, absent-minded sort of way. It had seemed to her that he loved his work more than anything.

She might've resented this more if she hadn't had a daughter and her own career. And friends like Annelise Delgado. Eight years ago they'd met in a Miami Beach kick-boxing class led by an enthusiastic sadist Kay thought of as the Gym Teacher From Hell. Both had sneaked out the back door one day, spotted each other slinking through the parking lot, and burst out laughing. Half an hour later, over hot fudge sundaes, they'd become friends.

Annelise owned a shop on Grand Avenue in Coconut Grove. At first a tax shelter, it had taken off and become outrageously successful, carrying one-of-a-kind clothing created by local artists out of cloth, vinyl, leather, and anything else they found. The shop had an ideal location, sandwiched between a Haitian art gallery and a French bakery, though Mike Delgado complained that his wife sometimes came home smelling like a giant croissant.

For Kay, all this had been enough. Jack began to seem more like a visitor, a pleasant overnight guest who dropped in at odd hours.

Was a life that ran so well without one of the participants warped in some way? Chloe idolized Jack but filled her time with friends, schoolwork, her cat, and playing with the paints and chalk in Kay's studio. If she'd felt neglected by a father figure, it hadn't shown. When home he was always attentive but vague. Kay had suspected his mind had been somewhere else, planning the next office plaza or restoration project. If it was neglect, it was the benign sort. Chloe was lucky to have a good home, and two parents at least some of the time. Many of her friends' parents were divorced, some several times over. A few hadn't seen one parent or the other for years, or only at holidays, loaded down with presents and guilt.

So life had continued without much effort until the day of the accident. The restoration of a lovely stucco-walled Spanish-style mansion built during Miami's first boom years. Three weeks into the project, a retaining wall had collapsed. It left four workmen injured, one hospitalized . . . and Jack dead. Perhaps, had he not been so preoccupied— but all that made no difference now.

At first Chloe was devastated by her father's death, and refused to believe he was gone. Then one day, while putting towels in the linen closet upstairs, Kay had overheard her daughter talking with a friend.

"I'm not sad anymore," she was saying, "because I'll see Daddy again someday. In another place."

The other child's reply was too low to make out, but Kay was surprised. Neither she nor Jack had attended

18

church, nor taken Chloe to Sunday school. She wondered where her daughter had come up with this theory of an afterlife. Perhaps she'd picked it up at the Palmwood School, where a strong Episcopal influence might still lurk beneath a sleekly refurbished facade.

Whatever the reason, she was glad Chloe was adjusting. Because bad dreams still poisoned her own sleep. The once-loved studio felt cold and unfriendly. When she sat at the drawing table to work, she fidgeted, sighed, stared off into space, drummed her fingers on polished wood. Wishing for a Marlboro Light, even though she'd quit smoking ten years ago, before Chloe was born.

The project she was supposed to be working on, watercolor illustrations for a book of eighteenth-century British nursery rhymes and ballads, was something she'd always wanted to do. Before Jack's death it'd excited her. Now, looking over preliminary sketches, she felt an odd numbness where eagerness had been — like a dead spot. But she'd committed to the contract, and the deadline, like London Bridge, would soon come crashing down.

This sense of panic and helplessness had been the final push to leave Miami. She'd closed up the house, packed their summer things, some linens, pots and pans, and of course Gus. And now they were on this endless back road in north Florida, headed for a new place that she hoped would be more conducive to work. Or more restful, at least.

I'd settle for that right now, she thought. A full night's sleep.

They reached Tallahassee an hour later and settled on a Friday's for dinner. Chloe had two scoops of vanilla with hot fudge for dessert. She carefully scraped the bottom of her bowl, and seemed happy enough. When they returned to the car, she made a fuss over Gus, petting him, bestowing some limp fried clams she'd saved from her dinner. He seemed unimpressed with the offering, and resumed caterwauling when they pulled out of the lot. Kay turned up the radio, but nothing could drown the furious howls echoing from the tiny plastic prison in the back seat.

TWO

The roadside was a carpet of red clover and heat-faded wildflowers. Overhead the thick branches of aged water oaks met in a green barrel vault, a fresh-air cathedral arch. Passing beneath these leafy canopies, Kay thought, was like driving through a cool green cave.

"Isn't it nice here?"

Chloe only shrugged, but Kay felt excited now by whole stretches of green pasture, acres of pecan groves, oak trees and meadows unmarred by a single condominium or fast food franchise.

Soon Chloe fell asleep. The drive, the heat, and no doubt the double ice cream had finally taken their toll. Even Angus had ceased howling.

The summer night was taking its own good time in arriving, though. The day-long drive had been hot and sticky from the start. In early afternoon shimmering heat waves had risen off the asphalt road like departing souls. A dilapidated clock on a bank in Green Cove Springs had claimed 101 degrees at five p.m. Despite the Volvo's air conditioning, Kay felt an occasional trickle down her ribs beneath her t-shirt. But a rain shower outside Tallahassee had finally cooled the air.

Now, as her daughter slept, Kay glanced briefly at the printed directions Mike Delgado had given her. The attorney had helped her with the move, obtaining directions to the town, contacting the only motel as well as the local realty office that had looked after the house for many years. She didn't own a GPS but in any case a bemused Mike had told her it didn't seem to have an actual 911 address. Comparing his directions to the MapQuest ones, she saw they should be close to the town now.

Chloe groaned and mumbled, "My butt's asleep," before sinking back into the effortless unconsciousness of childhood. Kay hoped the first night in a new town would give her even a fraction of that dreamless escape.

After a few miles she slowed, expecting one of the occasional side roads to be marked with a green highway sign showing the turn to Abaton. As the miles passed, so did a boarded-up gas station and a deserted produce stand. Her eyes scanned the darkening pavement. No mileage sign, no turnoff. Frustrated, she switched off the air conditioner and rolled her window down, as though the glass were hiding what she wanted to see.

Outside the frog and cicada chorus was loud as a gospel choir. After another mile crept by on the odometer, she passed a rutted clay road. "That can't be it. There's no sign," she muttered. "It's not even paved."

Of course, no one had promised it would be.

She pulled off, made a u-turn on the narrow grassy shoulder, and drove back. She stopped at the rough intersection, letting the engine idle as she consulted the directions one more time, squinting in the dim interior light. It looked like they'd come the right number of miles for the turnoff to the town, anyhow.

Alleged town, she thought. Perhaps this was just another of her horrible dreams, and soon she'd wake in a sweat, back in Miami. Or perhaps Abaton had moved and left no forwarding address. She preferred that absurd idea to the sudden, uneasy thought that they could be lost.

She opened her car door, got out, and walked a few yards up the clay road. She peered down it, squinting, but saw only that it disappeared around a bend into dark trees. No lights, no town were visible. On the way back to the car she stumbled and almost fell into a ditch full of overgrown weeds. Eyes on the uneven ground, she picked her way more carefully toward the Volvo.

Just before she got in, the dull shine of cheap metal caught her eye. She stopped and flipped over a flat, dented object with the toe of one shoe. Flaking white letters on a green background suggested *ABA ON 5*.

"Wow. The highway department spares no expense out here." She snorted and got back in the car, then pulled back out onto the highway, headlights sweeping an even deeper ditch filled with greenish-brown water. The brackish stink of algae drifted through the open window. "Ugh," she said. "Glad I didn't fall into that."

She turned onto the unpaved road. Five miles turned over on the odometer without a sign of a house, though, much less a town. She felt anxious again. They were down to less than a quarter of a tank. The road looked so damned empty.

Chloe whimpered in her sleep. If it was a nightmare, she should probably wake her. As she gave Chloe a gentle nudge, her eyes left the road for a moment and the car drifted slightly left. When she looked back there was a shape, a flurry of movement, a quick flash of white directly in front of the car. Kay gasped and pulled the wheel sharply right. Too late. She felt a muffled thump as the left wheel passed over something. "Oh no," she gasped. Shocked and guilty, she brought the car to a stop.

Chloe was wide awake by then. "What? Mom, are we there yet? What's wrong—Is it awful?"

"No." She gripped the wheel, trying to work up the nerve to get out and see what must be lying in the road behind them. Some poor, suffering animal . . . she looked over at Chloe. "I'm afraid, I mean, I think we hit something."

"You mean like a dog? Oh no!" Chloe was out her side in a flash, the car door swinging open on darkness.

"No—wait, Chloe!" Kay fumbled with the handle. Now, of all times, it was locked. Her Miami training. Muttering, "Shit, shit!" she yanked on the handle and scrambled out.

Chloe was standing in the middle of the road, bathed in a red glow from the Volvo's tail lights. She turned and looked back, puzzled. "But there's nothing here." She sounded almost disappointed.

Kay ran to her side. The night air suddenly seemed closer, more humid. She felt sick.

Chloe pulled at her arm. "Mom, what was it? What kind of animal?"

"I . . . I don't know. Didn't get . . . a good look." Her voice sounded faint. She felt a little dizzy.

"Maybe it was hurt and crawled away," Chloe was saying. "We should look for it." She let go of her arm and ran toward the tangled grapevine and bushes at the side of the road.

Kay swallowed back nausea. "No. Just get back in the car." Suddenly the dark, the trees, the deserted road, it all frightened her for some reason. Not wanting to scare her daughter, though, she added, "If we'd hit it hard, it couldn't have run away so fast. Probably just grazed it."

Chloe turned reluctantly from the woods and they got back into the car.

She locked all four doors. "So you won't fall out," she told Chloe, and got an astonished look in return. Then she put the car in gear.

Half a mile later, Chloe pointed ahead. "Look, there it is! A-B-A-T . . . that's us. Kinda cool, a whole town named after us, even if it is spelled wrong." She paused, frowning. "Or are we named after it? Maybe we're the ones who can't spell."

"The other way around," Kay replied absently. Her eyes kept returning to the rearview mirror. The road behind them was empty.

Chloe must've noticed her backward glance. "Don't worry," she said, patting her arm as if, Kay thought, I'm eighty. "You probably didn't hit that animal, Mom. But if you did, probably it was really old anyhow. Much older than you."

"Thanks," said Kay wryly. A larger sign for Abaton's town limits flashed by. She smiled over at her daughter. "Though I wonder. Could anything be that ancient?"

It must've been, though, because—if her brief impression was accurate—the thing hadn't had much fur on it. Almost like—God, what an imagination. She shook her head at her own foolishness. And yet . . . small, a flash of brown and white, a face glimpsed in a split-second that'd been almost human-looking.

No, come on. Stop right now.

"Well, honey, we actually found it," she said, dragging her thoughts away from the morbid impressions her brain was still trying to force to the front. "Now you be my navigator. See if you can spot a place called the Waverly Inn."

***

When the woman and child had finally disappeared inside the brick motel unit, and didn't reappear for another suitcase or forgotten bag or yowling cat in a box, the little girl crept from her hiding place at the edge of the pines.

She wore a striped brown tee shirt, torn and stained, and white panties, and moved in a breathless rush from the line of trees to the edge of a carp pond set in the middle of the motel yard.

Stopping to look for a moment into the still flat water, with a soft cry she struck at the surface, shattering her reflection into fragments like a thousand dark jewels. A hand reached down to finger a rip in the shirt, and the flap of flesh that hung bloodless and quivering within. On one side of the cloth was a distinct imprint of tire tread.

The dark figure scooted from the water's edge to the car, then peered around the edge of a back fender as if playing hide and seek with an unseen friend.

When the moon emerged from behind a torn flag of storm cloud, a small object glittered on the ground, briefly, then winked out like an extinguished star. A hairclip with strands of curling reddish-brown hair caught in one plastic hinge. She scooped it up, crowing with delight. Small feet danced over the grass, back to the sanctuary of the trees. Dark eyes gloated over the trinket for a moment before a grimy brown hand stuffed it greedily into one tattered pocket.

A rustling in the wild azaleas as a rabbit slipped from cover, intent on the clover dotting the motel grass. A sharp cry. Small strong hands closed around its neck. And then, as it struggled and thrashed, back paws drumming on emptiness, dirty nails crept over its face, found an eye, and plunged deep into the socket, cracking bone. Blood and brain tissue oozed in a trail down the frail dark arm that held the still-twitching animal.

The limp warm body bumped across cool grass, past the black pool. The soft burden came to rest gently, reverently, on the doormat of the motel room where the woman and child would be sleeping.

But still the small intruder lingered. She pulled the hairclip from one pocket, turning it over in the moonlight, again admiring the glitter. Frowning, she moved the rabbit left, then a little bit right. Turned it over to hide the gaping hole that had once been part of its face. The dead creature flopped bonelessly as it was spurned by a bare foot. At last, with a sigh, she jerked the stiffening bundle of fur roughly from the hemp mat, dragged it back across the lawn to the woods, and abandoned it beneath a stunted oak.

Flies began to buzz before the dark figure had disappeared back into the trees.

***

The old woman in the narrow cot stiffened as a weight depressed the ticking mattress. There came a soft scuffling, as if a small animal had just burrowed beneath the covers to join her in the bed. She relaxed then, at the smell and feel of the familiar. "Baby Doll. Where you been off to so long?"

She sat up and pulled the little intruder onto her lap. "And your clothes in a fine mess." She shook her head in mock anger. "What I gonna do with you, un-uh." Dark gnarled fingers lovingly stroked the slight shoulders of the child who snuggled into her lap, then froze as they felt a wound beneath the torn cotton shirt. "Who done this to you?"

One diminutive fist opened to disclose a faint gleam. But when the old woman reached for it, the child bit her sharply on the hand, then scrambled to the floor, protesting with shrill, incoherent cries.

The old woman sighed. "All right, all right. Let it be. Never mind, Gramma Mattie fix you up, yes ma'am. As good as new."

THREE

Kay woke to the faltering drone of the motel's ancient boxy air conditioner. She swung her legs over the side of the bed, feet sinking into soft gray carpet, and sat for a moment staring down at it, unseeing, not moving. Frozen there by her recollection of the dream she'd just had. So like, and yet unlike, life.

She'd been on the road to Abaton again, in it, looking for a sign for the town. There'd been a jolt, as if the car had struck some large object. She'd slammed on the brake, turned to Chloe and said, "I think we hit something."

Except in this dream version, Chloe wasn't there.

Before she could react, there came a scratching on the grille of the car, a rough scrabbling sound. Her head snapped back around to the windshield in time to see some . . . thing pulling itself up onto the hood. Her hands gripped the wheel so tightly it hurt. But she couldn't let go, or look away, or move.

A brown, wizened creature was dragging itself over the hood of the car, toward the windshield. Toward her. Head down, ragged nails digging grooves in the paint, it hauled itself laboriously up to the glass. Raised one paw and shook it. Bloody droplets spattered the glass. The thing then had reached out and smeared the drops in a wide red arc.

28

It looked up at her then, and Kay had seen it wasn't an animal at all. The creature had the face of a child—save for the pointed baby teeth bared in a dreadful grin. Skin hung from its body in dry, peeling strips, and shredded away in the light summer evening breeze like dead petals from a dried flower. And then, as her dream-self had sat there, trembling, the creature raised a paw—a hand—and dragged the shape of a large letter C through the drying blood.

And then an H.

"No," she'd whispered. And closed her eyes, but somehow through her lids had still been able to see finish the next letter, a large L, one sharp nail lingering on the smeared glass.

"No!" She'd screamed then and pounded a fist on the windshield.

Those feral eyes under glass had glittered like glass shards on a dark road. Then, with a howling laugh the creature sprang off the car and had vanished in the rustling weeds on the side of the road.

That had been all—the end of the dream. She wasn't ready to interpret what it might mean, yet.

Her left foot was asleep, prickling with pins and needles. She stood awkwardly, limped halfway across the room, then stopped. Chloe's bed was empty. Her cotton nightgown lay on the floor halfway between her rumpled bed and the open bathroom door. Discarded items of clothing, like a trail of oversized breadcrumbs, let to the black and white tiled bath.

Kay laughed at herself, rubbing her face. Chloe had obviously gotten up earlier, just as she always did at home. But she wasn't in the bathtub, so where had she gone?

Kay crossed back to the large front window, and pulled the drape aside. And yes, there was Chloe, bent over the back seat of the Volvo, burrowing like a badger into assorted boxes and bags. Kay's good-morning wave went unnoticed.

"Whatever," she murmured, and padded back across the thick soft carpeting. That, and the air conditioner, were the motel's only concessions to semi-modern living. The rest was all 1930s Deco. At the foot of the bed, she stopped to pet Gus' orange-striped back. The cat had slept quietly all night. Exhausted, hung over, or resigned to his fate. On the way to the bathroom, she scooped up Chloe's clothing-trail.

The bathroom was Depression-era porcelain and tile, clean as an old Disney movie. At the pedestal sink she washed her face, brushed her teeth, and tugged a comb through tangled curls. "God, I need coffee," she breathed, squinting sleepily at the mirror. The shadows under her deep-set brown eyes seemed lighter today, though, despite the horrific dream. Their contrast with the light skin she'd always shielded so carefully from the killing rays of South Florida sun was less noticeable. I look almost well, she thought. Almost . . . happy.

Moving back to the bedroom she unpacked a white cotton shirt, shorts, and sandals. She dressed quickly, noticing how loose the khaki waistband had become.

Then she opened the curtains again. Their room had an excellent view of the parking lot and a small blue-tiled pool, but now Chloe was nowhere in sight.

"What the hell?" She wrestled with the sticky door for a second, its real oak swollen with humidity, wondering how Chloe had even managed to get out. It opened suddenly, nearly throwing her backwards, and she went out to check the car. No sign of her daughter. Worried now, she walked quickly to the motel office, a squat stucco and brick building in the center of a chain of units like a child's set of Lego blocks.

The place could have been really awful, but was saved by lacy wrought iron trim and a cool green draping of live oak and dogwood trees. Red salvia and impatiens bloomed like bright confetti in terra cotta planters on each side of the office door. These, and the tiled pool where a silly blue frog on a green enameled lily pad spouted a trickle of water, made the motel seem less like an oversized brick bunker.

Kay opened the office door. "Hello?" she called. "Have you seen my—"

There was Chloe across the room, waving a doughnut as she talked, sprinkling powdered sugar on her shirt. A white smudge dusted one tanned cheek. A large glass of milk sweated beads of humidity in front of her. She was at a gate-legged table across from Mrs. Waverly, the plump, gray-haired owner who'd checked them in last night.

Chloe looked over at the door. "Hi, Mom," she said, a little sheepishly, lowering the doughnut. "You were still snoring, so I got dressed real quiet and went outside. Mrs. Waverly invited me in for breakfast."

Snoring? "But I don't—I mean, are you sure the invitation wasn't the other way around?" Kay smiled apologetically at the older woman. "I hope she hasn't put you to any trouble."

Mrs. Waverly beamed back, round and pink-cheeked. There was a stack of vintage-looking movie magazines at her elbow. "Please," she said. "Sit with us. I'll get you a cup of coffee. Made fresh. Maxwell House," she added, as if that would surely lure anyone in.

"Well, if it's not too much trouble." The brewed coffee did smell wonderful. Soon she was sipping it from a handmade mug, eating warm doughnuts, and questioning a big-city suspicion that strangers didn't go out of their way to be nice to you on purpose.

The innkeeper fidgeted with the stack of magazines. Some actress with a swept-up Forties hairdo was on the cover. "Miz Abbot, I hope it's not too nosy to ask what brings you all here. You're not just passin' through, are you? We don't get much business these days, not since the interstate."

"Well, no. We may stay a while. My husband—I mean, we own a house here in town, and came to, um, see about it."

"You don't say! How nice. You and your husband bought a home here? We sure could use some new folks to liven things up. You know how dull small towns get. Not much to talk about. Though folks will gossip anyways. Now I don't go in for it much myself."

"Actually, it's just my daughter and me. I'm a widow. We're here for a little peace and quiet. I've got some work to finish, and this seemed like a good place to get it done."

"Honey, you come to the right place, indeed. It's quiet as the grave in—oh dear. I am sorry!" She picked up her coffee cup and set it down again, red in the face.

"Don't apologize." Kay liked the older woman; her inquisitive chatter was actually sort of endearing. So far. "We're pretty well resigned to it now."

Mrs. Waverly looked relieved. "More coffee?" she offered, handing Chloe another doughnut.

"No thanks." Kay pushed back her chair. "I really ought to get into town and see about the house. You could give me directions to Blunt Realty, though, Mrs. Waverly. That'd be a great help."

"It's only a hop and a skip up the road. And please, honey, call me Myrna. You know, like Myrna Loy."

"All right, Myrna. Then I'm just Kay, please."

Myrna Waverly beamed. "Like Kay Francis! It's a deal. Now, you just head straight on down this very road, and you can't miss Blunt's. But if you do, stop in at any old place. Everybody knows the Blunts, 'cause they own pretty near everything in town."

"I see," said Kay, filing this information away under Minor Irrelevancies. "We'll be on our way, then. I'm going to leave our stuff in the room for now, since we don't know what shape the house is in. May need to stay on here a little longer."

Myrna looked thrilled at the prospect. "Fine with me, sugar. It's all on the credit card, anyhow. Plenty of rooms. You all are the only ones here right now. Oh, 'cept for old Judge Davis. But he lives here, so that don't really count."

"I see," Kay said, though she didn't. "Fine. We'll be back later. Thanks for the coffee."

Chloe tugged at her sleeve. "Where're we going now, Mom?"

"Just into town. Mr. Blunt's supposed to show us the house today. It will be exciting, seeing where your father grew up."

Chloe did seem excited, a welcome change from the day before. Her curls bounced as she skipped along, turning from time to time to walk backward so she could look up at Kay as they talked. "Yeah, I guess. It's not too bad here. Not like I thought it would be. Myrna's nice."

She started to remind her of proper etiquette, but hated to spoil her mood. "Oh, well . . . in small towns, honey, if children call adults by their first names, they say "Miss" in front of it."

"Right," Chloe said. "Miss Myrna. Her doughnuts were good." She stopped to lean over the water and touch the spouting blue plaster frog. "Cool, isn't it? Can we get one for our new house?"

"Maybe. Let's wait and see what else we need first, okay? It might take more than a plaster frog to fix the place up."

Chloe looked up, brown eyes serious. "No. We're going to like it here, Mom."

Kay smiled. "Thank you, Madame Chloe. Now hop in the car and let's get going. Before it's time to feed you lunch, too."

Laughing, her daughter scrambled into the front. Kay got in with more dignity, having seen the motel office curtain twitch. Myrna Waverly was probably watching.

The heart of town lay about a mile up the road, just as Myrna had said. The main street, imaginatively named Main Street, was lined with a variety of small shops. Some were empty, windows curtained or boarded up. Some were occupied but had clearly seen better days. Yet most were well-kept, with attractive signs, built of brick, stucco, or whitewashed wood.

On the left side sat a clothing store, a barber shop, a fabric store, and a small, old-fashioned hardware store. On the right a mom-and-pop grocery, a craft shop, and—

"Oh, rats! That was it."

Playing tourist, she'd just driven past a carved wooden sign with engraved gilt letters which proudly announced: *BLUNT REALTY—Selling the South.* Kay glanced up at the rearview. Not another car in sight, so she backed up quickly and pulled into the shell-paved lot.

No wonder I missed it, she thought. Doesn't look much like an office. The free-standing two-story Victorian house had a small turret and two bay windows. Its wraparound porch was flanked by crape myrtles, a dogwood tree, and fronted with Mexican marigolds and snowy tobacco flowers. Together it all hinted that a good deal of money dwelt behind that facade. The Blunts must be selling a lot of the South these days.

Chloe was out first and charged ahead up the wide steps. Kay followed, admiring the carved posts and curved arches of white-painted gingerbread trim and lattice that adorned the yellow clapboard house. The sign hanging over the leaded glass of the front door read *OPEN*, so she turned the knob. The door swung silently inward on well-oiled brass hinges.

She and Chloe both stopped on the threshold. Stretched before them, a rich golden oak floor had been polished to rival a mirror. The sash windows were hung with white muslin curtains, below diamond-patterned stained glass set in the arch above each. An oak roll-top stood on one side of the front room. A smaller mahogany Queen Anne secretary faced it. The red papered walls were hung with old engravings and watercolors. Beneath them stood glass cabinets full of curios and a Jenny Lind bed piled with cushions, in use as a sofa. Kay felt they'd stepped back a century—into someone's home.

Chloe found her voice first. "Cool!"

Kay had expected another brick and concrete block building, full of polyester, chrome, and maybe orange shag carpet.

Chloe pointed. "Oh my gosh, look, Mom!"

A Victorian dollhouse stood in one corner on a table. As they stepped closer for a better look, Kay realized it was a replica of the house they stood within.

"My husband's great-grandfather made that," said a female voice. They both jumped like guilty children. Kay turned to see a smiling woman in her late thirties, with shoulder-length blond hair and blue eyes pale as aquamarines. Petite, very thin, and dressed in a raw silk suit that Kay suspected had cost more than most people made in a week.

"Oh, hello. We're here to see . . . " Kay felt her face heat up with embarrassment as she realized she'd forgotten the realtor's first name.

"You must be here to see Slocum."

"Yes," she said gratefully. "I'm Kay Abbott. This is my daughter, Chloe." Who was still gazing, moonstruck, at the elaborate dollhouse. Kay nudged her.

"Hi," Chloe said shyly, coming out of her trance. "I like your house. The big one and the little one."

The woman nodded. "You have good taste, then. I'm Bonnie Blunt, Slocum's wife. Afraid he isn't in yet. Had a closing over in Grand Ridge. He should be back soon, though." She glanced at the gold Rolex on her left wrist. "Like to wait? The sofa's comfortable. I'm sure he'll be back any minute."

"All right." Kay took a seat on the Jenny Lind, sinking further into the down pillows than she'd expected. Like quicksand, she thought. Chloe remained in front of the dollhouse, discovering new delights through each tiny window.

"I'm making coffee in the back," Mrs. Blunt added. "And I have some wonderful, chewy chocolate chip cookies."

Chloe's attention snapped away from the dollhouse at the mention of food. Kay shook her head in disbelief. "That's very kind of you. Just coffee for me, please."

The woman disappeared down the hallway, returning quickly bearing a silver tray with coffee pot, cups, and a loaded plate. She poured a cup of steaming, chocolate-scented coffee. Kay finally gave in to one delicious-looking Tollhouse cookie. Mrs. Blunt put three on a green majolica saucer and carried it over to Chloe.

But her daughter barely acknowledged the offering, so caught up was she in the spell of the little house. Kay began to apologize, but the other woman shook her head. "I'm happy when someone enjoys my things as much as I do. You do like it, don't you, Chloe?"

"I've never seen anything so . . . so cool before."

"Then you'd definitely better look at this." Mrs. Blunt opened the hinged front wall of the house to reveal the interior. She showed Chloe how to turn on the lights, and tiny ceiling fans which revolved lazily, just like real ones.

Kay watched with gratitude and relief. She wanted very much for Chloe to be happy here, because she didn't think she could face returning to the house in Miami right away.

In the end they waited for almost an hour. To entertain them, Mrs. Blunt had shown them through the whole house, upstairs and down. The sunny, enormous kitchen and mosaic-tiled bath had been left old-fashioned, though the stainless-steel restaurant stove and huge Subzero refrigerator were new. One downstairs room was an unexpectedly modern study in expensive beige leather, glass, and chrome. "Slocum's office," Bonnie said tersely, with a hint of distaste.

Upstairs, two rooms had been converted into meeting rooms, with dark wood wainscoting and Italian marble fireplaces. But the third and largest was still furnished as a bedroom, with a sleigh bed of golden pine at the center.

What caught Chloe's eye, though, were the large, built-in oak cupboards. The doors had been removed; their shelves loaded with a collection of antique pull toys. Painted goats, dog carts, and ponies with real horsehair manes were all mounted on spoked wooden or metal wheels.

"These are really my favorites," said Bonnie Blunt.

The toys looked fragile and valuable, but Mrs. Blunt seemed eager to have them handled and admired. And clearly Chloe could've happily done so for the rest of the day. But it was getting late and Kay wanted to get something accomplished.

As if she sensed her growing impatience, Bonnie suddenly said, "Sorry, I can't imagine what's keeping him so long. Tell you what. I'll find the keys and take you out there myself."

They went back downstairs, and she rummaged noisily in the top drawer of the secretary, sorting through what looked like thousands of keys, old and new. "Aha! Here they are." She held up a brass triumphantly. "Come on, let's go."

Her Mercedes SUV took them out of town by what she called "the old River Road." Along the way, she relayed some local history, pointing out stands of scarred old pines where turpentine men used to notch the trees and hang buckets to catch the oozing sap. "Those collapsing wooden frames there, in the overgrown field? They used to hold muslin to shelter shade tobacco. A big staple industry in the past, here."

They rattled over a small plank bridge. "That's Blackwater Slough, it runs into Black River."

She turned left onto a narrow red-dirt road. The clay soon turned to gravel, which became a semi-circular drive before a white clapboard plantation house set on a couple of acres of immaculately-mown lawn.

Kay gasped, "Good grief. I mean, it looks . . . very nice. I really didn't expect—"

Bonnie laughed. "Well, of course Slocum sees the place is kept up. His daddy was Leila Abbott's—your husband's grandmother's—attorney. She had it in her will particularly that the house would always be taken care of. Been over fifteen years now. Of course, look real close and you'll see it's not perfect. Needs a little paint here and there, on the trim. But it's still quite livable."

"Quite, I'm sure," Kay muttered.

FOUR

A s they stood in the wide entrance hall at the foot of the stairs, Kay did feel a little dismayed, though. The house was in good shape, considering its age, but clearly no one had lived in it for a long time. It was furnished, she noted, though she wondered what the vague shapes beneath yellowed cotton sheeting were like. A fine layer of dust covered everything, including the chair rail she'd just run a hand along. Motes drifted in golden streamers of light through the wavy old window glass. She took a deep breath, and sneezed. The grimy rail topped the wainscoting which ran around every visible wall. Its half-paneling looked like mahogany, but it might be white birch under the dust. Now she saw endless days of cleaning, dusting, polishing, and more sneezing ahead. Less time to work.

"My, it really is a . . . a very big house," she said.

No doubt it would be worth it. The high ceilings had heavy exposed beams. Floor to ceiling windows saved the front rooms from the gloom she'd always associated with old houses. The rooms they walked through were often not exactly square, but rather octagonal, hexagonal, or held interesting little nooks that encouraged exploration.

In the parlor Mrs. Blunt paused to examine a brick and tile fireplace. "I'd just kill to have this in my house."

"It's all wonderful," Kay agreed. "But it looks like a major cleaning project. And, well—I was hoping to move in and get right to work on a book."

"Well, old wood-frame places like this don't seal like Tupperware. Dust and dirt get in, filter down from the attic or warped window frames. Of course, in this case . . . well, it's not just due to those things."

Bonnie lowered her voice as if someone still lived there and might overhear. "Old Mrs. Abbott was a little, you know, eccentric. She had two or three servants who'd worked for her since before the Flood. But she outlived them all, then refused to have anyone else in to do for her."

"Really? I wonder how she managed, after having people wait on her all her life," Kay said, meaning to be ironic.

The realtor's wife shrugged. "Frozen dinners, I guess. She didn't have many visitors, either. You know, it's funny. In her will it specifies that the outside of the house is to be kept up, painted and so forth, but the inside was to be left exactly as it was, including the dirt."

Kay gaped at her. "It said that?"

Bonnie shrugged. "Well, no, not exactly. But that's pretty much what happened. As if she wanted it to stay just the same, like . . . like a . . . "

"A shrine? But for whom?"

Bonnie shrugged. "Whoever it was, I don't think they ever made it back."

When Kay laughed, the echo in the big house was unnerving.

"Leilah Abbott was always a little strange," Bonnie added. "None of what she called 'riffraff' would have ever gotten in off that porch without permission when she was alive. Guess she decided none would get in just because she was dead, either."

"Well, I never got to meet her," said Kay. "She died a couple years before we got married." She was trying to imagine Jack living in this dusty cloister with a querulous, demanding old woman. "My husband never talked much about, about family, really."

Now, though, his refusal to visit his birthplace made a little sense. It must've been overwhelming to live in the shadow of such a domineering figure as Leilah Abbott.

"I'm not too surprised. Not the type to bounce grandchildren on her knee. And not the least bit fond of her daughter-in-law, that's for sure. At least she was known to say so often enough—and in public. Maybe you're lucky you never met her. But don't get depressed about all the cleaning. That's easy enough to fix."

"You must be a world-class housekeeper." Kay shook her head. "Not me. I'm here to finish some illustrations, not to scrub woodwork all day."

Bonnie snorted. "Honey, I don't know floor wax from ear wax. But I do know a woman who'd be happy to tackle it for you. Why, you won't have to dirty your little finger, if you don't want. She's good and real professional."

Kay has always done her own housework in Miami. It had never been her favorite activity, though. "One woman, to clean all this?"

"Oh, you don't know Perdita," said Bonnie firmly. "She's real serious about her business."

Chloe skipped through, humming as she traced arabesques through the dust on a sheeted tabletop.

Kay gave in. "Well, if you think so."

"I know," said Bonnie firmly. "A clean house makes life worth living. Especially if you can pay someone else to do it."

***

Together they made a list of cleaning supplies and tools, noted some obvious repairs, then Bonnie drove them back to the office. Still no sign of Slocum Blunt, so Kay and Chloe left in search of lunch. The Landmark Diner's daily specials sign advertised honey-fried chicken, turnip greens and yams. But she let Chloe choose, and they were soon seated in a red vinyl booth, Formica top sticky as the flypaper strips dangling from the ceiling of the town's only drive-in burger joint.

The thick cheeseburgers had grilled onions, an indulgence Kay figured she'd regret later. Afterward, leaving the car in the restaurant lot, they walked down Main Street to check out the local stores. She was hoping it wouldn't be necessary to drive to Tallahassee every week for supplies.

They went inside Blunt's Grocery first. Kay smiled, recalling Myrna Waverly's remark about the elusive realtor's extensive property holdings. The fresh vegetables looked too large to be real and wore no second skins of plastic wrap. The butcher counter in back, with its whole chickens and huge roll of brown wrapping paper, reminded Kay of long-past shopping trips with her own mother. A small frozen food section stocked with Boston Market and Fridays entrees was an almost-jarring reminder of the present.

Chloe checked out the snack aisles, and was even satisfied with the ice cream selection. "We'll come back to shop later, when the house is clean and the refrigerator's turned on," Kay promised. She picked up apples, tortilla chips, and a few Hershey bars.

She bypassed the hardware store, feeling it would become a second home soon enough, but was pulled in to an arts and crafts shop next door. She needed oil pastels for herself, and silk floss for Chloe's latest passion, embroidery. With no patience for needles and thread herself, Kay was amazed that an energetic child could sit still long enough to work minute stitches into a complete design. True, these were sometimes a bit crooked, but Chloe had finished several, proudly mailing off one design worked on a pillow to Gramma in New York, last Christmas.

A brass bell above the door jangled as they entered.

A tiny woman with pale blue hair and the pink myopic gaze of a white mouse scurried out to greet them. "Hey there," she squeaked. "You all got to be the new folks come to live in the Abbott house. Myrna told me about you and your sweet little girl, so sad about your late departed husband, what can I do for you today, sugar?"

The tendrils of the local grapevine were clutching at her ankles already. "Nice to meet you, Mrs.—?"

"Lord, honey, just call me Minnie. Minnie Sutton. We're not formal around here." She patted her pastel curls.

Oh dear. Those shoe-button eyes, the polka-dot dress. Minnie Mouse Sutton ought to be easy enough to remember. To stifle a giggle, Kay said quickly, "Myrna told you about us?"

Minnie's 78 RPM laugh shook her small frame. "Sure did. Now don't be offended, honey. That's just our way, mine and Myrna's, everybody's around here, really. We been friends since we were eyelevel with a possum. Got no secrets from each other, you can believe that."

Kay did. She saw her quiet, productive stay turning into a backwoods social whirl. "Well, I hope she put in a good word for me. I may be needing some things you don't normally stock."

"No problem, sugar. My baby brother Tal, Talmadge Sutton, he owns a frame and art supply store over to Bainbridge. Tal carries every kind of paint, pencils, paper, and brushes a body could ever need, and just what kind of work do you do, in the art world, if it's not too bold of me to ask?"

Kay sighed. "Not at all."

Minnie continued to chatter as she wrote up their purchases. After the sale was rung, on an ancient punch-key register, Kay inched toward the door, promising to come by another time to talk. They stepped from the cool, dim interior of Minnie's shop into a wave of heat rising off the sidewalk, so humid it felt like the caress of a huge damp hand.

"Whew," Kay breathed, just glad to have escaped.

"Yeah, it's hot," Chloe agreed.

"Not the heat, I meant . . . never mind." They might both be suffocated beneath all the Southern hospitality before summer's end.

Next they passed a hair salon with *RUBY'S BEAUTY SHOPPE* scrolled grandly across the big front window. A chemical stink of bottled curl briefly enveloped them. We Specialize in Curly Hair, proclaimed smaller gilt letters below. Kay put a hand up to her head involuntarily as they hurried past.

Only an auto parts store and a chicken take-out place remained. They crossed over and turned back toward the car, encountering another chicken place and two more auto supplies in the process.

I see what passes for entertainment in this town, she thought. Parts and poultry. But she was pleased to also see a florist, a book and gift shop, and a small clothing store. At least emergency purchases of red roses and new underwear would be possible.

The next block was entirely taken up by a brick warehouse. Crude block letters across the front announced *SAT NITE AUCTION 7PM JESUS SAVES*. The corner housed an empty Christian Supply Store—whatever that was; crosses and communion wine?—and the sign beseeched *PRAY FOR US AS WE MOVE TO OUR NEW LOCATION*.

As they passed, a number of shopkeepers and customers waved or nodded.

"Do all these people know us?" Chloe asked at last, looking puzzled, as she waved back yet again.

Miami had not prepared her for this. "No. It's just, this is a small town, and I guess everyone knows everyone else. So they know that we're new. They're just being nice."

"But they don't even know our names yet."

She wouldn't have taken bets on that. "You and I are used to a big city. People aren't as friendly there because, well, they're afraid—"

Chloe looked alarmed. "Of what, Mom?"

She frowned, wondering how to change the subject. "Well, you know, afraid they'll be friendly to the wrong person, I guess."

"Like a murderer or a robber?" Her daughter's eyes sparkled with morbid childish interest. "Or a monster. Or maybe they're afraid they'll get scraped. Like Jenny Goldstein's mother said."

"What?"

"Once she told the maid to be sure and lock the door or somebody might come in and scrape her."

"Um, sure. Maybe," Kay said, thinking fast. "Or just afraid of talking to someone who's not, you know, very nice to other people. In a small town, where you know everyone, you don't have to worry as much about things like that."

Then they were at the car and Chloe lost interest in discussing the prevalence of contemporary violence.

The inside of the Volvo felt hot enough to fire pottery. "Thank God for air conditioning." Still, Kay fried her bare legs on the hot leather seat. "Better get back and see how Angus is doing. He's probably used all the towels and called room service for dinner."

"Don't be silly." Chloe snorted. "They don't have any room service. I checked."

45

FIVE

A bank?" Myrna nodded. "Sure, used to be there was one right down on Main Street. That got bought up ten, twelve-odd years ago by the big savings and loan over to Marianna. So now it's out on the Old Town Highway, we call it the River Road? In a new double-wide. Pretty white vinyl siding. Can't miss it, right next to the Baptist Church like it is. That's fitting, since they got a lot in common."

"Who has what in common?" Kay frowned. Had she missed something? She'd asked directions so she could open a local account.

"The bank and the church, they got a lot in common," Myrna explained. "Blunt money, honey. It built the one and fills up t'other. Get it?" She laughed heartily.

Kay wondered at this hostility toward the Blunts. The rest of the town must be envious, she supposed. "Well, better get going. Thanks again for keeping an eye on Chloe. She's so sick of the car. Wanted to play outside today. And the cat — you've been so nice about Gus, too. I appreciate it, Myrna."

"Oh, it's nothin'." The motel owner's pink cheeks deepened to rose. "Why, he's no trouble. Cats are cleaner than people, my mama used to say. And I do love kitties. But keepin' company with the Judge, and all his allergies . . . well, just can't have one, anymore."

Back in her room, Kay gathered up her purse and the list of things to buy. When she came out again, Chloe was out by the fish pool. Last year's faded swimsuit showed white crescents of untanned skin. She's growing too fast, Kay thought. If only there was a way to slow down the process. Her daughter dangled her bare feet in the pool, wiggling her toes in the lukewarm water, unconcerned about runaway maturation. Beside her, Angus' jade gaze was intent on the murky depths, as if hoping to spot a prospective fish dinner.

Following Myrna's directions Kay went through town and turned off Main Street onto the Old Town Highway. The road was in bad shape. The car rode smoothly for a quarter mile or so, then suddenly bounced and lurched over cracked pavement and potholes. She slowed down to avoid shaking anything important loose. So far there appeared to be no Volvo mechanics in Abaton.

Just ahead, a large truck with wood-slatted sides pulled out onto the road. The open bed was padded with straw. Nestled into it, piled like green treasure four and five deep, were glossy striped watermelons. A shabby couch leaking gray stuffing, pushed against the back window, held a frail, elderly black man, fine hair a yellow-white halo around his weathered face. He wore dark suit pants, narrow blue suspenders, a thin black tie, and a starched white shirt. His legs were crossed genteelly at the knees, a Panama hat on his lap. A battered red plaid thermos rolled precariously beside him on the sofa. He looked so regal sitting knee-deep in watermelons, she smiled and waved. The old man nodded back solemnly.

Two buildings coming up on the left fit Myrna's description of church and bank. As she slowed to turn the truck rumbled on out of sight.

She stepped carefully across the uneven lot, but still got gravel in her sandals. Past the big plastic *FIRST FOUNDERS SAVINGS AND LOAN* sign, she climbed broad wooden steps to the front door. She pulled on the handle. It was locked. Her watch said five to ten. They can't be closed on Tuesday, she thought. Was it a local holiday; the Cucumber Festival or something? Surely Myrna would've known. She seemed to know everything.

Kay cupped her hands to make a sun visor, peered through the tinted glass, then gasped and stepped back. Someone inside was staring back.

The lock rattled, the door swung open. A pale, thin young man with spiky hair stood there, squinting against the sunlight like a nocturnal zoo animal. He blinked and slowly focused on Kay. "Can I help you?"

"Yes, I hope so. This is the bank, isn't it? I mean, are you open?"

He blinked again. "It's Tuesday."

"I know that." To her annoyance, a hot flush of embarrassment was creeping up her neck, toward her face. "But what the heck, I'd like to open an account anyway. If you don't mind. May I come in?"

His eyes opened a little wider. Faint lines creased his forehead. "Oh, I see. You're from out of town. Of course, come on in."

"Thank you." She tried not to sound too grateful.

"You see, it's Tuesday," he repeated, walking her over to a big mahogany desk in the center of the room.

"And so—?"

"And we always open at ten on Tuesday."

"Why is that? Your hours say nine to four on the door sign."

He looked momentarily distressed. The creases in his forehead marched upward again. "Why? Well, just tradition, I guess. Unwritten policy. We're also closed all

48

day Wednesday. But of course, he added, waving a hand, "we're the All-Day Saturday Full-Service Bank."

"How nice," she said drily. "Now, how do I go about opening an account?"

"Just see me. I'm in Accounts."

Of course. And it was Tuesday. "Fine, Mr.—?"

"Reed. Oliver Reed. I can take care of that for you, Miss—?"

"Abbott. Kay Abbott. And it's Mrs."

He stared. "Not . . . of the Abaton Abbotts?"

"Well, yes. That is, my husband was one. We're just visiting."

"Taking a vacation in Abaton?" Now he sounded faintly amused.

Kay only nodded, feeling she'd said more than enough already. Soon Reed was offering Kay many other exciting banking services, including certificates of deposit. "Thanks, but I intend to spend every penny in my account by the end of the summer." She smiled at his scandalized expression. "It's so much easier that way."

As he tapped information into the computer, she looked around. The carpeted floor vibrated underfoot, giving it the shaky feel of a mobile home. Opposite them, at a long Formica counter, a female teller counted stacked bills industriously. More Blunt money, no doubt. Another teller was filing nails like red talons. Kay wondered how safe money could be, kept in a glorified trailer.

As if he'd heard her last thought, Reed looked up from his screen. "We have an armored safe that's absolutely state of the art, Mrs. Abbott. The Brink's truck comes every week from Marianna. Your money is as safe here as it would be in any bank in Miami."

Perhaps he didn't realize what a doubtful assurance this sounded to her. At any rate, next he asked if she wanted her husband's name on the checks.

"No," she said quickly, determined not to explain. Let the local grapevine work for its material. She decided instead to have Chloe's name added below hers on the account. After signing at least six times on various lines, she received a firm, hearty handshake.

"One other thing," she said, slipping a folder of temporary checks into her purse. "Could you direct me to a drugstore? I'm still trying to find my way around."

"We don't have one, exactly. You might try Monk's. Go down the road a bit, till you see a wooden sign where Hank's Fish Camp used to be. Turn right there. Go about two more miles, past the old tobacco barn foundation—and there you are. Can't miss it. He'll probably have everything you need."

"Uh, thanks," she said, trying to hold all those rural landmarks in her head. She had no desire to get lost around this neck of the woods again.

This time getting there seemed simple enough. She turned at the fish camp, feeling good about her sense of direction for almost a mile. Until she saw a body lying on the right side of the road. She hit the brakes, then lifted her foot. What should she do out here in the middle of nowhere: stop and get out to help? Call 911? She groped in the center console for her cell phone.

NO SIGNAL.

Now what? She'd read often enough in the Miami Herald about people who'd been tricked into stopping, then robbed. About women alone who'd been—

The ragged figure raised a head. Or rather, the enormous buzzard crouched over the carcass did. It pulled a long, bloody ribbon of flesh from the body of the dead doe, whose sightless eyes were dull with road dust. Kay shuddered, quickly rolling up her window as the stench of death penetrated the car's interior. It seemed to cling to the upholstery, coat her nose and throat. So it was a double relief to see a large hand-lettered sign announcing:

MONk's cORNeR Rabits Live or dreSSed Cricketts anD wiGGlers Drugs sundrys

Just past it a young dark-skinned boy was trudging doggedly up the road, cradling an armload of clanking glass soda bottles. Did they still give back deposits on empties, she wondered? Or had she simply gone back to the past, and was now stuck in a time warp?

"Whatever," she muttered. This place was certainly . . . different.

It was also a place built with no discernible plan. Now large and aimlessly rambling, the original structure must've begun as a one-room log cabin. Over the years additions had been tacked on using an eclectic assortment of building materials.

Jack would've stared in architectural amazement. One wing was unpainted cinderblock, one was brick, another dully shiny aluminum siding. The main building had two small plate glass windows covered with fancy scrolled iron bars. She parked and, after some hesitation, headed for what she thought must be the front door. It boasted a garish red-and-yellow sign which asked, *FEELING L A Z Y ? Eat RED ROOSTER Pills*. A crude line drawing of a psychotic-looking chicken illustrated the advertisement.

Two geezers were parked on a wooden bench by the door. They wore faded overalls, looked closely related, and both smiled toothlessly at Kay as she passed.

The first room held a glass-topped counter crammed with fishing tackle, cartons of cigarettes, a dozen brands of snuff, batteries, penny candy, and many boxes of Juicy Fruit gum. A wire rack of dusty bathing beauty postcards, circa 1950 by the swimsuit styles, and a cash register sat atop it. Gaping game fish and severely-truncated wild animals hung crookedly, decorating the back wall. One open doorway led right, another to the left. A whiff of the

51

scents drifting in from the right side convinced her that the crickets, wigglers, and dressed and undressed rabbits must all be stored in there. She quickly went left.

The large room on that side—the brick addition—did seem to be a combination drug and general store. Canned goods, cake mixes, and carb-rich junk food filled the first two aisles. Five kinds of Oreos alone.

"Why not just put crack cocaine on the shelves?" Kay muttered, and hurriedly turned down the next aisle to flee temptation. There she found a cornucopia of laundry soap, sewing thread, shampoo, cosmetics, and at least ten kinds of hair curlers. The last aisle held more wire racks full of comic books, magazines, paperback westerns, and romances. It appeared e-readers had not caught on yet in Abaton. In the back another counter stood before floor to ceiling shelves of aspirin, cough syrups, cold remedies, bandages, heating pads, and trusses. OK—the pharmacy.

She picked up a battered wicker shopping basket from a stack by the door, and browsed the aisles, gathering up things they'd need at the house. Spray cleaners, bath soap, aspirin, toothpaste, needles and thread. When the basket was overflowing she heaved it up to the counter.

Behind the counter a chinless woman with limp dark hair seemed to be having a serious relationship with Danielle Steele. She dragged her head up reluctantly and shook it. "Ya need t' take all that up front. T' the register." Her eyes dropped like lead sinkers back to the creased paperback book.

Kay sighed. Well, at least the staff could read. She wrestled the heavy basket back down the aisle and through the side door. Braced it against a shelf, took a firmer grip, and hauled it the rest of the way to a register at the front counter.

As she dumped the load there she spotted a long red drink cooler. A cold Diet Coke would be nice. She walked over, lifted the lid, and stifled a scream in her free hand.

Instead of Coca Cola, the frigid metal box was packed full of pink flayed bodies. The 'dressed' rabbits were actually quite naked. And what were those larger, rat-looking things? She decided she didn't really want to know, and slammed down the lid.

As if the dull thump was his cue, a grizzly bear of a man charged out of a back room. He lumbered over to the register, knocking over a wire rack of faded bandannas, righting it again, all in one motion. "Good day, young miss. Didn't hear you come in. Got yourself a load, doncha? Well now, let's see."

He rang up her purchases with astonishing speed and a great deal of noise, pounding the keys as though he had a long-standing grudge against them all. He wore big gleaming dentures, a short-sleeved plaid shirt, a faded Falcons cap, and blue Levis with a tarnished Schlitz belt buckle nearly eclipsed by gut.

Somewhat recovered from her cooler encounter, Kay smiled. He grinned back between ringing up prices. "Nice day, ain't it? Hot, sure. 'Course, it's always hot 'bout this time. Fish won't even get up to bite. Just got to expect it. The heat. You need anything else, young lady?" He knocked over the rack of scarves and missed righting it this time, littering the pine floor with a rainbow assortment of cotton bandanas.

"N-no." His sheer bulk felt benignly overwhelming, like a Buick-sized teddy bear. "No, I guess that's all for now."

"Sure enough," he agreed, putting her purchases into tattered cardboard boxes. She dug for her wallet and produced four twenties.

He scowled at her outstretched hand. "Here now. What's all this?"

She glanced at the numbers that had popped up in the little glass window of the old register, then down at the money in her hand. "$76.84 . . . isn't that right?"

"Hell's bells, missy. You don't pay me now. Not time yet! That'd mess up the books real good. I'll put this on your account. Bill comes end of the month, like everyone else's. Don't want to do things different now."

"Account? But I don't have one."

"Course you do. Miz Blunt said open you one. So I done it. You'll soon catch on to how we do things here."

"Well, I suppose." If she kept the cash, she could give it to the house cleaner this afternoon. "I guess it'll be handy. Like a local charge card."

He frowned, furry brows almost meeting over his lumpy nose. "Never thought much a' them little plastic cards." He scrawled a notation with a leaking pen into a black ledger, wiping ink-stained fingers on his shirt. "There you have it. Miz Abbott. $76.84. Bills come out end of the month. Like I said."

"You know my name. I guess you must be Mr. Monk?"

"Just plain Monk'll do." He heaved the boxes off the counter. "Tote these out for ya." He carried them with one hand like a single tiny parcel, kicking over a floor display on his way out. Vienna sausage cans rolled everywhere. Kay paused for a moment to hold the door for the little boy with the armload of soda bottles, who was just coming in.

Halfway to the car she stopped. A young man in a fluorescent green shirt was leaning against it, gesturing and shouting at something or someone. "Yeah? Yeah? Man, you gon' be sorry. Yeah, I see you sucker. You'll be sorry, man. I'm gon' kick—"

Kay froze, thinking of the meth junkies back in Miami, the armed crazies in search of a victim. She began to back up a step slowly. The storekeeper snorted. "Don't worry none about him. Ain't dangerous, just been in the 'shine again. His mama'll be here any second to fetch him off."

A large woman in a dress and house slippers sailed around the building just then, collared the cringing teenager, and dragged him out of sight.

"Happens every other day," said Monk. "Kids."

"I know that's right," piped a high voice behind them. The child with the bottles. He tugged on Monk's pant leg. "Got me some more, Mister Monk."

"Be there directly, Eddie." He dropped the boxes with a thud in the trunk of Kay's car.

"I didn't know they still paid deposits on glass bottles," Kay remarked. "In Miami we just recycled everything."

Monk shrugged. "They don't. But Eddie don't know that. And his family can use the cash. Now, you come back any time, young miss."

He turned and lumbered back toward the store, Eddie clinging to one pant-leg, trailing in his wake like a tiny tugboat after a supertanker.

SIX

Kay took Chloe for a late lunch in town, intending to change into old clothes at the motel afterward and go out to the house. But hours of sun and swimming, plus three pieces of fried chicken, had taken their toll. Her daughter collapsed, fully dressed, on the bed and was instantly asleep. When she tried to rouse her, Chloe muttered groggily and pushed her hands away.

She sat at the foot of the bed listening to soft, even breathing. She didn't want to leave her alone at the motel again. Of course Myrna had said she didn't mind keeping an eye on her, that it was a pleasure. Nor did she want to impose, but Bonnie Blunt had arranged for her to meet Perdita Woodberry, the housecleaning wizard, at three o'clock.

Gus jumped up on the bed and arranged himself next to Chloe in a rubbery cat-contortion, all four feet pointing in different directions. Kay leaned over and smoothed damp curls from the girl's sun-freckled forehead. Kissed her cheek, then quietly left, closing the door softly behind her.

She stopped at the office to tell Myrna. "She's asleep. I'll only be gone an hour or so. She may not even wake up before then."

"If she does, I'll keep an eye on her. Good company, that sweet little thing."

Kay turned onto the River Road, wondering again if she'd made the right decision, moving them up here, even for a while. Had she been too hasty, deciding which direction their lives would go without giving her daughter a choice? But Chloe was only nine.

The Volvo's new radials hummed on baked clay, then grated on gravel. The sight of the big weathered house pleased her. Parked on one side of the half-circle drive was a vintage VW Karmann Ghia in great condition. She pulled in behind it, a little surprised. Having already imagined Perdita Woodberry as a large, well-muscled cleaning machine, it was hard to picture her folded into this little red sports car. Of course no law said a person couldn't be both big and sporty.

She walked up the drive to the house, then climbed the porch steps. The floorboards creaked underfoot. She stopped at the front door, lifted a hand and knocked.

You twit, she chided herself. It's your house now. Feeling silly, hoping Perdita Woodberry hadn't heard, she let herself into the front hall.

At first glance, everything looked the same. Kay heard someone humming in the kitchen. A sad, slow song she didn't recognize.

"Hello?" she called. "It's Kay Abbott. Hope I'm not late, but—"

She stopped in the kitchen doorway. A slender black woman was vigorously scrubbing the tile countertop. The kitchen looked spotless now. No dust, no pots-and-pans clutter, no dirt. Kay wasn't sure which shocked her more— that, or the realization that one woman had accomplished it in less than an hour.

"Hi. You're Mrs. Woodberry, right?"

"Please, call me Perdita."

"All right. Perdita, the difference in here is amazing. Wonderful. Incredible." The glass-front cabinets were filled with sparkling china. A few polished copper pans hung from a rack over the stove. Blue tile gleamed everywhere.

The other woman's face, which had at first looked a bit melancholy, lit up in a wide smile. She set her sponge on the sink and wiped her hands on a dishtowel. "I always do the kitchen and bathrooms first. To me, they're most important, since people got to eat and ought to wash. Then the bedrooms. Isn't too bad here, considering the time gone by. Lot of dust, though." She shook her head.

"You must have help with you, right?"

"I have a couple others who work for me. But no, this sort of old-house job I like to do myself."

"Oh, I see." Kay nodded, trying not to stare. The real Perdita was so opposite of the one she'd imagined. Almost frail. Skin that looked velvety and smooth as light mahogany. Curly hair cut short. Skinny faded jeans, a white cotton shirt with rolled sleeves, white sneakers. Most amazing, she too appeared spotless, even after all that work. Her subtle herbal scent reminded Kay of fresh-cut flowers. Yet the day was so hot, she herself felt damp and sticky merely standing still.

"Wow. How'd you manage to stay so clean? I just walked through and I'm already smudged."

Perdita laughed. "You know, dirt just rolls right off me. I don't like it, so maybe it doesn't care for me, either."

She took Kay on another tour, explaining what remained to be done. "Tomorrow morning I'll sweep and mop floors. That means more cleaning supplies . . . a mop, vegetable oil soap. Paste wax for the floors and woodwork."

"Sure. That's no problem." Kay felt pleased to be one step ahead for a change. "Of course I have an account at Monk's. I'll get those tomorrow."

"That's fine, Mrs. Abbott."

"Oh, please. Kay."

An uneasy expression flitted across Perdita's face so quickly Kay wasn't even sure she'd actually seen it.

"All right then . . . Kay. I'll have the upstairs finished by Thursday afternoon. If you like, you can move in then. Then I could keep working downstairs."

"That would be great. It's not a bad motel, but I've already memorized every crack in the plaster and pull in the bedspread. It's time to move."

"You'll be much more comfortable here."

"I'm counting on it. Oh, wait. What about sheets, towels, stuff like that? Is there a laundry in town? I guess I should buy some. I brought towels, but I didn't know the sizes of the beds."

Perdita shook her head. "No need." She led the way to a door in the upstairs hall. "Look in there. See?"

The white porcelain knob was cool in Kay's hand. The door creaked open and the scent of cedar filled the hall. She thought of a Murphy chest she still owned, packed with all the sweaters and down comforters she never got to use in Miami.

Perdita reached up and pulled on a string and an unshaded bulb lit the walk-in closet brightly.

"Goodness. It's a whole room lined with cedar." The small space had floor to ceiling shelves stacked with folded linens and towels. Kay touched a white flannel sheet. Soft and clean, not the least bit dusty. Fragrant with the good, clean smell of cut and sanded redwood.

She smiled at Perdita, who was clearly pleased with her discovery. "And Bonnie told me old houses don't seal out dust."

Perdita shrugged. "Guess this room did. It's a good omen. And such a good smell. You don't have to worry about doing laundry, either. There's an old Sears Roebuck wringer washer in the utility room. And a dryer. Not the latest, but they run fine."

"Good. I hate Laundromats. Every pervert in the world always does his wash the same day as me. I'd rather go down to the river and slap my clothes on a rock."

"Not this river, you wouldn't," said Perdita.

Back downstairs, just as they reached the front hall, someone banged on the front door.

"I'll get it." Kay reached the door first and opened it wide, feeling a little more like the homeowner now.

On the porch stood a beefy, red-faced man wearing . . . could that really be a blue leisure suit? Plus a gray pompadour and a grin.

"Miz Abbott? Slocum Blunt, ma'am. Just wanted to apologize about not being there to welcome you to town on Monday. Had out of town business that just wouldn't quit. Know what I mean?" then, to her amazement, he winked.

"Um, sure. Well, would you . . . like to come in?" Somehow she wasn't really sure she wanted him in the house.

"Tickled to." He breezed in past her. "Old place looks better already, and I bet I know why. Hey there, Perdita. Anybody could make this place shine again it's you, honey."

"Afternoon, Mr. Blunt." Perdita's voice had gone flat, as had her expression.

"It's Slocum, honey. You know that. Thinks she has to pretend she knows her place with me."

"I really have got to be going," Perdita said quickly. "My daughter's babysitting in town. I need to pick her up now."

"Oh, sure. Wait a second. I have a new account, but I thought you might prefer cash?"

"That's fine."

Kay got her purse and paid for the day's work. Slocum followed them out onto the front porch.

"See you Thursday afternoon, then," she told Perdita. Now that Blunt was here, she felt reluctant to let the other woman go.

"Yes, ma'am."

"Kay."

A smile tugged at one corner of Perdita's mouth. "Isn't that what I said?" She started down the steps.

"Look here. Believe we're about to have more company." Slocum Blunt shielded his eyes with one hand, watching a slight teenager coming up the drive.

"Perle!" Perdita called. "What're you doing out here? Something wrong?"

The girl laughed and ran the rest of the way up the drive. "Nothing's wrong, Mama." she said, a little out of breath. Uncle Patrick just gave me a ride, on his way to work. Thought I'd surprise you."

"That you did, young lady. What if I'd already left? Then you would've been the one surprised. And in a fix, too."

Perle darted a mortified glance at Kay and Slocum. "Mama, please. I'm not three."

"Well, that's true." Perdita sighed. She turned to Kay. "This is my daughter Perle Woodberry. Perle, Mrs. Abbott. She and her little girl will be staying in Abaton for a while."

"Hey there, Perle." Slocum Blunt said, and whistled. "Sure getting to be a big girl."

"And you know Mr. Blunt, of course," Perdita said stiffly.

"Hey, Mr. Blunt," said Perle, dimples framing her smile.

"We've got to be going now." Perdita said abruptly, turning away. "See you Thursday," she called over one shoulder, pulling Perle along to the car. The engine revved like an angry sewing machine. Wheels spit gravel as she pulled out.

"Fine-looking little lady, there," said Slocum to Kay.

"Yes," Kay agreed reluctantly. "Perdita is an attractive woman."

He frowned. "What? No, I mean the little one. Perle." He rolled the last words on his tongue like hard candy.

Ugh, she thought. "I'll going to lock up and get back to the motel. Thanks for driving all the way out here just to say hello. By the way, how's Bonnie? She was so helpful when we arrived. You're lucky, such a lovely wife."

"Yeah, aren't I though," he said. "Wait one second, I'll check the back door for you."

Kay waited impatiently on the porch. The pine floor boards seemed to shudder as he plodded down the hall to the kitchen door. The back door rattled loudly.

"Something wrong?" she shouted.

He reappeared. "Not a thing. Just checking that lock. An old one, for sure. Young widow, all alone, you don't want nobody sneaking in your back door at night, do you?" He winked again, closing the front door behind him. "But I think she'll hold."

God but his casual lechery annoyed her. "No, I certainly don't. I really hate unexpected company late at night."

Slocum laughed. "Nothin' to worry about, then, is there?"

He followed her down the porch steps and over to her car. Waited while she got in and started it. "Sure was a pleasure," he said.

At least he didn't wink again.

She smiled coldly as Blunt got into his Mercedes. The pale blue paint job almost matched his suit, if you overlooked the clay splashed over wheels and fenders. He must drive it through the woods, she thought.

The diesel engine growled and Slocum made a u-turn, revving the motor ostentatiously. He drove off fast.

Kay sat for a moment, allowing the distance to grow between her and Slocum Blunt. She didn't even want to be near him on the road. "Bonnie Blunt lives with that pig?" she muttered. "Unbelievable."

SEVEN

K ay drove with the windows down, enjoying the resinous scent of sun-warmed pine, the deep blue of the afternoon sky. The temperature had actually fallen below eighty—rare and cool for a summer day in Florida. She pulled into the lot, thinking perhaps she'd invite Myrna out to dinner with them. When she turned the engine off, she heard Chloe. The door to their room was open, and the screams from within sounded hysterical, raising the hairs on her bare arms. She lunged out of the car and sprinted through the door of their room.

Chloe was on the bed, face swollen and red, arms and legs thrashing. She was screaming in fear or pain, but what horrified Kay was the sight of Myrna bending over her daughter, holding her down. The dim glow from the bedside lamp threw grotesque shadows on the wall and shaded Myrna's face into that of a storybook witch.

"Let go of her!" Kay shouted, shoving Myrna away from the bed.

The older woman staggered bask and sat down abruptly across from them, on the other mattress.

"But I didn't—I was only—out by the pool, I heard her scream. Came in and she was havin' a regular fit there. I was afraid she'd hurt herself. Swallow her tongue, fall off or . . . or something. I'm so sorry. Wasn't tryin' to . . . to hurt . . . " A tear trickled down one pink, wrinkled cheek, leaving a glistening trail through her face powder.

Kay tried to listen and also restrain Chloe. How difficult it was to hold her still, gently yet firmly. The piercing screams went on as if she'd never stop.

"Chloe, it's me, honey. You're having a bad dream. Come on, wake up!" Her face was an alarming shade of red. Just as Kay had given up and was about to slap her, Chloe subsided into harsh sobs.

Kay pulled her onto her lap, rocking. "See? You're okay. I'm here. Tell me what scared you, what happened?"

Chloe's sobs diminished to small hiccoughs.

Kay sneaked a guilty look at the motel owner sitting across from them, still wringing her hands. "Myrna, I'm sorry. And . . . so embarrassed. But I heard those screams and just . . . "

Assumed the worst.

Now she felt ashamed of her reaction. What Myrna had said was no doubt true, and she'd only been concerned about Chloe.

Her face grew hot. "I don't know why I shoved you. I'm so sorry."

Then, to her further mortification, her eyes filled and she too began to cry.

An hour later, they were all seated at a picnic table inside the Shady Rest Barbecue, a family-style place halfway between Abaton and the larger town of Marianna. Myrna's suggestion, after Kay had asked her to join them for dinner. It was the best apology she could think of, and as Myrna had promised, the best barbecued shrimp she'd ever tasted.

But it was difficult to keep her mind on food. The scene at the motel kept creeping back. Was Chloe's bad dream reminding her of her own nightmares? And how, for heaven's sake, could a little girl sit and stuff herself with fried oysters so calmly after such a violent outburst?

Between bites of barbecue, Myrna was rattling on about something Minnie had told her about somebody's sister's affair with someone else's husband. " . . . and so then, just when they were checking into the Paradise Fish Camp, the trashiest place in the county—they rent by the half hour—who should be driving by but Reverend Otis Almond from Written Word Holiness. And he saw them there in the parking lot, just as plain."

Really?" Kay murmured, trying to look interested. "What happened?"

"Well ma'am, he called out the little girlfriend at the Wednesday night Bible supper, and do you know what she said?" Myrna paused to take a lusty bite from the rib she'd been stabbing into the air for emphasis.

Kay, thinking about the bad dream Chloe had described, shook herself. "No, what?"

"And right in front of Trey Cotton, he's a deacon, she said it was none of his blessed business and that she guessed she knew what he must be doing driving around a motel parking lot in the middle of the afternoon and it wasn't baptizing motel clerks. She called him . . . Reverend Peeper!"

Kay had to laugh then. "Guess it's hard to keep anything secret in a town small as this."

"Well, yes and no. All the little stuff, like who's stepping out with whom and how often—sure. The whole town knows all that, sometimes before the people involved. Or fills in the parts they don't know. But tell you what."

She leaned closer.

"There's big secrets here too. Stuff that stays a secret to most. Until it doesn't. And then—well. Things happen." She shook her head.

"Things happen," Kay repeated, drawing circles on the damp tabletop with the bottom of her ice tea glass. "Like what? What would be a big secret here? I mean one from long ago, of course," she added, not really wanting to hear anything disgusting about someone she might've just met.

"Now honey, that'd be telling." Myrna winked, reminding Kay for one unpleasant moment of Slocum Blunt. "Truth is, I can't tell you any of that stuff, anyhow."

"Why's that?" Kay asked.

"Because if I knew, then they wouldn't be secrets now, would they?"

"Myrna, leading me on . . . you have no shame."

"Not a lick," she agreed.

Kay turned to Chloe. "You're so quiet. But I see your appetite's still healthy. Now that you've made a piglet of yourself, are you ready to go?" She scrubbed at the girl's milk moustache while Chloe squirmed in protest. "We certainly don't need dessert tonight."

"Right. I don't."

"Aren't you even going to argue a little bit? I better take your temperature when we get back."

"You shouldn't do that, Mom." Chloe looked suddenly serious. "Because there won't be enough room in my mouth for a thermometer and the chocolate bar I hid under my pillow."

"I should've known." She made a grab but Chloe was already skipping away out of reach, to wait for them by the cash register.

**

"Chloe, are you awake?" Kay whispered across the darkened room, a little after eleven.

"Uh-uh."

"Oh. Well, feel like talking in your sleep?"

A muffled giggle. "Want to tell me about your dream. The one that upset you."

A sigh. "I already did."

67

"I know, I know. But now that it's just the two of us."

"But that's all, what I told you before. In my dream I was asleep, too. But someone was there. Out in the hall."

"Which hall, where?"

"Don't know. It was too dark. Maybe back home. Then I got out of bed. But the floor was wrong."

"Wrong how?"

"Cold. And hard. Not carpet like at home. And I went out in the hall. But no one was there. I walked a long, long way, out the door."

"You went outside?"

"Yeah. First I just saw regular stuff. Trees, you know, and . . . and the dark."

"But then you saw . . . something scary. Or someone?"

Chloe hesitated. "Uh-huh. A man. I didn't tell before because I wasn't sure. But—"

"But what? Tell me now."

"It was Daddy. Standing out there in the dark. Waiting, for me. And first I was glad. I ran up to him. His back was turned. And then—"

Her voice was shaking now. Kay got up and knelt beside Chloe's bed. "It's okay, honey. That's enough. Thought it might help to talk about it. But I don't want you all upset again."

In the dark the faint gleam of tears made silvery tracks down Chloe's cheeks. "Mom?"

"What, baby?"

"I understand that Daddy's dead. I used to pretend he could come back. But that's a baby wish?"

"No, Chloe. Not really. I wish the same thing."

She took a shuddering breath. "But I'm not a baby. I even knew that in my dream, before he turned around. That he can't come back." She sighed. "He looked the same, but . . . not the same." She clutched at Kay's arm.

"What, honey?"

"I want to sleep with you tonight."

68

Chin resting on her daughter's head, Kay smiled. Finally, something useful she could do. "Not a problem. Come on."

After they both had settled into Kay's bed, Chloe said, "Mom?"

"Mm-hm?"

"If somebody dead tried really hard, because they really wanted to . . . could they come back? Just for a little bit."

"No." Her tone sounded sharper than she'd intended. "No, baby. Not even for a little while."

After that, Chloe fell asleep almost immediately.

But Kay was still lying awake an hour later, eyes wide, staring into the dark.

EIGHT

Kay put the last of the clean lunch dishes in the drainer and wiped her hands on an old chef's apron found in the linen closet. From the window over the sink she could see most of the back yard.

Chloe sat out beneath an old fig tree whose branches draped to the ground like an arched green canopy, with a book in her lap and the cat under one arm. She was apparently trying to interest Gus in a story. He tolerated literature class for a minute or so, then squirmed free and stalked off, tail twitching. Through the open window she heard her daughter yell, "You stupid boy. It's a good story. You're just too dumb to appreciate it!"

The cat's tail gave a final disparaging twitch before he disappeared beneath a row of azalea bushes.

"You could read it to me," Kay called.

Chloe's sunburned cheeks turned a ruddier shade. "Oh, hi Mom. I was just kidding. I know cats don't like listening to stories."

"Not usually, no. But we could sit out on the sun porch with the book, and have mint tea and cookies."

"Deal." Chloe closed the book and rose to come in.

They'd been living in the house for a week. Things seemed to be going well. Chloe hadn't had another nightmare. Maybe it had simply been too much sun and fried chicken. She still worried her daughter would be lonely, the only child, with only her mother and a cat for company. She'd taken a real interest in the house, though. As soon as they moved in, she'd claimed the front bedroom and set about redecorating, drafting Kay and Perdita to push larger pieces of furniture around, rejecting one arrangement after another, until her sweaty mother finally snapped, "For God's sake, Chloe, make up your mind first. Then we'll move the stuff!"

Unruffled, she'd changed her mind again. Then, when everything was finally satisfactorily in place, she pulled down the flowered cotton drapes. "But what will you use to cover the windows?" Kay asked.

"I don't need curtains. There aren't any neighbors. Anyway, I like to see the tops of the trees. See? There's a bunch of big fat squirrels living in that one."

The argument seemed logical enough, so Kay relented. On their next trip to town, Chloe chose some lavender paint at the hardware store and did a nearly drip-less job of painting the bedroom walls, leaving the trim white. She spent an entire afternoon arranging her stuffed bear collection, her needlework supplies, and her favorite books on tall shelves.

She'd coveted this room as soon as she'd seen its bed: a curved sleigh of carved, light pine. She'd run in, dived onto it, and shouted, "It's just like a boat! We have to take this back home to Miami with us."

Back home. Miami. Kay preferred not to think that far ahead yet.

Making a raid on the linen closet, Chloe had wrinkled her nose at the strong cedar scent. She'd found a Jacob's Ladder quilt, only slightly faded, and spread it on the bed. Then sat down and declared, "OK, now I'm finished."

"I'm impressed," Kay had told her, and meant it. This child had been born with a true sense of style. She sometimes felt dull and sloppy by comparison.

The sound of a horn jerked her back to the present. That would be Bonnie Blunt, bringing Perdita's teenage daughter, Perle. Kay had asked Bonnie to tell more of the family's and the house's history. But Bonnie only shook her head. "History was my worst subject. You better come visit my mama, May Olive Reed, instead. Anything you want to know, she can tell. She never forgets anything," she added, with a slightly martyred sigh.

Kay had also discovered that Oliver the Banker was Bonnie's younger brother. Maybe the old cliché about people in small towns all being related was true.

In any case, Bonnie was now knocking at the front door. So Perle would stay with Chloe while they went visiting.

***

May Olive Reed's pace was an old Florida-style house—a large one-story white clapboard bungalow with a steep tin roof. The veranda was lined with clay pots of begonias, geraniums, and ferns, and one entire side yard was an herb garden. Before Bonnie and Kay reached the porch steps, a tanned, elfish woman with short gray hair flung open the front screen door.

"Bonnie! And you must be Miz Abbott. Come sit on the porch. It's cooler out there. Been baking all morning, and it's Hell's basement in that kitchen."

When she came out to join them, she walked with a cane. It didn't seem to slow her down. She moved quickly to one of the big painted rockers set around the porch. They took others on either side of her.

"Whew! Got to quit firing up that stove in the summer. A fool's errand. Getting too old for the heat." She fanned herself with a creased People magazine. "Bonnie, go get us some ice tea. In the icebox. Blue pitcher. And mind you don't spill it on my clean floor!" she yelled after her. She turned to Kay."I love the girl dearly, but she's the messiest thing."

Bonnie returned with three tall, sweating glasses on a tray. "Now Mama," she said, passing out the drinks and settling back. "I promised Kay you'd tell her all about the house. And the Abbotts."

"All the illustrious relatives I never got to meet." Kay sipped some tea and suppressed a shudder. It was fresh and minty, but sweet as cane syrup.

"Illustrious, pshaw!" exclaimed May Olive. "Ain't no illustrious folks in Abaton. Past or present . . . especially present."

"Now Mama, you know that's not so. What about Lou Ellen Parker? She represented Crane County in the Miss Florida pageant ten years ago. Sang 'I Gotta Be Me' in the talent competition. Swore she'd of won the swimsuit competition if she'd only stuffed her bra like her mama told her to, but—"

May Olive had been tapping the porch floor with her cane and blinking impatiently through this speech. Finally she broke in. "Lot of good it did her. What does she do but up and marry an exterminator from Quincy and start breeding right and left. Any more kids and that husband'll have to start sprayin' for em. Saw her in the Walmart over to Marianna last week, and she's grown a behind like a twenty-dollar mule." She sipped tea, nodding emphatically. "A woman's got to have brains, not boobies, to make something of herself in this world."

"Mama." Bonnie rolled her eyes. "Kay doesn't want to hear about old Lou Ellen's behind, or her boobies."

Kay straightened in her rocker. "Oh, well—sure I do."

"No, no. Tell her about the Abbotts. About your best friend Miss Leilah. You knew all of them. Go on and tell her. She's dying to hear."

73

NINE

hloe got up off the living room floor and tugged at Perle's sleeve. "Hey, let's go outside. I'm tired of watching this show. And if I eat one more Ritz cracker with peanut butter I'll throw up."

Perle Woodberry clicked off *The People's Court* regretfully. Her mother never let her watch it at home, and the auto mechanic from Kansas City had been about to describe the sex-change surgery that'd transformed his life.

"OK. What you want to do instead?"

"Go for a walk. To the river. More fun than sitting here."

Perle frowned. "Uh-uh. Not down there. Your mama doesn't want you near that. It's kinda dangerous. Bet she told you not to go."

Chloe looked down as if suddenly interested in the pattern of the couch upholstery. "She never told me that."

"Well, she must not know much about it, then. It's real deep and runs fast. Plus there's gators. It's not safe for a little kid to play down there."

"But I don't want to go in it. I just want to look at it."

"Oh yeah? Well, it's . . . just . . . like . . . WATER!" Perle lunged, grabbed Chloe, and tickled her.

The younger girl gasped and shrieked.

They fell off the couch and she finally squirmed out of reach.

"No fair! I'm too ticklish. Oh, come on, Perle. Please? We can just take a walk. Not all the way to the stupid river."

"Well . . . we could go down that little path out back. But that's all! Your mama and Mrs. Blunt will be back soon."

Chloe flung a cushion, which bounded off the side of the babysitter's head. "Last one out is a monkey turd!"

She dodged and raced past Perle, then through the kitchen, slamming the back door behind her.

"Girl, your language." Perle rolled her eyes. "What're they teaching kids down in Miami?"

***

The afternoon was locker-room steamy, but once beneath the shadowed coolness of the pines surrounding the Abbott property it was easy to forget the heat. Chloe and Perle scuffed down the winding path, kicking up pine needles in gold, green, and brown.

"So what's so scary about this river?" Chloe asked.

"I didn't say it was scary. I said dangerous." Perle was braiding a pine-needle chain as they walked.

"Okay, then. How come it's so dangerous?"

"You're stubborn like a bulldog, aren't you? All right, I'll tell you. Because people been drowned in it. Grownups. Little kids, too. Looks shallow on the edge, but it's not. There's a big drop-off about three steps in. Current's so fast, it'll carry you all the way to Ibo Key before anybody knows you're gone."

Chloe frowned. "To where?"

"That's where the river ends up, way out to the ocean, in the Gulf of Mexico."

"Oh." Chloe shuffled along silently for a bit, imagining being swept out to sea from her own back yard.

"There." Perle regarded her handiwork with satisfaction. "Put this on." She'd braided a green and brown coronet out of the fallen needles.

"Oh! That's pretty." Chloe held still while Perle fitted it around her head.

"There. Just wait a second." Perle picked a handful of wildflowers from beside the path. "Now you hold real still while I do this."

Chloe obediently held her breath.

Perle deftly wove the blossoms into the headpiece. "The star-shaped one's columbine. Those tiny white flowers are trillium." Then she stepped back to admire the effect. "Cool. You look like a princess in a picture book."

"I want to see!"

"You can look in the mirror when we get back."

"But I don't want to go yet. Let's walk a little more. Then we'll turn around." She took Perle's hand and they continued down the path. "So how many people drowned in this river?"

Perle sighed. "Like a dog with a bone. I don't know! Maybe six or seven. Maybe a hundred. Mama says lots. But then she doesn't want me down there. Because once I saw—well, never mind. I guess really on account of what happened to Lala."

Chloe looked up, confused. "What's a la-la?"

"Lala's not a what. She's my . . . my second cousin, I guess. See, her mama went off and never did come back. Don't know who her daddy is. So Aunt Mattie—well, she's not my aunt, she my mama's aunt, I just call her that—she always took care of her from the day she was born. She's little for her age. And acts kind of silly. Real cute, though. Aunt Mattie calls her Baby Doll."

Chloe's head spun as she tried to take in this convoluted family tree. "But . . . what's all that got to do with dead people in the river?"

"I didn't say there were dead people in the river. I mean, they pull them out and . . . you know. Well, back when Lala was real little she fell in and almost drowned. I was there, but I couldn't reach her. Aunt Mattie heard me screaming. She jumped in and pulled her out and doctored her. Then she was fine. Guess we were lucky, 'cause the same day a little boy disappeared, too. Fell in, I guess, but they didn't know until they found his body. Weeks later, so they weren't sure what happened."

Chloe shivered with a pleasant thrill of fear. "Then what did they do?"

"Buried him, I s'pose."

"We buried my father. In Miami." She was silent for a moment. Then, "Hey, Perle?"

"What?"

"Do you think the river's haunted? I mean, by all the kids who drowned in it?"

"Girl, please! You get the strangest ideas. Now I never did hear of a haunted river. Did you?"

"Well, no. But—"

"But nothing. Maybe, just maybe, there's some haunted houses. But haunted water? Fool!" Perle rapped her knuckles lightly on the top of Chloe's head. Her laughter echoed through the woods.

Chloe flushed hot with embarrassment. She did not like being made fun of by anyone, even an older person. And now, beneath Perle's laugh she could hear another sound. The rush and gurgle of swift-running water. She realized the older girl hadn't noticed yet, but they must be close to the river.

Without a backward glance, she took off down the path, giggling.

"Chloe! What're you doing? You get back here right now!"

Enjoying the note of panic in her babysitter's voice, she ran on.

"I mean it," shouted Perle. "You come back right now, or I'll – "

Chloe glanced back once, and saw her still standing in the middle of the path, hands on hips, as if imitating an outraged mother. Shouting, "You just get yourself right back here, young lady. Wait 'til I get my hands on you!"

Chloe just turned and ran on. The dull thud of shoes on pine needles meant Perle had finally taken her seriously.

"Now don't you make me run after you," Perle gasped.

Chloe dashed on, around a bend.

"Your mama and my mama are both gonna kill me!" Perle shrieked.

Chloe ducked under loops of grapevine, skimming over the ground, heedless of stickers and thorns.

She burst out of the woods into a clearing, and skidded to a stop.

A few inches past the scuffed rubber toes of her purple Sketchers, the bluff dropped steeply away to a churning rush of water the color of Coca Cola.

When something white nearby flashed out of the reeds she gasped and nearly went over the edge.

An egret took flight, flapping away ponderously as a giant wind-up toy over the water.

Chloe laughed a little shakily and looked down at the water again. She couldn't remember ever seeing a river as big and wild as this one. The water dark as tar, with silver foam here and there, it gave back a such a pretty reflection of sky and trees you almost forgot the night-color at its heart.

Back in Miami there'd been the ocean, but this was different. No crowds of sweaty people in bathing suits. No regular blue waves pushing rafts and surfboards. No people at all. No hotels or beach houses. Just silent, green, insect-clicking woods. Old crooked oaks dripping with Spanish moss. Swirling muddy water below, strange birds above. And just now, a faint splash Chloe imagined must be an alligator. All of this was practically in her new back yard. Almost like it belonged to her.

Used to be my father's, she thought. Now it's all mine. Well, mine and Mom's.

Out in the middle, drifting in the current, there came a small red skiff with two men in it. She raised an arm and they both waved back.

She suddenly felt generous. "It's my river, but you can use it!" she called.

But they didn't answer. She guessed her words had gotten lost in the roar and splash of the water.

A moment later Perle charged out of the trees, nearly colliding with her. They clung together for one terrible breathless moment, teetering on the edge of the bluff. Chloe recovered her balance first and ran away again along the bank, jumping cypress roots, dodging vines.

"Come on, catch me!"

"You are crazy!" Perle shouted after her. "There's water moccasins in those trees!"

Chloe slowed a bit. "You mean, like, snakes?"

"I'm not chasing after you anymore," Perle added, folding her arms, scowling. "Now get your tail back here before one of us gets in big trouble."

Chloe whooped and hollered her way back along the bank, flowery crown falling over one eye. She darted back into the trees again, away from the water and snakes. "OK, I'm not running any more. I'm tired! Just one game of hide and seek, then we can go back. I'm hiding now. You come find me."

"Uh-uh," Perle said. "I'm not playing any more games. You don't play fair."

"I'm no cheater! If you find me, I'll come out and we can go home. Okay?"

Perle sighed loudly, a sound that Chloe knew often preceded a personal victory for her.

"But as soon as I find you, we go back. Or else I'll have to just leave you for the gators!"

Chloe squealed. Now that was more like it. She squirmed deeper into the huge clump of wisteria chosen as her first hiding place. Perle's footsteps were already crunching into the woods. She went the wrong way, Chloe thought smugly. She shifted to squat in a more comfortable position, and a cobweb brushed her face, tickling her nose.

"Oh, gross." She swatted it away, rubbing at her face. But her nose itched and her eyes began to water. If she made noise now, the game would be over. She clamped both hands over her face to contain the coming sneeze.

Footsteps crackled over dry needles, right toward her. She held her breath, squeezed her eyes shut, and thought: Go away, go away!

The steps circled, stopped, then moved away.

Safe.

Just then something touched her shoulder from behind. Chloe screamed, sneeze forgotten.

"No fair, Perle. You tricked me." She turned to stick out her tongue, but the face looking back through the leaves was small and dark, not Perle's.

"What . . . who are you?"

The little girl giggled. She stuck one pudgy finger in her nose.

Chloe lost her fright. "Eew. Don't do that. It's not nice."

Now she felt grumpy, ashamed she'd been scared silly by such a little girl.

The child giggled again. She removed the finger and clasped both hands behind her back. Her large brown eyes stared without blinking.

"It's not polite to stare, either," said Chloe.

The little girl pulled a branch aside and came in to squat next to her on dirty, sandal-clad feet. Her striped sundress rode up so high Chloe saw white cotton underpants.

"You shouldn't sit like that in a dress. Boys can see your panties. I'm Chloe. What's your name?"

The girl's grin exposed a gap where two front teeth were missing. She tugged at the hem of her sundress, but didn't answer.

Chloe frowned. "What's the matter, don't you have a name?"

"Lala," the child lisped.

"I hear you now, Chloe," Perle's voice called triumphantly. "Now, who you talking to, yourself? I am never gonna take you for a walk again as long as I—oh! There you are."

Chloe squirmed out of the wisteria-choked bush and stood, brushing at her shorts and tee shirt. Perle stooped to help, slapping at her back and sides until Chloe cried, "Ouch, not so hard!"

"Sorry, but we better hurry. Your mama and Mrs. Blunt are probably back, wondering where we are. Come on now, let's run."

Chloe pulled back against Perle's grip. "But what about Lala?"

"What about her? I already told you what happened."

"No." Chloe dug in her heels harder. "I mean I just talked to her. She crawled in with me to hide. Maybe we better take her home first."

Perle cocked her head and stared. "What are you talking about? Aunt Mattie wouldn't let that child come out here all by herself."

"She is, too. I just talked to her. She's still hiding. Hey you, Lala! Come on out."

No answer.

Chloe pulled at the branches, trying to peer into the dim interior of the bush. "But— I don't see her." She looked back, bewildered.

Perle sighed. "'Course you don't see her. She's not there! Now come on, I'm tired of your tricks. Let's go."

"But . . . " Chloe's lower lip trembled. "She was there. I talked to her, Perle. I did!"

"Oh, all right. I'll look inside this stupid bush and show you. I'm telling you she can't be in there."

Perle knelt and pulled back some branches, peering into the tangled depths. "See—nobody."

"But Perle!"

"Okay, okay. Lord, I don't believe I'm doing this." She squeezed further into the leafy maze. "Ouch! Now I got a sharp stone in my knee. Okay, I'm right in the middle and there's nobody here but me."

"Are you sure?"

"Am I sure," Perle muttered indignantly. "All I see is a orange and white crab spider. Talk about ugly." Perle scrambled out of the bush on her hands and knees, shuddering. "I can't stand it when they start rocking the web like that."

Chloe was jumping impatiently. "Did you see her, did you?"

"I looked, Chloe," she snapped, brushing dead leaves and cobwebs from her hair. A thin trickle of blood threaded down her left knee. "There was nobody in there. Just one big ugly spider. Now I'm a sorry mess, too. I should throw you in that river myself."

"She ran away, then," Chloe said. "But she was there. She had on a little striped dress, and white sandals, and . . . and no front teeth!"

Perle stopped in mid-brush and looked at Chloe sharply. "I told you that," she said uncertainly. "Now look here. You been running around like a stone fool in the sun. No wonder you're seeing things. Let's get you home before you get heat frustration."

"But Perle—"

"No buts, girl. Mind me now." She collared and herded her back up the path. Chloe went reluctantly, looking back over her shoulder for a flash of white panties or a gap-toothed grin. Finally she shook off Perle's grip. "I'm coming, I'm coming," she muttered. "And I did too see her," she whispered to herself.

TEN

May Olive Reed was still warming to the subject of the Abbott ancestry as she rocked with Kay and Bonnie on her front porch.

"Me and Leilah Abbott was good friends. As good a friend as you could be, at least, to Leilah."

"What do you mean?" asked Kay.

"Now don't get me wrong, sugar. I probably loved her better than anybody else in town. But Leilah Eugenie wasn't a warm person. Lots of folks thought she was mean. Why, she had no more meanness in her than my old tomcat. She was stiff, true. But that wasn't her fault. Raised that way, you know. Her daddy being so old-fashioned. A rich old tobacco planter."

Bonnie looked surprised. "I thought he was just a drunk, Mama."

"That was later." May Olive frowned at her daughter. "But first he was a tobacco man with, oh, a thousand acres. A place so big it ran almost to Pleasantville. 'Course, he'd invested in Coca-cola stock, like lots of other folks around here. Town banker, Slocum's grandaddy, wouldn't loan anybody a nickel 'til they did. They grumbled and thought it was a big risk back then. But Lord did they feel good about it later."

"Anyhow, he was a poor old boy who made himself a rich old man. They're the worst kind. He only had the one girl, Leilah, and he was determined she'd be a real lady. Not shame him or his money. The mama died of consumption when Leilah was just a baby, so she was raised by the hired help. Then he sent her to finishing school in Atlanta, like Scarlett O'Hara in the movies. But before that, she went to school here in town. That's when we got to be friends."

"If you knew her when she was young, you must've known Jack's father. And all the relatives after that?"

"Sure did. I was there the night Leilah met her husband. It was all on account of the tent revival."

"You mean . . . one of those religious shows in a circus tent?" Kay blurted out, then blushed, hoping she hadn't offended May Olive.

The older woman guffawed and slapped her knee. "Circus is good a word as any. That's what Leilah's father called it. And worse! Said no daughter of his would be seen at such a thing. But she was tired of her daddy always pulling on the reins. Had a mind of her own, even then. Made me promise to help sneak her out of the house to go. Not that either of us was devout, you understand." The tanned skin around May Olive's blue eyes crinkled in laugh lines. "It was just something to pass the time."

"Mama, you were such a devil!" Bonnie laughed, spilling tea in her lap. "Ooh, darn it."

"Maybe it was the devil." May Olive handed Bonnie a napkin absently. "But out we went anyway, through the window of her room and down the old magnolia tree. We like to burst, trying not to giggle or rustle those leathery leaves. Neither one of us cared the least bit about bein' saved. It was an adventure. At least to me that's all. So we run off in the dark, giggling like ninnies, to the scandalous tent show.

"It was that, all right. Reverend Nathan Shivers was a Primitive Baptist. Oozing hellfire and damnation out every pore and handsome as a gypsy. It was early March, still airish out, but that preacher had already worked up a sweat by the time we got there. He was struttin' back and forth in front of the crowd like a barnyard rooster. You could smell the sulfur in the air.

"I leaned over to Leilah and said, 'Don't he remind you of my mama's old Rhode Island Red?'

"But one look at her and I knew she wouldn't laugh like she usually did. It was plain she was took—just that fast. She never pulled her eyes off him. Not for one second.

"Well, that was trouble. She was almost eighteen, but her daddy had yet to allow her on a date even with a town boy they knew. He'd kill her dead afore he'd see her take up with a traveling preacher with nothing to his name but a tent, a piano, and a hell machine."

Kay blinked. "A what?"

"A lantern-show with a Victrola for sound effects. Slide pictures of sin, destruction, Sodom and Gomorrah, Judas Iscariot, New York City, and such as that. Played records of screechy music, sounds of people moanin' and groanin'. And all of it glowing red like a sunrise in Gehenna."

Bonnie snickered into her glass.

"It was right scary back then, miss! Folks cried and screamed and shook and prayed. Women fainted right in the aisle. Men too."

"A lot of people came to see these shows?" Kay asked skeptically.

"Why, sure. Weren't any picture show here. No television or video games and such. Of course not everybody went. Big shots like old Mr. Abbott sure didn't. Mostly cracker farmers, sharecroppers and their wives. Turpentine workers all dressed up in their Sunday best. And all the black folks, just about. At that time they had to sit in back, separate. They made the most noise, though there was plenty of carrying on from all sides."

"Tell her what they do at those revivals, Mama." Bonnie leaned over to pick up Brothercat, May Olive's fat arthritic old tom, who'd just brushed by her legs. "She's from the city, up north."

"I'm getting to that part," her mother replied crossly. "Just give me a minute." When she gulped tea, beaded moisture from the outside of the glass dripped down the front of her cotton dress. She sighed and patted her mouth delicately with a linen napkin.

"I recall they'd already sung 'The Old Rugged Cross' and 'Jesus Is Coming Tomorrow.' The lantern-show was over and the preacher was hollering about how Tallahassee was the Sodom and Gomorrah of north Florida, what with the crooked politicians, godless liquor stores, short skirts at the girls' college, and all the Ford cars with fold-down back seats. I was a bit put out with that, since my daddy had just bought us a new Ford.

"I can still see that man a-yelling and sweating. One lock of long black hair kept fallin' over his eyes. His shirt was unbuttoned well-nigh to his th—"

"Mama," said Bonnie hastily. "Too much information."

"Well, I guess he saw his words were having a prime effect. He called on all the sinners and backsliders to come up and repent. Two colored women in the back got up, but one fell out right there in the aisle. Rolling on the ground, grinding her teeth, speaking in tongues. Or so Shivers said. Sounded like gibberish to me. But somebody shouted, "It's a sign!' Then people jumped up right and left, marched on up like a flock of sheep.

"I looked over and like to died. Darned if Leilah wasn't gettin' up too. I grabbed hold of her arm and set her back down in the folding chair. Well, ma'am, she give me a look that chilled my bones. Like she didn't know me and would be pleased to kill me if I didn't let go. Then she threw off my hand and went right on up with the others.

"She pushed her way through the sharecroppers and farmers wives, right to the front. Planted herself bold as brass before Shivers. He bent and took her hand, like he'd done with those who'd come up first. I couldn't hear what he was saying, but I saw how he looked. Like he was the collection plate and she was the offering.

"Leilah wore a pale blue linen dress bought in Atlanta. Hand-embroidered, with these little flower cutouts. Her red-gold hair was loose and curled. She was like a painting that night, one of them Leonardos. And he was takin' it all in—especially the big diamond lavaliere that'd been her mama's. He knew she wasn't no farmer's daughter. He was counting her up with his eyes. Made me afraid of what would happen next.

"Eventually she came and set back down. We went home together and on the way I tried to laugh and talk, like always, but she was somewhere else. Climbed back up the magnolia to her open window without saying another word. Next night I stayed home, but all that week she sneaked out and went back. I know, because she told me later.

"I saw her the last day of the revival. She told me that the night before, this preacher-man Shivers—only now she called him Nathan—had healed two people. 'With his divine gift,' if you please! 'He's going to be a great man, May,' she said. 'He has a calling.' May Olive snorted. 'But that was just so much twaddle. I knew what his `divine gift' was, and it hung right between his—"

"Jesus, Mama!"

"Well, that's the truth, if you want to hear it," May Olive said primly. "and I'll thank you not to take the Lord's name in vain on my front porch."

"And what happened?" Kay asked. "After that."

"She'd tried to have him to dinner earlier in the week, but her daddy said he'd fill his butt and his bible full of buckshot if he stepped into the front yard. Leilah argued and cried and said he was ruining her life. But Mr. Abbott never gave a hoot for women's tears. So, on the last night the show was in town, Leilah sneaked out for the last time with one packed grip, and a wad of her daddy's money. She left Abaton with her preacher."

"They eloped?" Kay exclaimed. "But . . . but she must've come back. She raised my husband here, later."

"Oh, she came back. Three months after, wearing a cheap black dress. Telling how her husband—for they'd got married in Augusta, she claimed—had took sick and died of pneumonia. Her daddy had gone half-crazy when she left, so he took her back in. She was all he had. And six months later, she had a baby. A little boy."

"Jack's father. But if she married this Shivers guy, why wasn't that Jack's last name, instead of Abbott?"

"Old Mr. Abbott took her in, but on one condition. She had to change her name back to Abbott. And when the baby was born, she had to call it an Abbott, too. Especially if it was a boy. Oh, and she could never mention Nathan Shivers' name again. To her father, her son, or anyone else. That way the old man got an heir, preserved the family name, and erased that preacher like he'd never existed."

"Three birds with one stone," Bonnie said admiringly. "Tough old bastard."

"That's right. But a few months later, old man Abbott took sick, and pretty soon died. Doctor said it was a wasting disease. But I believe he died of a broken heart."

"Why would his heart be broken?" said Kay. "He got his daughter back. And a grandson."

"But Leilah wasn't the girl he remembered. She'd become a grown woman with a sharp tongue and a thick skin. Except for the conditions he put on her return, he couldn't tell her what to do anymore. Nobody knows what really went on in the house after that, except the servants, and they were all close-mouthed. But Leilah bloomed, while her daddy took up drink and declined. Just stopped eating one day, shriveled up like a dried cornstalk, and died."

"And running off with a preacher, then being widowed changed her so much?"

"She was always stubborn, but then she realized how far she could go. Most people believed the story about the dead husband. Or were smart enough to pretend so, since a lot of 'em worked for the Abbotts. But some didn't believe, and of course they were right.

"I talked to Leilah after she'd just come back, before she knew if her daddy would even see her. She was scared silly, because then there'd be nowhere to go. She was in such a state, she let the real story slip out."

"You mean they weren't really married?" Bonnie squeezed the cat so hard he squalled. "You never told me that before."

"Well, they ain't your relatives. No need to know. See, Leilah thought they were. They'd had a ceremony before a justice of the peace in Augusta. Then traveled on, through Atlanta, on up to Charleston.

"But on their third night there, after the tent show, a woman came up to the trailer. She banged on the door and Leilah let her in. Sometimes people would turn up after to witness or make donations. But when Nathan Shivers saw this skinny little woman standing there he went pale and sick-looking. Leilah said the woman started whining at him about desertion and children and support. But she didn't believe it 'til the other woman pulled out a marriage license and pictures of five pasty brats from her wallet. Nathan Jr. was the very spit and image of him.

"They argued and Leilah left. The first wife stayed. Shivers tried to make Leilah stay too, but she slapped him and spit in his face. 'He made me his whore, and a cheap one, too,' she said. That's the only time in our lives I ever saw her cry.

"They'd spent all the money Leilah brought, so she sold her mother's diamond necklace for enough to get home by train. She'd suspected her condition earlier. By the time she got off the train in Tallahassee, she was sick as a dog and sure of it.

"At first she didn't know what to do. Then, seeing a couple of widows traveling alone, waiting in the station, she hit on that idea. She liked it—especially the part about Nathan being dead. Had a lot more appeal than going back and looking for a bigamist, since she didn't want him anyway by then. Or telling her daddy she'd been ten kinds of fool. So that was her story."

"Then she had a baby boy, her crotchety old daddy died, and she had the place to herself. She was surely no dummy." Bonnie's eyes glittered. Kay wondered what was behind that look of smug satisfaction.

"Indeed she wasn't. Ran that farm better than any man ever had—and enjoyed it. But she loved that baby more than anything. And then, after the accident—'

"I know about that," Kay broke in. "Jack told me about the train, how it hit his parents' car, and—well." She shrugged. "He never really knew them. Only his grandmother. Leilah."

May Olive gave her a puzzled look. "The car . . . well, I . . . anyhow, she loved him just as much as she had his father. Too much, I suppose. They say on the talk shows these days that's not healthy. I don't know. I think she meant to keep him to herself. Though of course in the end she couldn't."

"Oh my lord, will you look at the time!" Bonnie gasped just then. "I promised Perdita I'd have Perle home by four. We really got to run." She jumped up, dumping a startled Brothercat on the porch floor.

"Of course," said Kay, though she felt disappointed to leave the story hanging there. "Mrs. Reed, I enjoyed the family history. It's fascinating."

"You'll have to come back soon to hear the rest. Just any time at all, hear? And stop being formal. Call me May Olive. Then I won't feel so old. Bonnie, mind you don't step on that cat again."

"He gets underfoot!" Bonnie complained, but she kissed her mother goodbye. "What are you doing tonight, Mama?" she called back up, before she and Kay got into the car.

"Your baby brother is bringing an old friend to supper. Now what's his name . . . Tony, that's it. The musician. Such a polite young man. Too bad he wears those skin-tight pants. You and Slocum are welcome, too."

Bonnie rolled her eyes. "You know how he gets around Oliver's friends. Some other time, Mama."

"Oliver's or anyone else's," May Olive shot back.

"Oh Mama, you're a mean one." Bonnie laughed and slipped into the driver's seat. She glanced at Kay as she was backing out. "Might as well tell you right now, my little brother is as gay as the day is long. Mama doesn't have a clue."

"Would it matter?" asked Kay.

"Probably not. But Slocum, he's kind of . . . well, funny . . . about that sort of thing." Her eyes clouded as she turned out onto the highway, but she said nothing more about it.

ELEVEN

Kay worked all through the next morning on illustrations, until she got hungry and realized it was past time for lunch. She frowned and set aside the fine sable brush she'd been using. Where was Chloe and what had she been doing all this time? She went to the window and squinted out against the harsh early afternoon sun.

Her daughter was nowhere in sight.

Or no—there she was, crouched in the shadow of a camellia bush, back bent in concentration, hands busy in the rich black dirt, apparently unfazed by the moist, sticky heat. Angus lay at a safe distance, his look of disinterest betrayed by the twitching tip of his tiger-striped tail.

Mud pies, Kay thought. Thought we were past that stage. Shaking her head, she returned to her makeshift drawing board on the dining room table. Watercolor tubes, chalk, and Conté pencils were heaped in pastel confusion on the oak tabletop. The portable easel she'd packed into the Volvo's trunk now held the third sketch she'd completed this week. She eyed it with mixed feelings. A rosy-cheeked girl in Elizabethan dress stooping to stroke the arched back of a tabby cat. A formal English flower garden and a carved stone bench formed a misty background.

The galley sheet for the book's facing page read:

I love little pussy,
Her coat is so warm,
And if I don't hurt her,
She'll do me no harm.
So I'll not pull her tail,
Nor drive her away,
But pussy and I
Together will play.

She'd given the child Chloe's red-brown curls and hazel eyes, but had decided against Angus as a model, instead making it a grey tabby. She wasn't entirely satisfied with that cat, though. Did he need longer whiskers, a kink in the end of his tail?

She yawned. What I need is more coffee, she thought. So tired . . .

She returned from the kitchen with a turquoise Fiestaware mug from the Depression-era set that had probably been Leilah Abbott's everyday dishes. In front of the drawing once more, she sipped and made a disgusted face. The pot had been on since early morning. "The lazy woman's espresso," she muttered. "Ugh." And set it aside.

She gazed idly at the sketch until the lines began to blur. What were her friends back in Miami doing this morning? Making plans for dinner. Working at well-planned careers. Driving their kids to softball and gymnastics and pottery class. With the exception of Mike and Annelise, all had ceased to call or visit after the first few weeks of her widowhood. As if they blame me, she thought. As though I carelessly misplaced Jack somewhere. Or perhaps they feared loss was contagious. Well, she didn't want to be a spare part at dinner parties. Anyhow, she still had her work, a beautiful daughter, her own home.

Homes, she amended. No husband . . . but if Jack were still alive, the odds were they'd have divorced eventually.

She sat her mug on the table abruptly, shocked. But it was true. And so things would have ended the same. Almost.

She knew what Annelise would say. She'd laugh as she attached another heart-stopping price tag to some new metallic, silk, and plastic creation. And tell Kay that it had been long enough. "Time to meet someone."

But she had been certain she didn't want to Meet Someone, back in Miami. It was too soon, and anyhow that took time and energy she simply didn't have to spare right now. She shuddered, remembering the crowded bars in the Gables and the Grove. Could she see herself at such a place, cozying up to some slick lawyer in an Armani suit and enough gold to sink a scuba diver?

Maybe she'd tell Annelise she'd met a nice farmer here. That should keep her at bay a while. Though Annelise was married to a very nice attorney.

Mike Delgado had been Jack's best friend as well as his lawyer. Kay missed all three of them now.

Her phone rang shrilly, and the watercolor girl and cat jumped back into focus. Funny if that's Annelise, she thought, rising. It would be just like her to call on daytime rates.

She picked up the cell. "Hello?"

Beneath the brushfire pop of static she heard a male voice. Definitely not Annelise. "Sorry, you're breaking up. We have a terrible signal here. Try calling back," she shouted.

" . . . hang up . . . wait . . . second . . . An . . . back!" Then just the crackling. She shrugged and punched END.

It rang again immediately. "Hel-lo."

"It is you! Hear all that noise? Thought I'd dialed the wrong number."

95

"Mike!" The next best thing to Annelise. "I was just thinking about Annelise. And you, of course."

"I always knew you guys had something going on. So go ahead. Rub it in. Taunt the deceived husband. How are things in the north forty? Miss the crowded beaches, the drugged vagrants, the surfing South Americans? You can tell Uncle Mike."

Kay laughed. "None of the above. I kind of like it here. For now. It's different."

"I'll bet."

"So, what's the occasion? Have you discovered a rival heir to the Abbott estate?"

No reply.

"Mike? I was kid—"

He huffed a slow breath. "Well, as a matter of fact, I am calling about the will, Kay. There's sort of a . . . problem. We need to do something about it right away."

"What . . . did I forget to sign something?"

"No. Nothing that easy. It seems that, well, a few days ago . . . "

She wished people would stop trying so hard to spare her feelings and just act . . . normal. "Come on, Mike. Spit it out."

"There's actually another will. Not Jack's. This one was made by his grandmother. Leilah Abbott? I never saw it until day before yesterday. Wasn't part of the papers and stuff he kept here in the safe. And he never mentioned it. Of course, he couldn't have known it would matter so soon."

"Please, Mike. Cut to the chase. You're killing me."

"Hobdy, Kirby, and Hamby, a firm in Tallahassee, sent it down. They were notified by the realty office in Abaton that you were taking possession. The firm thought we should have the original of Mrs. Abbott's will, which was kind of embarrassing, since we didn't even have even a photocopy or a digital file to begin with. So I get this will,

read it, and find out that the old lady—your grandmother-
in-law—put some peculiar conditions on her grandson's
inheritance."

"What sort of conditions?"

"Apparently old Mrs. Abbott was some sort of Mrs.
Havisham wannabe. In the will she deeds all her property
and other assets to her grandson, Jacob Parker Abbott, with
these stipulations, and I quote: 'For possession of the
described inheritance, said heir must reside in the domicile
on the property, or failing that, must be interred at Abaton
after his death.'"

"What?" She pulled the phone away from her ear to
stare at it. "Are you serious?"

"The old lady definitely was. Unless one of these two
conditions is met, then Jack no longer has a claim to the
inheritance. Which means it's not his to will to you and
Chloe. Leilah the Terrible had some other provision here to
cover that occurrence. Let's see. . . " She heard papers
rustle furiously. "Where the—oh yeah. Here it is. 'In the
event that said conditions remain unfulfilled, the properties
described herein, the buildings, and their furnishings, shall
be deeded to the township of Abaton, to use for the public
good.'"

She felt as if she were hearing his voice from a much
greater distance than Miami. For instance, hell.

"But—I don't believe it. This can't be legal. How can
some dead woman—a stranger—make me dig up Jack and
have him hauled seven hundred miles just to bury him
again? That's insane!"

"Please, Kay. Try to calm down. You don't have to
worry, I can make all the arrangements. You won't have to
deal with any of it. It's awful, but even stranger things than
this happen."

She paced back and forth in front of the dining table.
"What if I refuse?"

"Then you'd lose. It might take months of litigation, but in the end you and Chloe would lose the house, the inheritance. Or at least be liable for a sizeable cash settlement to the town. And you don't have that much money. I should know. No doubt this all sounds wild to you, but I checked the statutes, case law, everything. It's perfectly legal to put conditions on an inheritance. Of course, we can't violate the rule against perpetuities, but—"

"What does that mean?"

"Well . . . say you inherit some property from a long-lost relative, and later on you sell it. But the will says the property can only be deeded to family members for all time. Forever. That's not legal, because it doesn't set a time limit on that condition. It would affect the property and its heirs for all eternity. Any conditions imposed must have a specific time limit in which they can be fulfilled . . . here, listen to this: ' . . . the vesting of the title of any estate cannot be postponed, upon a condition precedent, for a longer time than the life or lives of persons in existence at the creation of the estate, and twenty-one years thereafter.' But Leilah Abbott's condition placed on the transfer of the property could've been fulfilled during Jack's lifetime, or right at his death, so it doesn't violate that rule. Like I said, and I wish it wasn't true, this is perfectly legal."

"But we'll have to go through the whole awful thing, the funeral, everything . . . all over again."

"No. We'll do it low key. I'll make all the arrangements, talk to the cemetery people here, the local authorities there."

"And I suppose you'll explain it all to Chloe?" She found she was crying, and brushed the tears away angrily.

"If you really want me to," he said uncertainly. "But . . . but she should probably hear it from you."

"Yes. I know, I know. I'm sorry. You're right." She fumbled awkwardly at a roll of paper towels by the sink.

"It's just . . . I thought we were finished with all that. And now you tell me it's not really over."

"A shock, I know. A goddamn fucking mess. Pardon my language. And please don't cry. If 'Lise finds out I made you cry, my life will be worth nada. Don't worry about Chloe. Kids are tough. Still young and energetic enough to bounce back. Unlike us old folks."

"I suppose." She felt sick and empty enough for both of them, at the moment. "So . . . what exactly have I got to do right now?"

"Just relax. I'll call back after I've made the arrangements. I'll make it as easy as possible. You don't even have to be there. Take a weekend trip and I'll have it all done when you get back."

"Relax," she said bitterly. "Forgive me if I sound ungrateful, Mike. I'm just . . . in shock."

"I'd be surprised if you weren't. Think nothing of it. We law dogs are used to having scorn heaped on our heads."

She managed a faint, obligatory chuckle. "Goodbye, Mike. Tell Annelise I'll call her."

Back at the table again, she stared listlessly at the sketch. Rotten picture. Girl looks mental. Cat looks stuffed. The child's smirking mouth was crooked, her eyes crossed. Even the flowers were stupid. Overblown. Like a gaudy display at a tasteless funeral.

She snatched up the heavy Morilla board and tore it across. Once, twice, three times. Dropped the pieces on the table and rested her hot forehead on the cool oak surface. It felt good. *Maybe I'll just stay like this forever.*

"Shit," she said.

A muted giggle.

Kay jerked her head up.

Chloe stood in the kitchen doorway, one filthy bare foot resting on top of the other. Dirt smudged her nose, cheeks, elbows, and tee-shirt. Her knees and lower legs were absolutely black.

"Hi, Mom. Look what I found." Chloe held out a tiny, stiff grey bundle. A dead field mouse.

Kay swallowed a shriek. "Chloe—"

But then another child, doll-like in her smallness, hair braided with red yarn, peeped around from behind Chloe. The giggler.

Chloe rubbed at her face, distributing the dirt more evenly. She glanced down at the smaller girl. "Oh, yeah. This is Lala. What's for lunch? Can she stay and eat with us?"

***

"All right, girls. Let's graze." Kay turned from the stove with a steaming pan of chicken and stars soup in one hand, and a wooden ladle in the other. I'll be cheerful now, she thought grimly, and tell her later. Much later, after her little friend's gone home. No sense ruining their afternoon. She spooned soup into green and blue bowls and set them on scrubbed pine.

In a burst of giggles, Chloe and Lala tumbled together out of the tiny bathroom off the kitchen. Her daughter held out a pair of somewhat cleaner hands, shaking off water drops.

"Chloe." Kay raised one eyebrow. "Dogs do that. People use towels."

"Sorry." She looked meek, but still on the brink of giggles.

"Now, let's sit down. There are tuna sandwiches—toast with no crust, Chloe. The soup's real hot, so be careful. And to drink . . . what would you li—" Kay stopped, staring at Lala. "What's wrong?"

Chloe looked over, too. The other little girl was standing in the middle of the kitchen, lower lip pushed out in an exaggerated pout. She held the hem of her short blue sundress away from her body with both hands stiffly, as if the material were on fire. "No good," she lisped solemnly, shaking her head.

"Why, what's the matter? Is there something wrong with your dress?" Kay knelt in front of the frowning girl.

Lala pulled the dress out even further. "See?"

"There's really nothing there. Just a few spots of water."

Another head-shake. "No good."

"Oh, water!" said Chloe. "She hates to get wet. Won't do anything until it dries." She smiled at Lala with the affectionate disdain of an older sister.

Lord, what next, thought Kay. "No problem. I'll just put it in the dryer for a minute. Mind if I—" She touched the hem.

With a shriek of delight, Lala jerked the dress over her head and let it fall. In white cotton panties, pigtails bouncing, she climbed up nimbly into a chair and inspected her quartered sandwich.

Startled, Kay lost her balance and sat down hard. After a stunned moment, she laughed. "So, a topless lunch. Sit, Chloe. I'll be right back."

When she returned from the laundry room, her daughter was eating her sandwich. Lala was stirring lazy circles in the soup. "Everything all right?" Kay said brightly as she took the remaining place at the table.

Chloe nodded.

"Well, Lala. So nice to meet you. Where do you live?"

The little girl turned a gap-toothed smile on Kay. "Gamma."

"She lives with her grandmother. Over that way." Chloe gestured vaguely at the line of trees visible from the kitchen window.

Kay nodded. The child seemed young to be out wandering the neighborhood—such as it was—on her own. Maybe she'd better call her family. "What's your grandmother's name?"

"Gamma," Lala repeated patiently.

"It's Mattie . . . Mattie something." Chloe lowered her sandwich. "She's related to Perle. Well, sort of. Her grandmother is Perle's old-aunt." She frowned. "I mean, great-aunt."

Lala lifted the top of her sandwich and eyed the filling. She touched a finger to the mayonnaise, then put it in her mouth.

"It's just tuna salad." Kay smiled encouragingly, taking the child's hesitation for suspicion, or a dislike of fish. "Tuna and mayonnaise, plain. Whole wheat bread. Nothing else. Don't you like tuna?"

Lala looked over at Chloe, as if for advice. "Like tuna," she repeated agreeably.

"Oh, she likes it all right." Chloe shrugged and started on her soup.

"That's good," Kay said doubtfully. As far as she could tell, the child hadn't eaten a bite. And she'd just noticed a faint, peculiar odor. Spoiled-fruit sweet, musty. Unpleasant. Surely Lala was housebroken? She looked far too old for diapers.

Then, feeling rude for staring, she looked away, swallowed a spoonful of soup, and gasped. Too hot. She quickly sipped some tea, wondering why this small child made her feel so uncomfortable.

"Hey, Mom," said Chloe suddenly. "What's a root . . . a root doctor?"

"An herbalist. A sort of . . . unofficial doctor who uses plants and flowers and bark and things to make medicines. Not a regular doctor. Why?"

"That's what Lala said her grandma is. And that she does Hoodoo. So is she a . . . a Hoo-dist?"

Kay frowned. "She must've meant Buddhist, honey. You know, like your friend Mai, back in Miami?" She turned back to Lala, who was climbing down now, rocking the chair precariously. "Finished? Hope you had enough." The sandwich lay dissected but uneaten on the plate.

102

"'Nough to eat." She returned Kay's smile with the same gap-toothed grin. It was pretty cute. "Like tuna."

"Well, good. I—"

"I'm done too, Mom." Chloe pushed her chair back. "Can, I mean *may* we please go back outside?"

"I don't know . . . I've got to go to town in a bit. To the post office. And do a few other errands. Could you try to stay a little cleaner this time?"

"Yes, ma'am. I promise."

"What're you guys doing out there anyhow, to get so dirty—making mud pies?"

"No! That's baby stuff. We're making frog houses."

"Frog houses? You mean, houses for frogs?"

"Yes," she said slowly and patiently. "You put your foot in a shallow hole in the dirt and then pack mud all around it. Then you pull your foot out. Real slow, so the roof won't cave in. That's a frog house. After dark, frogs come to live in them. Mothers and fathers. Whole families. That's what Lala's grandmother told her."

"Well then, it must be true." She ruffled her daughter's glossy brown curls. "But finish the housing development another day, all right? Otherwise I'll have to wash you and put you in the dryer with—oh, Lala, wait. Your dress!"

The little girl was almost out the kitchen door, still in just underpants.

"Wait a minute. You can't go out like that." Kay dashed into the laundry room, and returned quickly with the dry sundress. She helped Lala pull it over her head and then turned her around gently to button it up. "There you go. Good as new. And very dry."

The child reached up and kissed her on the cheek. It was so unexpected she almost flinched away. The kiss was damp and cool, and she smelled of earthy musk, forest leaves and grasses. And that same odor, sweetish but less pleasant, that Kay couldn't place.

103

Moments later the two girls were back outside, swinging on the low-hanging branches of a fig tree, throwing the green fruit up at passing, out-of-reach birds. As Kay cleared the table, there came an insistent scratching at the back door. She opened it and Angus strolled in, mewing.

"Hungry, boy?" She stroked his sleek orange back. "Wait a second. Have I got a treat for you." She picked up Lala's uneaten sandwich and scraped the tuna into a bowl, as the cat wove a figure eight around her ankles, purring.

"Look—your favorite thing in all the world." She set the bowl down on a vinyl placemat that served as the cat's dinner table.

He darted forward and stuck his nose into the dish. But instead of wolfing the food with his usual gusto, Angus merely sniffed. An eerie moaning rose, faint at first, gradually filling the kitchen. The cat backed up a few steps and crouched low, growling at his food.

"Gus, what in the world?" When Kay stepped toward him, Angus hissed and ran off, pupils huge, tail an outraged bottle brush.

She shook her head, picked up the bowl and sniffed. It smelled like plain, freshly-made tuna.

"Is the world coming to an end?" she muttered. First that awful phone call, and now this. "Everything's going weird on me. Even the cat."

TWELVE

Granite slabs and marble crosses gleamed bone-white under the bright Miami sun.

"Damn. This cement gift box don't want to be transplanted." A sweating black gravedigger, bare chest glistening, stood a few feet from a newly-opened plot, kneading the biceps of one muscular arm.

"Christ in Hell, John." His freckled, red-haired partner grabbed at the hoist. "Get your ass back here. If we drop this bastard, old man Lunquist will be on us like shit on a shoe."

John grimaced and tossed a mock salute. "Yessuh, Boss Jimmy." He struck an exaggerated cast-iron jockey pose. "Dang. Now where I leave that old hoss?"

The other gravedigger snorted. "Fuck you and the horse. We both know you could kick my ass anytime you want. Just mind that hoist, man."

"Where's this bastard going?" asked John, as he took over the hoist again. "We gotta dig a new hole somewheres else cause his old lady got mad at him postmortem or something? Or did the family just not pay the bill?"

"Big words, man." Jimmy laughed. "Nah. It's going up north, to some hick town. Miami dirt ain't good enough, I guess."

And then they both returned to work, sweating and swearing, as a concrete vault emerged slowly, slowly from the ground.

THIRTEEN

Kay shifted her chair to take advantage of the afternoon light filtering through the dining room windows. She was sketching on a large vellum pad. "Perdita?"

"Hmmm?" The other woman was rubbing at a stubborn spot on one already-shining dining room window.

"How long have you lived here? In Abaton, I mean." She set the chalk aside, flexed that hand, then cautiously lifted a yellow mug of steaming cinnamon coffee. Fresh this time, thanks to Perdita.

"Most all my life. Except for two years at school, in Tallahassee."

"You went to Florida State? So did I! We have a lot in common. Same college, daughters . . . "

Perdita looked down at her hand, holding the polishing cloth, and smiled. "Oh, you think so?"

Kay flushed. "I only meant, same school, same type of family . . . " She watched Perdita start on the next window. "Did you ever want to live somewhere else? When you graduated FSU, did you plan to work someplace like a big city?"

Perdita folded the dust cloth and laid it down on the window sill. "You want to know about me?"

"Well, only if you want to talk. I've told you a little about Jack, Miami, my work. But we never talk about you. Don't think you have to, though, if you don't want."

Perdita's sigh was almost inaudible. "I don't mind. Not much to tell. I went to high school in Pleasantville. Got a kind of minority scholarship, senior year. A grant." She picked up the cloth again and moved to the next window. "So I went to the college in Tallahassee for almost two years. Studied art."

"Like me. But why'd you quit?" Kay blurted, then wanted to take back the words. "Sorry. That was nosy."

"I don't mind. Nothing I'm sorry about. It was because of Perle."

"You mean you had her there with you? That must've been difficult."

"No. I dropped out, end of my second year, because I was pregnant. Had to come home, back to my mama. It nearly killed her, I think. She had such big hopes for me."

Now Kay really regretted heedlessly trampling into the other woman's private life. "But . . . but she must've been proud of you. Look what all you've accomplished. A beautiful daughter, your own business—"

"I don't think this is exactly what she had in mind for me." Perdita smiled wryly. "Anyhow, who knows if I'd have made something of an art degree? I never drew a line after that. Strange . . . I never even wanted to. But Perle, she has a hundred times more talent than I ever did. Wants to design clothes."

She glanced up quickly, as if expecting Kay to laugh. "I work so hard mostly for her. Never thought of her as a mistake, as something to regret. Even when that law student told me he was too young to be a father. She's the best thing I ever made. Before college or since." Perdita looked away and began to polish the already-glowing oak tabletop fiercely.

"Well, she's a beautiful girl. Obviously no mistake."

Perdita looked up, smiling again. "But she's going to college all the way through. And then make a name for herself. We'll both see to that. Now, excuse me. I've got to get the dishes done so I can get to Mrs. Blunt's on time." She took the empty mug from Kay's hand.

Kay turned back to her drawing. She heard Perdita in the kitchen, talking. "You again. Lazy man. Hungry too, I suppose."

For a moment Kay tensed. Who was she talking to? Was a stranger in the house? Then she heard the screen door creak, and Gus's hoarse meow.

"I hope he eats better for you than he did yesterday," she called. "You won't believe this. He turned down a whole dish of tuna. And there were two dead rats on the back porch again this morning, disemboweled." She shuddered. "Of course he acted the innocent. Like he'd had nothing to do with all that."

"Really?" the other woman exclaimed. "Only time I've know a tomcat or a man to turn down food was if it was spoiled. Even then sometimes the man won't notice. But if a cat didn't catch something himself, he won't want anything to do with it. They're particular that way."

Kay rose and came to stand in the kitchen doorway. "But the tuna wasn't bad. We all ate it, and didn't get sick."

Perdita was bent over, pouring dry cat chow into a bowl. "Well, he's sure got an appetite now. Don't you? Just sleeping, and eating, and laying around the house. How can you get so hungry doing nothing?"

"He lies around now. But he used to stay out all night and half the day, fighting other cats."

Perdita snorted. "Looking for lady friends."

"That too," Kay conceded. "He used to come home all beat up. Ran up vet bills, especially after he almost lost an eye. Then I decided I couldn't afford his lifestyle and had him neutered. Now he's a homebody. Never even hunted, 'til we moved here."

"Could do that to some men," Perdita said in a low voice. "Keep them home nights."

"Whoa. That seems a little drastic." Kay went back to the table and picked up the chalk again. Suddenly the grinning image of Slocum Blunt came to mind. She frowned, shook her head, and began sketching again.

Chloe was out back. Through the open windows, Kay hear her singing in a high thin soprano.

William, William, trimber, trucker
He's a good fisher
Catches him hens
Puts them in pens
Some lays eggs
Some lays none
Wire, briar, limberlock
Three geese in a flock
One flew east
One flew west . . .

Must have learned that one from Lala, Kay thought. She'd never heard it before. Well, at least she knows now that all kids don't go to private school in expensive cars wearing hundred-dollar pre-ripped jeans.

She flipped to a blank page in the sketchbook. Perdita's remark stayed with her, though, making her uneasy. Now even Puss 'n Boots looked kinky, in those tall black leather boots.

FOURTEEN

'm not pleased." Wilfred Lunquist said, as he paced the sterile white tile floor of the Lunquist Mortuary and Memory Garden. "A cracked vault. An improperly sealed casket. And now this." He held up a silver-framed photograph. The glass covering the picture of a dark-haired woman and a little girl had shattered into a web of cracks. "What if the relatives had wished to view the loved one before re-interment? Stranger requests have been made. A fine sight this would've made."

He carefully shook the knife-edged shards into a wastebasket. "Herbert!"

The slight, white-coated man who'd been hovering near the open doorway rushed over. "Yes, Mr. L?"

"Have this glass replaced immediately. Oh — and do something about that sand dollar."

The other man's eyes widened behind thick wire-rimmed specs. "The . . . the sand dollar, Mr. L?"

Lunquist snorted. " 'The sand dollar, Mr. L,' " he mimicked in a falsetto tone. "Don't parrot my words, Herbert. The sand dollar that was on the bod . . . on the deceased Mr. Abbott's chest. It was placed there, I assume, by a grieving relative, during the first viewing."

111

"But what should I do about it, Mr. L?"

"It's shattered, you idiot! Find another one. That shouldn't be too difficult in Miami Beach, should it? You know how distraught relations get when anything is missing. And stop calling me 'Mr. L'. I despise nicknames."

"Of course, Mr. L-lunquist." Herbert scurried away.

The funeral director jammed his fists into the pockets of his second-best black suit. He scowled at the casket sitting on the trolley. "A simple disinterment, bungled. Breakage. Incompetents. No wonder I'm not a well man." He fumbled in one pocket, popped a chalky white tablet into his mouth, then jabbed an intercom button. "Rosa!"

"Yes, Mr. L? *Que ese es?*"

He grimaced. "Check that plane reservation for the Abbott re-interment on Friday. And get me that—what was his name?—that lawyer fellow on the phone. Delgado. That's it. Quickly!"

He slammed the receiver down on her "*Si, claro*. Right away, Mr. L."

"Don't call me that," he snarled at the casket.

FIFTEEN

hloe kicked at the damp cotton sheet until her legs were uncovered. She sighed and turned over for maybe the fifth time. "It's too hot," she whined. The revolving fan her mother had put on the dresser only stirred the humid air around. A full moon shone streetlight-bright on her face. Her Wonder Woman pajamas felt damp and prickly. A bead of sweat trickled slowly down one cheek and into her ear. That did it.

She sat up, wide awake and miserable.

***

Down the hall, Kay slept, undisturbed by moonlight. The ceiling fan above her bed turned lazily, but even without it the air in her room was cooler. She turned over, frowning, clutching at the sheet, twisting one corner. Dreaming.

***

Chloe slid out of bed. The polished pine floor was cool under her bare feet. She tiptoed to the middle window of three, carefully avoiding the one loose board that always creaked. She climbed onto the window seat, pushing stuffed animals aside to make room, and rested her arms on the sill beneath the raised sash. A slight breeze rattled the leathery magnolia leaves into muffled applause. Even this too-warm air felt good on her flushed face. At least it was cooler outside than indoors. No central air here, not like they'd had back in Miami. The afternoon heat stayed trapped on the second floor for most of the night. She was pretty sure it was cooler downstairs, too, by now.

***

Kay frowned and turned over in her sleep, mumbling. In the dream she was walking aimlessly through the woods. Lost. All around her a nightmare forest pressed. Fleshy green plants oozed blood-colored sap, dangled strings of moss over her face like cool dead fingers. She rubbed her nose, but didn't wake. In the dream she wasn't lost, exactly, but rather looking for something. Or someone? A dream-branch slapped back in her face and her fingers twitched and plucked at the sheet.

***

From her window perch, Chloe stared into the darkness of the backyard. The moon silver-plated the trunks of the crape myrtles, giving them the phosphorescent glow of movie ghosts. Branches cast spidery shadows on the grass. She felt a pleasantly safe shiver of fear, the same kind she used to get at a Saturday matinee in Miami Beach. In spite of the heat, she was really glad to be inside, with walls and doors between her and all the scary-looking stuff of night. Which was all fine from a distance, but not right with you, close up.

She rested her chin on her folded arms, thinking about her father. His funeral had been scary too, but a different, what-will-happen-now kind of scary.

***

In Kay's dream it was twilight, a time of day she hated. Hard to see well, but not dark enough for flashlights or headlights or porch lights to help. Someone was walking close by, beside or behind her. She was afraid to look too closely into the deepening shadows of this dream country. So she walked on, stiff with fear, until the woods receded and she stood in a clearing before a small frame house. The yard was crowded with pale shapes, more animal than human, their faces hidden by mist. The house's tacked-on porch leaned tiredly, needing paint and repairs. Red geraniums and orange marigolds in rusted Maxwell House cans lined its warped railing. Near the rough wooden door a seated figure rocked slowly. She was afraid to go closer to the house, and afraid to re-enter the dark woods behind her.

***

Chloe yawned. Her head drooped sleepily onto her arms. Then, outside beneath the crape myrtles, came a flash of white. Her eyes snapped open. She peered intently at the dark alleys between the ghostly trees.

There it was again, slipping from one tree to the next.

***

Kay moaned in her sleep. Her dream self refused to go back into the woods, so finally she went forward, toward the house. Steps dragging with the reluctance of fear. As she drew nearer the pale shapes in the yard all turned toward her, watching coldly. Now she could see the splintered porch clearly, rust flaking on the red and blue coffee cans, the moisture beaded on the petals of the flowers. The dark, knotted hands gripping the arms of the rocker. A pair of bare, calloused feet lifted from the porch floor each time the chair rocked back.

***

At the window, Chloe gasped. She covered her mouth and looked guiltily over one shoulder. But when after a few moments her mother didn't appear in the doorway to order her back to bed, she turned back to the window again. The flash she'd seen flitting through the trees ran out into the open, into a slice of silver moonlight. It wore white cotton pajamas, and waved happily up at her window. Its small round face flashed a gap-toothed grin.

"Lala," Chloe whispered.

SIXTEEN

Mike Delgado called back on Wednesday. Jack's coffin would arrive at the Tallahassee airport the following Monday, along with the director of the Miami Beach funeral home. Both would ride west by hearse, to Abaton. All the arrangements had been made through a local mortuary.

"You won't have to do a thing," he promised.

Mike's cheerful confidence was beginning to get on Kay's nerves.

Dread of the coming week had made her tense, and she'd snapped at Chloe more than once. The house felt like a cage she paced, drinking too much coffee, biting her nails, when what she really wanted was a cigarette. And there was no one to talk to about it. Not Bonnie. Not Myrtle. Certainly not Perdita, who'd no doubt think her weak and foolish. And of course not Chloe. She didn't want to renew grief for a lost parent just when her daughter seemed to be doing so well. One neurotic per family should be the legal limit.

Her work was too quiet, too introverted, to be a distraction for the mind. Company would have been nice. A whole group of people. Or at least one real houseguest to fuss over. But who did she know that would come up here?

At last she dialed Annelise's number in Miami. There was no answer at the house in Coral Gables, so next she tried the gallery.

"Clothed in Light. Can I, like, help you?"

Great. The ditzy assistant. She drifted away to summon Annelise, but was gone so long Kay began to fear she'd been distracted, like a magpie, by some shiny bauble along the way. Several minutes passed.

At last Annelise picked up the phone, out of breath. "Mrs. Delgado, may I –"

"Hi, Lise. It's me."

"Oh, Kay! So glad you called. I was just thinking about you and Chloe, stuck up there in Abbotville."

"Abaton."

"That's what I meant. How is she, not sick? You're not sick, are you? God, I sound just like my mother. I'll just shut up now and let you talk."

Kay laughed. "If you do, then I've just wasted a long-distance phone call. We're fine. A little homesick for familiar faces. Dreading the next funeral. And so I was wondering—"

"You're coming back and want me to pick you up at Miami International," said Annelise eagerly.

"Well, no. Not yet. I was . . . um, hoping I could persuade you to fly up here. To Tallahassee. Then I'd pick you up at the airport. I'm sure a trip out to the sticks probably isn't your idea of a good time, but—"

"Oh, double damn! I can't go anywhere in the world for the next few weeks. There are guest artists here from New York, and they're a little, you know . . . unusual. We're setting up their shows today. One's actually staying at the house. She has a morbid fear of hotels. And she goes in the kitchen and makes all these weird dishes with eleven kinds of sprouts—well, anyhow, Mike is about ready to divorce me. If I leave him alone with the sprout queen he will divorce me! I'd love to come up and escape the whole sordid affair, but . . . " She trailed off. "Now I feel like a real shit. Some friend, putting work before you. Hold on. Maybe I can get Lulee to cover for me."

"Deep-Space Lulee? Oh no, don't do that. Besides, Mike's taken care of everything. I can wait a few weeks. Don't worry, I'll keep 'til then."

She was proud of herself for even managing to sound cheerful about it.

"So, what's it like, this place you inherited?"

"You'd like it. The house, at least."

"Uh oh. Are the natives too . . . rustic?"

Kay sighed. "Well, there are some really nice people here. But then some others—God! You wouldn't believe how . . . how retro they are. And I don't mean in the good, fashionable way."

"Do tell," said Annelise. "Hold on . . . OK, I've got my coffee. So, shoot. All the juicy details."

After they'd talked for another half hour, said their fourth or fifth goodbye and then actually hung up, Kay picked up a paintbrush with good intentions. But an hour later, her spirits were as flat as the dried-out tube of cadmium yellow she was uselessly mashing.

"Mary had a little lamb, big fucking deal." She sank into the Morris chair beside the fireplace. When she'd felt depressed in Miami, she used to throw small dinner parties. Jack had always said that was crazy. But then he hadn't worked alone all day.

She sat up suddenly, thinking, Why not? If she couldn't lure a long-distance houseguest, she could still invite some locals to dinner. Temporary company was generally the best kind, anyhow.

The idea seized her like born-again religion.

Seated at the pigeonhole desk in the study, she began a guest list. Who did she know well enough here to invite?

There was Bonnie. That meant she had to invite Slocum, too. Well, she supposed she could stand him for a few hours. She scribbled their names at the top of the list.

Myrna Waverly. Though she'd only seen her in town once since they'd left the motel, Myrna was as pink and friendly as ever. Okay. That meant she also had to invite the mysterious Judge, Myrna's elderly, reclusive gentleman friend. She could invite Minnie from the arts and crafts shop, too. That made five, but she wanted more of a full house than that.

May Olive Reed was sure to be entertaining. She wanted to visit her again, but hadn't been out since the first time with Bonnie. May Olive was a widow, and had no boyfriend so far as she knew. And of course there was Oliver, Bonnie's brother. She'd spoken to him yesterday at the bank. He'd make seven. The Chinese said odd numbers were lucky. But who was she forgetting?

Perdita. And Perle, who was old enough to mix with adults, but young enough to keep Chloe occupied. And Perdita could bring her cousin . . . Patrick, that was his name. The psychologist at Naxahatchee State Hospital. That should be interesting.

Ten made a good number. Everyone would have someone to talk to. And the preparations would keep her mind occupied until Annelise could get away.

She already felt happier. Perdita was coming on Thursday. She had all day Friday to cook. Today she'd plan the menu, buy groceries, find a place to get flowers.

She'd filled up three days already. And all she had to do now was pick up the phone.

***

At five to seven on Friday night, Kay was just swirling the last spoonful of dark chocolate icing on the cake, when someone knocked at the front door.

"Chloe? Please answer that."

"I got it!" She heard thuds and thumps as her daughter galloped down the stairs, taking the steps two at a time. Risky in the ankle-length dress she'd insisted on wearing tonight.

Kay tensed, expecting a crash. "And don't run!"

She set the cake in the icebox, wiped her hands on a dishtowel, and went out to greet the first arrivals.

May Olive and Oliver stood in the front hall, smiling down at Chloe, who had just contacted the severe social paralysis of the young and gangly.

"Hi. This is my daughter," Kay said, coming up to lay a hand on Chloe's shoulder. "And Chloe—Oliver and Mrs. Reed. I'm so glad you could make it."

"We certainly didn't have a more attractive invitation," said Oliver. "Here, Mama. Let me take your wrap." He lifted a silky rose-embroidered shawl from May Olive's shoulders, then stood awkwardly holding it.

Chloe was staring at him, but not offering to take it.

"Here, let us help," Kay said, giving her daughter a surreptitious nudge. "Please come to the living room and make yourselves comfortable. I have hors d'oeuvres out there. And a tray of ice and drinks. Be right back."

"Are we the first ones?" asked May Olive. "That's not very fashionable, I suppose." She chuckled. "Now I must be getting senile to ask a thing like that. Did I see any cars out there but ours? Come on Oliver, help your old mother find a seat."

Cane in one hand, Oliver's arm in the other, she pulled him toward the other room. He smiled at Kay over one shoulder.

"Chloe, go in and make sure they get something to drink, and some food."

"He's cute, Mom."

"Who, Oliver?"

"Shhh! He'll hear you." She glanced wide-eyed at the living room. "Yeah. He's a . . . " She frowned, searching for some term. "Like the fifth-grade girls say. A hunk."

"A hunk, huh." She shook her head. Hunk, indeed. She went upstairs and laid the folded shawl on her bed. When she came into the living room Chloe was sitting on the mahogany platform rocker across from the couch, feet dangling. May Olive gave her a grandmotherly smile. "My word. Aren't you a pretty one."

Chloe blushed and ducked her head, giving Oliver a quick sidelong glance. Without looking up she said, "Thanks. The cheese and crackers are on the table over there. There's mushrooms and olives and some other stuff in those dishes. The smoked oysters are really gross, though."

Kay winced. "I see Chloe's been keeping you entertained. The others ought to be here soon. At least, no one's said they won't be coming." Just as she poured a glass of Chardonnay for herself, the hall phone rang. "Sorry—excuse me."

She picked up the heavy old-fashioned receiver. "Hello?"

"Kay? Bonnie. Sorry to bother you right now, but . . . "

"Don't tell me you're lost!"

Bonnie's laugh sounded forced. "I'm certainly not. But Slocum . . . oh, I could just kill him. His car's in the shop, and he took mine out on business somewhere. His cell just goes to voice mail. No telling when he'll be back. Afraid we'll have to take a rain check. Sorry. I was really looking forward to it."

"So was I. Hey, maybe Oliver could pick you up."

"No!" she said sharply. Then, in a lower voice, "I mean, I wouldn't want to interrupt other guests on my account."

"No trouble. Everything's ready and so far only Oliver and your mother are here."

"They are? Well, uh . . . I'm sure the rest will be along any minute. And . . . and I'm not even dressed. Please don't let me ruin things. I'm just going to take a long hot bath, and read a book, and sink my claws into Slocum when he drags in."

"Well . . . if you're sure."

"I am. Next time, though, I'll be there if I have to walk."

Kay laughed. "Surely that won't be necessary. And don't be too hard on Slocum on my account. Talk to you later."

"Right. 'Bye."

Kay went back to the living room. "That was Bonnie. She and Slocum can't make it."

Oliver and May Olive exchanged glances. "Is that right?" she said. "What a surprise." But May Olive didn't sound the least bit surprised.

Oliver cleared his throat, glanced again at his mother. "Oh well. Who else were you expecting?"

"Let's see—just Myrna Waverly, the Judge, Myrna's friend Minnie, Perdita Woodberry, Perle, and maybe Patrick Woodberry."

"Quite a party. Well, hope they get here soon. It smells wonderful."

"I'm sure they—" But Kay was interrupted again by the ringing phone. "Excuse me."

She picked up, expecting Bonnie with the news that Slocum had arrived after all. "Hello?"

"Hi, honey, it's Myrna. Myrna Waverly? Sorry, it's unforgivable to call at this late hour. But it's the Judge. He's in a state."

"I assume you mean, besides Florida?"

"No, no. He's taken one of his spells," Myrna explained. "He's a martyr to daisy pollen. Not a well man at all, and I just couldn't leave him like this."

"Oh dear, of course not. Anything I can do?"

"Heavens no. I'll just sit with him. I already gave him his pills, and set up a vaporizer. He'll be fine by and by. You can't take any chances at his age."

"Of course not. But what about Minnie?"

"Minnie?" A puzzled silence. "Oh! You mean Minnie. She's not here, honey."

"I meant, is she still coming to dinner? She was going to ride with you, wasn't she?"

"Say what? Oh—I could kick myself, I really could. She told me to be sure to tell you, and I forgot. Just plain forgot."

"Tell me what?"

"Minnie, she had to go on up to Bainbridge to see her brother. I do believe he's sick, too."

"It's beginning to sound like an epidemic."

"Oh honey, don't you know it. Well, I better get back to the Judge. Believe I hear him calling me. And I do apologize again for my terrible memory. You'd better get back to your guests. Don't let me spoil things."

"No problem." Kay sighed. "Please tell the Judge I hope he feels better soon."

Kay returned to the living room. "You won't believe this, but—"

"Myrna got car trouble, too?" asked May Olive.

"Now, Mama." Oliver nibbled a crab puff in small nervous bites.

"No. But the Judge is sick. Oh, and Minnie had to go out of town. Her brother's ill, too."

"Do tell." May Olive reached for the last stuffed olive. "Yet he passed away, I believe, in ninety-six."

Oliver rolled his eyes.

Chloe's eyes were wide. "Is the Judge going to die?"

"Chloe," Kay said. "Of course not."

May Olive looked unperturbed. "I believe I know what's—"

The phone rang again.

"Well, I wish I did." Kay got up again. "Excuse me."

It was Perdita.

"Hello, what a surprise."

"Afraid we won't be able to come tonight."

"Perdita, if you tell me your car is broken down or Perle has Legionnaire's Disease—"

"Perle and the car are fine. We just can't come. I'm sorry. But it will probably go better without us."

"Why? I don't understand what's going on. And so I guess your cousin Patrick isn't coming, either."

"He's not coming because I didn't tell him."

"You—but why not?"

"I thought about it. In fact, I was going to come."

"You said so Thursday."

"Yes. But when you told me who all was coming, I got to thinking. And I knew if I said anything earlier, you wouldn't listen. It's better this way. We'll come some other time."

"I really don't understand what's going on," Kay repeated, pacing back and forth in front of the phone table in the hall.

"You might if you'd lived here longer." For some reason, Kay could see Perdita smiling. "Tell me, who's there right now?"

"May Olive. Oliver. Everyone else, including you, has called to cancel."

"That sounds about right. Well, you'll have a better time with just the two of them."

"And you're not going to tell me why. Not even going to make up a reason?"

"I'll see you next Thursday."

"You're leaving me in suspense for a week!"

"I'm sure Mrs. Reed will explain. And I'm sorry to miss your nice dinner."

"Perdita!"

125

The only answer was a dial tone. Kay stood with phone in hand for a minute, then slammed it down. She returned to the living room and dropped into a chair. "That was—"

"Perdita Woodberry." May Olive said, ignoring Oliver's exasperated sigh. "Well, she was the only one left."

"That's right." Her dinner party was a disaster. She felt like a pariah. Or as if she'd been stood up for the prom. "Well," she said brightly, "let's go to the dining room. I believe this is the whole party." She offered May Olive a hand. "I know you're starved. It's this way. Of course you know that."

"I knew it twenty years ago." May Olive patted her hand. "But you go on and refresh my memory."

They walked through the arched entrance to the dining room.

Oliver stood and smiled at Chloe. She ducked her head shyly.

"Please, take my unworthy arm." He offered an elbow, and she took hold gingerly.

"Tell me," Kay heard him whisper. "Have you seen Paris?"

"Not yet," she told him. "I'm going to eat first."

***

"Most delicious meal in ages," May Olive declared. "Pass those little red potatoes, Oliver. I'm just a slave to any kind of potatoes."

"Glad you liked it." Kay felt better now. An appreciative audience helped. The food had turned out well: lemon chicken, new potatoes, green beans. Adding sautéed garlic to the beans had been the most daring touch.

"I haven't eaten this much since I got back from New York," said Oliver. "Those little Asian places always lure me in."

"Do you travel there a lot?"

He shrugged. "Some. Several times a year."

"Why, he has friends all over the big city," May Olive protested. "Mostly in theater. Hope to heaven I never have to count them all. Handsome boys."

Oliver cleared his throat, looking embarrassed.

"It's the truth. Why one was just here visiting him. What was his—"

"Heaven's sake, Mother. Kay's not interested in my friends' itineraries."

"How about dessert?" she said, gathering up plates. "I made a dark chocolate pound cake. With coffee? Not you, Chloe," she added, seeing a hopeful raised eyebrow.

A few minutes later, May Olive pushed away her dessert plate. "Those fools don't know what they missed."

"Thanks," said Kay. "I still can't get over the fact that no one else could come."

"Wouldn't come, you mean."

"It was just an unfortunate coincidence," Oliver insisted.

"Ouch! Don't kick my ankle under the table, young man." She smacked him with her dinner napkin.

Chloe stared in amazement.

"If you know what's going on," said Kay, "I wish you'd tell me."

"I just thought you should know why . . . probably . . . no one else showed up."

Oliver frowned at his water glass but said nothing.

"I suppose things are different in Miami," she added.

Oliver snorted.

"Ways and attitudes are changing here, too, but it takes longer in a small town. There's some haven't changed their ways in fifty years. And probably won't 'til the trumpet sounds on Judgment Day. What I mean to say is, by some standards, you made a fox pause tonight."

Kay was mystified. "A fox?"

"Faux pas," Oliver muttered darkly.

"Whatever, smarty britches." She looked at Kay again. "You invited Slocum, Bonnie, Myrna, Minnie, and Perdita and Perle all on the same night."

Kay froze as it dawned on her. "You don't mean they wouldn't all sit down together at the same table."

"Not the Judge. Not Slocum. Oh, I'm sure Perdita would, but she was just trying to save you some trouble."

"I don't believe it. You mean even Bonnie's so prejudiced, that she—"

"Bonnie's not," the older woman said defensively. "I raised her to be fair. To treat folks right."

Oliver coughed behind his napkin.

"But Slocum would rather cut his own throat with a butter knife than sit down to dinner with Negros."

"Negroes? I think you mean African Americans," Oliver suggested.

"I mean all of them. Any sort of black person. And to keep the peace at home, Bonnie will do whatever that . . . whatever he says." May Olive scowled. "Well, she's grown. It's her life and she seems to like it. At any rate, she'd rather not upset the apple cart now."

"Not with so many expensive apples at stake." Oliver said, then winced; apparently it was his turn to receive a sharp kick under the table.

Kay shook her head. "But . . . that's crazy. Perdita is . . . they all know her. In Miami, we had all kinds of friends. Jamaicans, Cubans, Filipinos."

"This isn't Miami." Oliver glanced up and then looked away. "People in small towns aren't always as open to differences. And they never forget anything."

"I see." Kay blinked. "At least I think I do."

"Well, I see it's time for us to go." His mother folded her napkin decisively. "When you get to be my age, it takes more than coffee to keep you awake after a certain hour and a fine big meal."

Oliver helped her up. Chloe dashed upstairs to get the rose-embroidered shawl.

"Don't judge us too harshly," said May Olive, as they stood at the front door. "There are a lot of kind, caring folks here."

Kay nodding, remembering the man at the Paradise store paying for bottles he didn't need, just so a little boy could take some extra money home. "Sure. I get that."

They waited until the Reeds' car disappeared around the bend, then went back inside.

"No dishes now," she muttered, passing by the stack in the sink. "Tomorrow," she promised, adding, to Chloe, "and you can dry."

Upstairs, as she pulled a red striped nightgown over her head, Chloe asked, "Mom, did May Olive—"

"Mrs. Reed, sweetie. Or wait—you can call her Miss May Olive."

"Did she mean nobody likes Perdita?"

How could she have forgotten her daughter was present at the conversation? "No, no, honey. That's not it."

"Oh." Chloe looked skeptical. "Do they hate Perle and Lala?"

Kay groaned. "Tomorrow, I'll try to explain all this in detail, OK? But right now I'm beat, and we both have to get some sleep."

"All right." Chloe sighed. "But Mom, I think I'm going to have inson . . . insome . . . "

"Insomnia?"

"Right. Like you have when you drink too much."

"What!"

"Coffee, I mean."

"Oh. Well, try to pretend like you're tired and you'll be asleep before you know it."

"Say what Daddy used to say."

Kay bit her lip. "You mean 'This bed's just right. Good night, Baby Bear'? But you were little when you liked that."

"I like it again." Chloe's smile was overtaken by a huge yawn. "Good night, Mama Bear."

In her room, Kay undressed quickly and pulled an old shirt of Jack's from the top drawer of the lingerie chest. She was exhausted and still incredulous about the no-shows. All right, so it wasn't going to be just a quaint southern paradise, full of brotherly love under the magnolias.

"At least it isn't Miami," she whispered, slipping under the cool sheet. Because she'd wanted peace and quiet. A slow-moving backwater village. At least for a while. She turned over, hearing the chirp of cicadas and, from the river, a bass and tenor chorus of frogs. She imagined a fat, curved finger of moon beckoning to her over the river, until its reflection was shattered by a rippling splash. And beneath it glowed alligator's eyes, the dull orange of pine embers in the dark.

In another minute, she was asleep.

SEVENTEEN

Warped wooden treads sagged and creaked beneath her feet. She mounted them slowly and stepped onto a sagging porch. She'd picked up a splinter in the sole of one foot, and felt its sharp insistent stab with each step. But she couldn't stop, or take her eyes from the face behind the screen door obscured by moon-cast shadows.

Like a distant observer she watched and heard herself speak.

"Where is she?" Or was it, Where is he?

"Not here. Not here." The cracked voice from the house made a nursery rhyme of the words.

When she finally touched the handle of the rusty screen door, it swung open wide with a dry screech of ancient, unoiled hinges. And then she saw –

Kay sat straight up in bed, gasping. The room was stifling; airless as a killing box. She peeled the damp sheet from her legs and lay back, staring at the motionless ceiling fan. Breathing fast, heart hammering at her ribs like a crazed carpenter.

A dream, she thought. Just another damned dream. Her eyes took inventory of the room just the same. What a coward I am, she thought with disgust. Afraid of a nightmare. She reached up and tugged on the tasseled cord hanging above the bed. The oak-bladed ceiling fan eased lazily into motion. Stirring the hot air made it feel instantly cooler.

She turned over and closed her eyes.

Creak.

Her eyes snapped open. Her heart leapt and took off again.

She sat up. "Chloe," she called softly. "Are you up?"

No reply. The faint creak came again.

"Shit." She swung her legs over the side of the mattress. Had it come from downstairs? She tiptoed to the door.

"Ouch, damn!" she gasped at a sharp stab in the sole of her foot, and hopped the last two steps. One hand on the doorframe to steady herself, she bent to look. Even in the faint dusk of a nightlight, she could see the inch-long splinter embedded in her heel. She used her fingernails to tweeze it out, hissing at the pain. A fat drop of blood welled up.

She tiptoed cautiously down the hall.

Chloe was still asleep, tanned arms and legs flung out in geometric disarray. If someone was prowling around downstairs, it wasn't her. Not Gus either. She'd put him out before she came up. Maybe he was scratching at the door, hanging on the screen like a big furry insect. She stepped back out into the hall. She would have to check downstairs. My kingdom for a husband, she thought.

A metal-tipped umbrella hung in the upstairs hall closet. She opened its door slowly to outwit the squeaky hinge, then groped inside. The umbrella fell with a loud clatter. "Damn," she muttered, reaching down to yank it out. Bending over reminded her that she had Jack's old tee-shirt on—and nothing else.

Feeling increasingly silly, she stepped quietly into the downstairs hall, sliding along the wall until she could peer around the corner. She gazed into the shadowed kitchen, gripping the umbrella tighter.

The back door was ajar.

She gasped, then clapped a hand over her mouth, thinking back desperately. Surely she'd locked it? A quick unwelcome flash to the day Slocum Blunt had rattled the lock and commented on its advanced age. Shivering now, she tried to remember events after the dinner guests had left. How Gus had cried to go out while Chloe kept talking a mile a minute about dinner and Oliver. She'd opened the door, the cat dashed out, then she'd closed and locked it, and turned to answer Chloe. She slumped against the refrigerator, weak with relief. So the unreliable old latch had apparently not held.

"Stupid thing." She crossed the kitchen and reached out to close it. A faint cry came from outside. "Gus?"

"Waoww." Definitely his whiskey-hoarse cry.

She opened the door a crack. "Kitty-kitty," she called.

But he didn't run inside, and there was no answering meow.

She stepped onto the back stoop.

"Psst. Here, boy. Come on, kitty!"

Another cry, but no sign of the cat. She scanned the bushes around the edge of the yard. A flash of white moved from one tree to another at the far edge.

"Kittykitty. Okay, last chance."

Anyhow, Angus was orange, not white.

She backed clumsily toward the kitchen, feeling behind her for the doorknob. Something soft brushed her bare ankles.

"Jesus, Gus!" She whirled to look, but the cat wasn't there. Instead she spotted the limp corpse of a young squirrel lying on the top step inches from her foot, split from chin to gut so neatly a pathologist would be proud.

"Waooww." An orange shape streaked across the grass toward her. Angus.

"Hurry up, you bad boy!"

The cat dashed past into the kitchen, and hunkered down by his bowl, greedily crunching Friskies.

She pulled the door shut hard and shot the bolt. It did seem loose. And what had touched her leg a minute ago? She thought of the dead squirrel, its soft brush of a tail. Ridiculous idea, it was long dead. A leaf . . . the wind? Her hand shook as she released the lock. She leaned the umbrella against the wall.

"Goodnight, Gus." You furry little bastard.

Back in bed, she resolved to double-check all the doors from now on, at night. And to get a new lock installed. Her big-city paranoia had taken a vacation, but was back on duty now. She used to lock up the house tighter than a bank vault, in Miami.

Soft thuds meant the cat must be padding up the stairs. Soon the bed quivered under his purring weight. In a minute, he'd be up trying to nest in her hair. Kay groaned and pulled the pillow over her head. "Go away."

Instead he walked over her legs and settled on her stomach, purring and kneading her belly with needle-sharp claws.

"No! Beat it, squirrel breath."

Gus rose as if offended and moved to the end of the bed. Kay punched her feather pillow into shape and settled down again to sleep.

She was entering that dusky zone between awareness and slumber when the cat let out a hair-raising yowl.

"God!" She sat straight up. "Now what?"

Gus was crouched at the foot of the bed, peering down at the floor, fur electric, tail bushed out. He sang out again, like a mad contralto practicing scales.

"Oh for—! Get out, you!" She kicked at him, and he flew off the bed. There he crouched, belly to the floor, still growling.

"Mom?" A sleepy voice from down the hall. "What happened?"

Terrific. Chloe was awake too. She swung her legs over the edge of the bed to go to her. But, instead of hard pine floor, her foot met with a soft, yielding object that breathed 'unnhh' as she stepped on it. Something sharp sank into her bare ankle, and she shrieked and lunged for the light switch. The bulb flared for a fraction of a second and then burned out, leaving her blinking at the red afterimage, blind as a new kitten.

"Mom? Mom! Are you okay?"

Kay gritted her teeth against the pain. "No—yes! Wait a minute. Stay there." She hobbled into the hall and flipped on the overhead. Gus was there now, crouched against the banister. Ears flat, glaring and hissing.

"You bastard," she said through gritted teeth. The cat turned and fled down the stairs.

"Mom, I'm scared!"

"It's OK, honey. Just the cat. I accidentally stepped on him and he bit me. Go back to sleep, Chloe."

Kay limped over and sat on the top step. She pulled her injured foot up across her knee to check the damage. Then felt lightheaded for a second, and had to put a hand on the banister rail to steady herself. But she couldn't so easily brace herself against the trembling that seized her as she stared numbly at the bite mark on her ankle.

It wasn't a simple puncture. Not a cat's bite either. Instead she saw a small, gapped impression of a set of human teeth, the indentions welling with her own blood.

EIGHTEEN

Bonnie Blunt dropped the rose-red lipstick back into her Coach bag and flipped the mirrored visor back into place. "Well, I just don't like it, is all. Mama didn't raise me to treat people like that."

"'Mama didn't raise me to treat people like that.'" Slocum mimicked in a whiny falsetto. He scowled. "Why don't you just shut the fuck up."

"Slokey, don't talk to me that way." Bonnie felt tears gathering and blinked rapidly to contain them. Her husband hated crying. "It's not—I don't mind skipping the dinner party for you. But I like Kay. Now she might not speak to me again. I don't have many friends so I can't afford to insult or . . . or lie to them."

"Blunts don't sit down to dinner with a bunch of spooks—with the maid, for Chrissake!" He stomped the accelerator, and the car surged forward. "That's the trouble with you. You don't understand how it'd look to the rest of the town. And you know what that is? Nigger-stupid, is what."

She gasped and blindly punched the button to roll down the passenger window. Then rested the side of her face against the frame to catch the cooling evening breeze. Wind stung her eyes, streaking the tears across her temples.

"Pull your head in," her husband growled. "You look like a goddamn dog."

She leaned against the headrest, rolled up the window, and sighed. "You think I don't know why you treat me this way, Slocum. But I do."

He steered with his left hand, the square-cut diamond on his little finger catching rosy fire from the late sunset. He rested his right hand on her thigh. "Oh you do, do you?" Just what is it that my little bride knows?"

"I know . . . I know all about that woman. The one in Grand Ridge. Your grass widow!"

He laughed heartily and unpleasantly. "My, my." His eyes widened in mock alarm. "Whatever shall I do now? So you know that. Well, that ain't much. Bet you didn't know a thing about the one in Marianna."

She gasped, "Marianna!"

"Lord God, I married a parrot. I said Marianna, didn't I?" His grip on her thigh tightened.

She lifted her chin and turned away. "I would've found out soon enough."

"Oh, I doubt it. You're really not too smart, sugar."

"I don't have to listen to—"

"Why honey," he said, giving a sharp squeeze just above the knee, where it hurt most. "Of course you do."

"Slocum, that—"

"Hurts, don't it? Oops. Sure don't want to bruise the little wife. Paid good money for her, didn't I."

"It's just . . . it'll leave a mark. I-I wish you wouldn't grab me like that."

"Like what? I'm entitled to my conjugal rights. Only want my money's worth. You got yours, so don't try to cheat me out of mine. Everybody in this car knows why you married me." He wiggled his eyebrows at the rearview mirror, reflecting an empty back seat. "Right, folks?"

"Slocum, let go of my leg. You're h-hurting me."

He relaxed his grip slightly. "Sure thing, sugar britches. Don't want to damage the goods any more than they already been. I know your sweet old mama has some sharp pair of eyes. 'Course they weren't so sharp, back when you were away at—"

"Stop it!"

" . . . back when her little girl got knocked up by a nigger at that fancy private school." He grinned, but his face had an angry flush. "I don't know what kind of a college credit you'd call that. Needed old Slocum to fix things up then—didn't you?"

"He was Indian, not—oh, what difference does it make." She began to cry again. "Why do you always do this to me?"

"'Cause I like it." His lower lip crept out sullenly. "You're my little woman. S'posed to offer comfort, and the right to use you as I see fit."

Bonnie lowered her head until a curtain of fine, wheat-colored hair hung before her eyes. She squeezed them shut.

"And you do like the money. Don't you, babe? So don't ever forget it was me made you the richest bitch in Crane County. You wanna keep on spendin' that money on them stupid toys of yours. Don't you?"

Her shoulders twitched.

"I didn't hear that. Don't you?"

"Yes," she whispered, louder. If she didn't say it now, he'd keep at it till she did. Sometimes it used to take days. But now—

He looked pleased. "All right then." He settled back into the soft leather. "Now when we get home, you remember that. There's something I wanna try out tonight." He slid the hand beneath her skirt and gave a last squeeze. "I got it in the mail."

Bonnie bit her lip and flinched. But she didn't pull away.

The road to Abaton was bathed in the dusky half-light that arrives briefly after sunset. Ahead, an early possum wandered out onto the asphalt, blinking in slow, marsupial confusion.

Beside her, Slocum tensed. The stretch ahead was free of oncoming cars. He turned the Mercedes' steering wheel a fraction. Enough to put the left front tire just over the yellow line, to score a direct hit on the possum. At the last minute he frowned and jerked the leather-covered wheel right. The breeze from the car ruffled the animal's dingy grey fur. It never paused in its amble to the other side.

Bonnie jerked her hands from her tear-streaked face and looked around in alarm. "What was that?"

"Nothing." He'd paid fifty dollars for that wax job back in Marianna.

His right hand gripped her left. He laid it on his swelling crotch. "Nothing at all."

NINETEEN

Kay frowned at the swollen ankle she'd just propped carefully on a cushioned footstool. Jack's second burial was scheduled for tomorrow. And she'd be hobbling to it on this grotesque, puffy ankle in the only dress shoes she'd brought from Miami, a pair of black kid heels. She had trouble on heels even with two good feet.

Perdita entered, balancing a plastic basin of hot water. "Here. Epsom salts." She set it on the floor. "Just soak it in that for a while."

Kay lowered the foot hesitantly, grimacing when the heat reached the open wound.

Perdita frowned. "Let me see that again." She cradled the ankle carefully in both hands, shaking her head in disbelief. "That no-account tom did this?"

Kay nodded. "He was the only one in the house besides us. I must've stepped on him."

"You're not sure?"

"Well . . . yes. I stepped on him pretty hard. Must've hurt, and he really let me have it." She winced as Perdita lightly traced around the bite with one finger.

"He surely did. Funny, though. Cats usually swat and scratch. It's dogs that bite. Dogs and little kids. Hmm . . .

this looks awful red and swollen. If you don't want to see a doctor, my Aunt Mattie could—"

"I don't need a doctor. I've got some antibiotics left over from an old prescription. Brought them along, just in case. Good thing, too."

"I guess." Perdita looked doubtful. She lowered the foot carefully back into the water. "You should stay off it today, anyhow, or Chloe and I will have to carry you around tomorrow."

Kay laughed. "I'm not that far gone. I can still hobble." She peered down at the water in the basin. "What is this stuff? Those little green and brown specks . . . am I getting feverish? Doesn't look like Epsom salts."

"Not just them. It's better. Old recipe of my mother's."

"Oh. Then I'll probably be all better by tomorrow, right? Mothers are notoriously good doctors."

"The best." Perdita smiled. "So . . . I'm going to finish up in the kitchen."

"Oh, Perdita. Wait."

The other woman turned back.

"Uh . . . about dinner Friday night. I . . . I understand the problem now. I mean, why you didn't come. And I don't blame you. Those people are despicable and ignorant. They—"

Perdita shook her head, looking amused. "What they are doesn't really matter. I choose to live here, you see. This is my home. I wouldn't feel right anywhere else. The foolishness of other people makes no difference to me unless I let it. So why should it worry you?"

Kay stared at her, unable to think of an answer.

"Those dishes are calling my name. You just sit back and read your book. Shout if you need anything."

Kay was astounded at such a cool reaction to the dinner incident. She was still fuming about it, herself. Okay, so she wouldn't tell Minnie, Bonnie, and the rest what she thought of them. If Perdita didn't care, why should she?

But she felt differently toward them all now. Things had changed. "They always do," she muttered, thinking of what lay in store for them tomorrow, at the Abaton cemetery. "Just when you think a thing is past . . . "

Still, she was determined to go, to at least give the appearance of being in charge. She'd usually let Jack handle anything terribly difficult or unpleasant. Now Mike had stepped in to take care of things. This seemed a good time to break the pattern and begin acting like a responsible adult. Whatever that meant.

TWENTY

A t his first glimpse of the cargo area of the small Tallahassee terminal, Wilfred Lunquist pressed his thin lips into a line resembling a paper cut. He glared at the dusty Cadillac hearse idling at the loading dock.

This is the limit, he thought savagely, mopping his forehead with a black-edged handkerchief. First a wretched seven A.M. flight from Miami. Before they got off the ground a half-witted flight attendant had spilled orange juice on his best black summer-weight suit. He tugged at one sticky sleeve irritably. Then this tiny excuse for an airport. The building was bad enough, not at all like Miami International. But the casual attitude of these sloppy baggage handlers—

"C'mon, Harvey," one man shouted just then. "Give us a hand. This stiff weighs a ton."

Lunquist shuddered. Insufferable. And now this . . . antique vehicle. The last straw.

A tall, handsome young black man unfolded himself from the driver's seat of the 1950s-era hearse. "Mr. Lunquist?"

A curt nod.

The man offered Lunquist a gold-toothed smile and a firm, slow handshake. "I'm Calvin Nester. Mr. Small sent

143

me. He's finishing up an early funeral this morning, over to Graceville. Sends his apologies for not bein' able to meet you here himself."

"Well . . . " Lunquist sniffed, slightly mollified. "I suppose he couldn't reschedule on my account." He tugged at the passenger door, flinching back when it sagged open with a bone-chilling screech. He sank into the seat, wincing at the jab of a rogue spring.

The younger man fitted himself back in a good deal quicker than he'd gotten out. "All set then? I gotta stop and put some gas in old Phaedra before we leave town. She's a guzzler." He patted the cracked dash, then pulled out at whiplash speed toward the exit road.

"Phaedra?" Lunquist gasped, clutching the armrest with desperate fingers.

"Yeah. A, you know, mythical woman. Some ancient mama. Mr. Small, he readin' that stuff all the time."

Lunquist frowned, unable to think of a suitable reply. Finally he cleared his throat. "But I assume this is not the only, ah, conveyance in Mr. Small's establishment?"

Calvin favored him with an 18-karat grin. "No, sir. Mr. Small, he has the new hearse over to Graceville today. Big old white one. He got Phaedra in 1962 from Superior Coach. Cadillac body on a limo chassis. Sweet ride. He won't give her up. Always tell me, he say, 'Calvin, she been more faithful and work one hell of a lot better than my ex-wife ever done.' He sort of attached to her, you know?"

"I can imagine." Lunquist mopped at his face; the humidity up here was incredible. "Suppose you could turn on the air conditioner?"

Calvin shook his head regretfully. "No sir, sure can't. Been broke since 1986. Crack that side vent, though, and you can catch a nice cross-breeze."

"Thanks." When he did, the resulting gale lifted his carefully-combed strands of thinning top hair and whipped them wildly around his head.

"Here we go," Calvin said suddenly, swinging across three lanes on Highway 90. With a squeal of balding tires, he pulled into an old Starvin' Marvin gas station complete with bays.

"Hey, Calvin." A grease-stained redhead, attractive despite the mechanic's coveralls, sauntered out of one of the bays, wiping her hands on a nasty rag. "Filler up?"

"Yeah, Cissy. With . . . let's see . . . Super this time."

As she unscrewed the gas cap she cupped a hand and peered through the back window at the casket. "Business still good, I see."

Calvin got out and reached for the squeegee, dunking it in a rusted bucket by the pump. "Yes ma'am. Outta town fella this time."

"That so?" She popped gum and eyed the box again. "Where from?"

"Mi-amah." He scrubbed at a stubborn bug spot on the glass. It left an ugly yellow smear of insect juice right in front of Lunquist's face.

"Geez," said Cissy, hanging the gas nozzle back on the pump. "Who'd wanna come all the way from there to get buried up here?"

Who indeed, thought Lunquist morosely, flicking an amorous pair of lovebugs off his sleeve. The insects, still linked, settled on the dash. He reached into his suit jacket pocket and popped three Rolaids into his mouth.

Calvin returned with a receipt for the gas. "All right. Now we talkin' business. Just one last stop. If you don't mind?"

Lunquist sighed and waved a limp hand to indicate he'd ceased to care much about anything at all today. He belched sadly, tasting potassium chloride.

The hearse eased out and executed a quick u-turn that left the living passenger breathless. They headed back toward Tallahassee. Lunquist shut his eyes, too exhausted to even fan himself anymore.

When the brakes shuddered he glanced up tiredly. His eyes bugged in horror. Now they were in line for the drive-through window of a vintage McDonald's, complete with gaudy yellow arches. "What—what in the world?"

"Oh, they got it all," Calvin said encouragingly. "What's your pleasure, Mr. Lunquist?"

"I? I—nothing!"

Calvin shrugged. "No problem." As they drifted nearer the buzzing speaker, he ordered hash browns, sausage, biscuits, eggs, and a strawberry shake.

Heavenly Father, thought Lunquist, sliding down. We are taking a loved one to the drive-through window. He tugged at his tie to loosen it. Suddenly the moist, heavy air seemed thinner. He felt like panting.

The line of cars inched forward with excruciating slowness. An old couple turned to stare, faces set and disapproving. A teenage boy leaned in the window and asked, "Yo, man. You filmin' a YouTube video?"

At the pick-up window Calvin took a white grease-speckled sack from a bored girl in brown polyester. He uncrimped the top and peered inside. "Well, dog. No hash browns."

Jaws working, she paused to blow a pink bubble, then handed out the forgotten potatoes, nearly dropping her gum into the bag in the process.

Calvin settled his breakfast on his lap and took a long pull of the shake. He sighed appreciatively. "We don't got a Mickey D's in Abaton."

Lunquist somehow was not surprised.

"Now we ready to really hit the road." Calvin gunned past a grinning fiberglass clown and turned west onto the asphalt.

Wilfred Lunquist removed his suit jacket, conceding defeat at last. He wondered if his antiperspirant would be sufficient for the day ahead. A vain hope, he was sure.

He sighed and glanced sideways. "Spare a few of those hash browns?"

TWENTY-ONE

Kay eased her foot slowly into the black shoe, breath catching as the soft leather pressed swollen flesh. She limped to the door, trying to get the knack of walking wounded on high heels.

"Dressed yet, Chloe?" she shouted down the hall.

A muffled reply came from her daughter's room. When she entered it Chloe was perched on the side of her bed, a white sandal dangling from one hand.

"Feeling okay?"

"I'm almost ready." She sighed and looked down at her lilac cotton dress. "Daddy liked this one," she said.

"Sweetie, maybe we should get Perle to stay here with you. I was letting you come because you insisted. And you said you weren't upset about the . . . about your father."

"I'm not a baby. I'm okay." She tugged up her white ankle sock and fastened the sandal. "I'm ready." She looked up with a slight, crooked smile.

At that moment Kay saw both herself and Jack in Chloe's face, familiar features merged into a new individual. Like her, yet unlike. Feeling something like . . . regret? She bent impulsively and kissed the top of that dark, curly head.

"Hey. I'll have to brush it again."

"No, it's fine. Come on, Perdita's waiting."

The other woman was standing at the bottom of the stairs. "Thought I heard you coming down."

"Sure you don't mind driving my car?"

"Of course not. No way you can drive with that ankle." Her gaze took them both in, an efficient once-over. "You both look just right. Pretty, but dignified. Well, let's go."

They both helped Kay hobble across the treacherous gravel drive. Chloe got in back, scooted to the exact center of the seat, and made a great to-do of smoothing out her skirt.

Perdita got in. "Cemetery's off River Road, about a mile. We'll be there in ten minutes."

"Good," said Kay. "I just want to get this over with."

***

Wilfred Lunquist was perspiring again, despite the excellent air conditioning in the Small Mortuary.

"Highly irregular," he repeated. "And most disrespectful. I've never experienced such . . . such casualness in the handling of a loved one. A drive through window, at a fast-food establishment." He shuddered. "Hardly the sort of endorsement one would wish for, in—"

"Now, Mr. Lunquist . . . Wilfred. May I call you that?" Bevis Small, snowy-haired and ruddy-faced in a light gray suit, didn't pause long enough for his colleague to answer. "Being in the same line of work, I appreciate your distress. I surely do. Bet they do things different down in Miami. But this is a small town, and I like to say we do things in a Small way." He paused, looking pleased with the word play.

Lunquist merely glared.

"I know how y'all are always in a nervous rush down there," Small added. "And I can see why, what with New

149

Yorkers, Spaniards, and other foreigners not always speaking good English and wanting to include voodoo chickens and such in the ceremony." He shook his head in commiseration. "Well, sir. It ain't like that here. Now I apologize if Calvin caused you any distress. But we're behind schedule. We got the body—Mr. Abbott, I mean— into the good wagon now. Grave was dug this morning, and we put the nice blue tent up. That lawyer fella said there wouldn't be no crowd, but you never can tell."

"No mourners?" Lunquist sagged. The man was so large, so loud, so healthy. It didn't seem decent. And that suit—why, almost pastel. "But I understood Mr. Abbot was quite an important personage, here in—"

Small gazed back unperturbed, smiling blandly at the panting Lunquist. "Widow's attorney told me there'd be only her, maybe one or two others. After all, it ain't the first time he's been –"

"—interred. I know, I know," said Lunquist, mopping at his face. "I just thought, perhaps, this being Mr. Abbott's hometown . . . "

"His kin are long gone. I did know his Grandmama. His mama and daddy are deceased, too. Miss Leilah really raised the boy. He sure was a one for fishin' on that river. Why, I recall—"

"Please," cried Lunquist. "It's ten minutes to one. Couldn't we reminisce later and just get on with it?" He fumbled in his pocket for an antacid tablet. Found a single dusty, crumbled one, glared at it, then popped the white disk in his mouth.

Small pulled a silver railroad watch the size of a travel alarm clock from his vest pocket. "Well, so it is. Calvin! Jabo! Gotta get on the road now." He beamed at Lunquist and opened the back door. "After you, Wilfred."

***

"Wait! Just a second," called Kay. "I can't take another step. Stand still a minute, Perdita."

Leaning on the other woman's arm, she bent to remove her shoes. "These things are killing me. Now maybe I can walk like a normal person."

The grass of the old cemetery was thick, cool, and springy beneath her feet. As they walked Perdita told them a little local history. The burial ground dated from the early 1800s. This final resting place for generations of Abaton was shaded with spindly dogwood, thick oaks, and twisted redbuds. A famous Civil War battle had been fought among its granite and marble gravestones; bullets had chipped some of them. Unpaved red-clay paths wound round the crypts and family plots planted with azaleas, camellias, and red and white day lilies.

Most graves appeared carefully tended, though some of the headstones weren't very elegant. The largest made of marble or black granite; others cruder, of plain cement. One section even had some markers that looked like home-poured plaster; a few graves were studded with crosses made of hammered tin. One crude concrete cross had been painstakingly inlaid with a design made of some child's cats-eye marbles.

"Maybe being barefoot isn't very respectful," Kay said as she picked her way carefully through the grass. "I'd better put my shoes back on before anybody sees."

"Doesn't bother me. Do you think your mama looks scandalous, Chloe?"

"No," replied her daughter earnestly. "You look like a princess in the forest, Mom. A big princess," she amended, stopping before a pink marble monument carved with dogwood blossoms. "This is pretty. Better than those little metal signs back in Miami. Like a stone flower garden."

It was true. The Abaton cemetery felt more real and substantial than the clipped, mowed 'memory garden' in

Miami. Jack would've liked it better. For the first time, moving him here seemed like a good thing to do.

Her thoughts were interrupted by a gentle touch on her arm. "The Abbotts are this way." Perdita led them left along a row of larger plots fenced with stone pillars and wrought iron. Delicately-carved angels' wings and thick granite obelisks cast triangular shadows. "It's the oldest, of course."

Kay read some of the carved stones as they passed.

Versaline Davis
1889-1943
Each Duty Done
Each Chore Complete
She Now is Gone
And Rests in Peace

How grim, thought Kay. Sounds like the poor woman earned it.

The next plot held three graves, one with a carved marble lamb atop the smaller stone. A mother, a father, a child? She squinted to read the worn, mossy letters on the tiny stone. *Cricket Yates 1953. Our little lamb of God.* "Oh, what a shame. Poor little Cricket," Kay said aloud.

She heard a muffled snort, and turned to look. Perdita's hand over her mouth, stifling laughter.

"How is that funny?" Kay demanded.

"Because Cricket . . . " The other woman burst out laughing again. "Cricket was . . . a dog."

Kay gaped. "In the family plot? But—can they do that?"

"I guess in Abaton, even a poodle can go to glory."

Kay laughed, too, until her eyes watered. "Oh, this is the silliest thing I ever—"

"Mrs. Abbott?" A solemn voice deep as the tolling of a church bell.

Kay gasped and dropped a shoe. "Yes?" She looked around but saw no one else on the path. Even Perdita looked startled. They all walked hesitantly around the next bend.

And there, no longer hidden by a massive stand of rhododendrons, stood two men, both in suits. The tall, pale, stringy one looked familiar. The other was cheerfully bulky and white-haired; a storybook grandfather. Behind them lay a large plot elaborately fenced with brick and wrought iron. The carved marble letters inlaid above the gate spelled out ABBOTT in chiseled gothic script.

The two little groups stared at each other for a moment.

Perdita broke the silence. "I do believe we're here."

"Mrs. Abbott," said the larger man. "I'm Bevis Small, from the local funeral home. This other gentleman is Mr. Lunquist, whom I reckon you know, come all the way from Miami. We're here to make sure things go just like you wish."

Oh yes, Lunquist. No wonder he'd looked familiar. The efficient but unctuous director from Jack's first funeral. She dropped her high heels to the ground, trying to re-shoe herself discreetly. When she nearly fell sideways, though, Perdita bent to help.

"I remember you, Mr. Lunquist," Kay said, struggling to appear dignified, leaning on Perdita's shoulder. "From . . . from last year." As Perdita forced the second shoe onto her swollen foot, Kay tried to disguise her grimace as a smile.

"I'm honored," Lunquist droned, "that you remember me from such a trying time. I've come to assure that, once again, your beloved husband will receive the utmost care at our hands. And—" He glanced at Small. "And those of—others."

"Ah, well. I'm sure you've done your best." She'd just noticed that, a short distance away through the trees, a white Cadillac hearse was parked. Two young men, one black, the other sun-burnt and blond, lounged against the car. She looked away, clearing a lump in her throat. "And this is my daughter Chloe, and Mrs. Woodberry, a friend of the family."

Small touched an imaginary hat-brim. "Miz Woodberry."

"How do you do," Lunquist countered smoothly. "Pleased to be of service. Striving for the best possible transition for the late Mr. Abbott. Now, if you have any requests—"

"No ceremony. Right, Miz Abbott?" the local undertaker interrupted. "No clergy. No service. Waiting on anyone else coming to pay respects?"

"Well, no." Kay suddenly felt defensive. "We've been through all that before."

The Miami director's lips compressed into a line thin as a paper-cut.

But Small only said, "Whatever you want, Ma'am. It's all up to you. We'll just get on with it, then."

Everyone's gaze shifted to the freshly-excavated space in the Abbott plot, a gash in the earth like a raw red wound.

She was mesmerized for a moment by that neat hole in the blood-red clay. Then her eyes rose to the granite headstones flanking it. *Davis, Jonah, Leilah, Abigail.* "Yes," she said faintly. "Let's get on with it."

Chloe tugged at her arm.

"What, honey?"

"Aren't we going to look at Daddy? We did last time."

That had been in the velvet-draped viewing room of the Lunquist Funeral Home, with a candelabra only Liberace could have loved, and the sick perfume of too many flowers from well-meaning friends and business associates. The open casket on draped risers, as she'd walked up to it, dreading what she'd see. The mortician had done good work, considering the accident—though Jack had looked rather stiff and white, like a large mannequin in the—

"No!" she said, tone more harsh than she'd meant it to be. She knelt and kissed her daughter's shocked face. "No, sweetheart. I'm sorry. This is not like last time."

"But Mom." Chloe's lower lip trembled. "What about the things I put in with him? Maybe they got broken on the way here. Or lost. I want to see!"

She remembered now. Chloe had insisted on putting some of her treasures into the open casket. A small gold-framed picture of the three of them—"so he won't forget us"—and a large, perfect sand dollar he'd found for her once, on a vacation in the Keys.

"Honey, I'm sure those things are still with Daddy," she said, thinking, please don't let anyone open it now. As if she, not Chloe, were the helpless child. Get a grip, she told herself. You are the adult here.

Perdita stooped to eye-level with Chloe. "Honey, your daddy still has all those things. Why do you suppose he wouldn't?"

She glared at Perdita tearfully. "You don't know."

"Young lady." Lunquist cleared his throat. "As a matter of fact, I happen to know that all your—your gifts—are there, right where you put them. Made sure of that before we left Miami."

"You did, for sure?" She eyed him with suspicion. "What did they look like?"

"A sand dollar. A photograph. A stuffed seahorse." Lunquist ticked off each item. "Everything as it should be. I always see to that."

"Oh." Chloe frowned, then nodded. "Well, I guess it's okay then."

The adults all exchanged relieved looks. No one, obviously, had wanted to explain to a child the real reason they didn't want to open the casket.

"Well now," said Small. "Since everything's in order, we can get on with the—"

"—interment," his big-city counterpart finished.

155

As if summoned by a spell, one of the young men pushed off from the hearse and walked around to the back doors. The other unfolded a wheeled trolley.

Kay took hold of her daughter' shoulders and turned her deliberately away. "Thanks for all your help. Both of you. I appreciate all the trouble you've gone to, to make this happen. If there are other arrangements needed, I'll contact you through Mr. Delgado's firm. And so, we'll be going now. The heat," she added apologetically.

Perdita stooped briefly next to the excavation for the grave. She touched the red earth there as if scooping something up, then rose and followed them.

Kay steered Chloe back up the path ahead of her. Pain gripped the wounded ankle like a fiery metal bracelet.

When they rounded a curve screened from the gravesite by a planting of camellias entwined with Confederate jasmine, Kay stopped abruptly.

"Just a minute. I've got to get rid of these." She kicked off the heels again. On the right side of the path lay a heap of trash—broken flowerpots, dead branches, mummified flowers—waited to be cleared away. She dropped the shoes on top. Suddenly she felt much better.

Perdita said nothing, as if it were the most natural thing in the world to toss away a pair of two-hundred-dollar heels in a cemetery; a proper offering for a second burial.

Chloe, wandering ahead, didn't seem to notice. Kay took the arm Perdita offered in support. They smiled like conspirators and walked on. Talking about the heat, about the advantages of well-worn flats, and what to do for lunch.

Still, instead of chicken salad and chilled cucumber soup, Kay was picturing a heavy mahogany casket being slowly lowered via hoist by two sets of sweating arms into the gaping maw of red earth.

"What did you pick up there, back at the grave?" Kay asked Perdita.

She shrugged. "A little dirt, is all. A tradition. A sort of…memento."

TWENTY-TWO

Back at the house Kay dropped into the closest chair and started sorting through the mail. She stopped at a letter postmarked with a New York zip code, and set it aside. From her agent. She felt a twinge of guilt.

"Always a relief to be done with things that stir up painful memories," Perdita agreed.

Chloe scuffed in. "Can I go out and play?"

"You mean, May I. Sure. Oh—wait. Change first."

Her daughter raced up the stairs two at a time. She galloped down a couple minutes later in a baggy Mickey Mouse shirt and red shorts. "Bye!"

"Chloe! Did you hang up your—"

The bang of the screen door cut off Kay's question.

"Never mind. Who cares. Screw the rules today." She hiked up her skirt and peeled off tattered pantyhose. The shredded feet were stained with red cemetery dirt. "Even Heloise couldn't find another household use for these." She dropped them next to her chair.

Perdita laughed. "I'm going to the kitchen for that peppermint tea I made yesterday. Want some?"

"You're wonderful." Kay tilted her head, frowning. "Oh. Did I just hear a car pull up?"

The distinct slam of two doors answered that question. Then footsteps on the gravel drive, and voices.

"Oh no. I don't believe it. Not today."

"I'll send whoever it is away."

"Thanks." She wiggled her bare, dirty toes, and slid lower in the chair, relaxing.

A rattle as Perdita opened the front door. A pause, then voices in the hall. Kay looked over. Bonnie and May Olive stood in the doorway between living room and foyer.

"Hey there, Kay. Brought you a little bit of pie," said May Olive. Bonnie just looked anxious.

"A-a pie?" She tried with one foot to shove the pathetic scraps of dirty nylon under her chair. "Well . . . how nice."

May Olive came in and perched on the couch. "Around here, if you don't bring a cake, or pie, or meat, or a casserole dish, it's a sin. The old funeral tradition." She held up one hand as if Kay had been about to interrupt, which she hadn't. "Now we know this here was not a regular funeral. But I swan, it still gives us a chance to visit."

"That's right." Bonnie came and sat next to her mother. "We wanted to, you know . . . cheer you up." She smiled, but didn't meet Kay's eyes.

"Now, we won't stay long," said May Olive.

That was when Kay realized this unexpected visit was a timid apology for being no-shows on Friday night. At the moment, she didn't feel mean enough to mention it.

"Well, sure." She sank back in her chair again. "I don't mind some company today. Besides . . . I still wanted to hear the rest of the Abbott family saga."

Perdita came back in silently, and reached for the covered dish still in Bonnie's hands. "I'll get tea for everyone."

"Don't forget the pie, honey. And I mean big pieces!" May Olive called after her. "My chocolate peanut butter cream."

"Sounds delicious." Kay suddenly remembered she'd had no lunch yet, and felt like she could eat it all herself.

"It is. Though deadly for the hips and thighs." Bonnie patted hers and made a face.

"Bother your skinny hips," her mother cried. "You're a toothpick. I should make you eat two pieces!" She turned to Kay. "Now where did I leave off, last time?"

"Let's see. You were up to Miss Leilah and her baby boy. Jonah, Jack's father."

"Yes. Jonah Jacob Abbott. Two Bible names. To rile her daddy, I imagine. So he couldn't ever forget who the father was. It did rile him, too. He took to drink around that time, anyways."

"Jonah Jacob Abbott," Kay repeated. "Very Old Testament. Jacob was my husband's first name, but he went by Jack."

"I don't wonder." May Olive nodded. "Anyhow, little Jonah grew up the apple of Leilah's eye. Nothing too good for him. That should've spoiled him rotten. But little Jonah, he was always the sweetest thing."

"Most boys aren't," Bonnie mused, staring into the empty fireplace.

"True." May Olive gave her daughter a narrow look. "But Jonah was. Some said growing up without a daddy would make him a Mama's boy. A sissy. And he did think the world of his mama, it's true. But he was no sissy. Old Mr. Abbott died when the boy was around eleven. When he got older, he helped run the tobacco farm. Went hunting and fishing like any good old local boy. The main difference between him and them was the way he treated women."

She paused as Perdita returned carrying a tray laden with tea and pie. "Now doesn't that look good!"

"Sit and have some with us," said Kay.

160

Perdita hesitated, then shrugged. "All right. But I still have lots to do." Still, she sank into the remaining chair and take a plate and fork from May Olive's outstretched hand.

A peace offering, thought Kay. It's that, too.

Everyone dug in eagerly as May Olive continued her story.

"All I mean is, he respected females of all ages," she said. "Wasn't no skirt-chaser. He stepped out with a couple girls in town, naturally. But for all the gossip, he never did any serious courting. Wasn't for lack of them trying, neither. Besides being the richest young bachelor in the county, Jonah was handsome as the devil. So his pa did leave something to him, after all. But he never paid those cow-eyed girls much mind. At least not until he set eyes on Louvinia Parker."

"So that's where it came from," said Kay. "Jack's middle name was Parker. But he never told me it was his mother's name."

"Well, now you know. The Parkers were an old family in town too. Way back, they'd even been wealthy. Nothing to touch the Abbotts, of course . . . but they'd lost all their money. All they had left by then was a big old falling-down house on the edge of town. Fact, it burnt down five or six years ago. Wasn't much left of it by then.

"Anyhow, Rueford Parker, Louvinia's daddy, was a good-hearted soul. Started the first fried chicken take-out in town, and kept his chickens—dozens of 'em—behind the house. Betts Parker, Louvinia's mama, now she was another story." May Olive lowered her voice as though the people under discussion might be lurking in the next room.

"Drank a lot, out in the speak-easies. And didn't mind paying the tab with other things when she was low on cash. A town scandal. Well, one of 'em, anyhow." Her eyes twinkled with mischief.

Bonnie laughed, a bit too loudly. "Some things in life could drive a person to drink." She met her mother's eye. "Well, it's true," she muttered, and looked away.

Perdita put the empty plates and glasses on the tray, and stood.

"Oh no, you don't." Kay shook her head. "You've got to sit here with us and get the rest of the scoop on the historical Abbotts."

"Yes, please stay," said Bonnie, cheeks flushing as she looked at the floor.

With a slight shrug, Perdita sat down again. "All right. But only for a minute. Then I need to finish up back there."

"Now then," May Olive resumed. "For some reason, Jonah took special notice of Louvinia, though he'd barely given the others a look. Some said it was on account of she resembled his mama, in a plain sort of way. Never saw it, myself. But he must've done more than just notice her. Because soon she had a loaf in the oven."

Kay was puzzled. "She what?"

"Knocked up," Bonnie interpreted.

"Now, instead of denying it or running off like some good for nothing, Jonah seemed tickled to death. He wanted to marry Louvinia. A lot of the other boys from town had already gone off to the war. He'd got some kind of deferment, I forget why. Some claimed, of course, that it was on account of Leilah's money. And I wouldn't put it past her to have pulled a few strings. Without telling Jonah, of course.

"Any rate, he decided to marry. And he went to Leilah and told her."

"And then the shit hit the fan, I'll bet," said Bonnie.

"You're not so big I can't still make you wait in the car," said May Olive, glaring at her. "Anyhow, nobody knows what he did or said to get Leilah to agree. The whole town already knew what she'd think of the idea. Smart money was on Louvinia being run out of town, with Leilah paying for the rail.

"But I expect he just stood up to her, for once. Maybe he told his mama they'd just leave town and do it anyways. She should know about that sort of thing. So there was a small, quick wedding. The mother of the groom wore black."

"Ouch," said Kay. "Really?"

"You don't know the half of it." May Olive laughed. "She wore black from that day on! And never spoke to her daughter-in-law, if there was any way around it. They could've lived in this big old house with her, but Leilah couldn't stand the sight of Louvinia, and I'm sure she was scared of Leilah. Who wasn't? But Leilah wasn't willing to let Jonah go too far off. She built them a nice little place a few miles up the road. And Louvinia had a girl six months and four days after the wedding. Little thing was a real beauty. Jonah named her Abigail Leilah."

"A girl?" Kay frowned. "But Jack didn't have any brothers or sisters that I ever heard of."

"Well, that's true, in a way. I've not finished the story yet. Now, Jonah loved his little girl more than anything. Took her along everywhere, from the time she was a baby. He loved Louvinia too, but when he looked at little Abby, he just lit up all over. And Louvinia was a jealous woman."

"Uh-oh," said Kay.

Perdita only sipped her tea silently.

"One day there was a terrible accident. Jonah was in town, buying a present for his daughter's fourth birthday. I don't know exactly what happened. He stepped out in front of a car down on Main Street. Was killed instantly."

"How awful!"

"More awful than you imagine. When they brought his body home, Louvinia seemed calm. Too calm. First, she burned that pitiful little birthday package stained with his blood. Then she refused to see or speak to anyone, including her own daughter. So they took the little girl up to Miss Leilah's place."

"How did Leilah take the news?"

"Like a stone," said May Olive. "She took her granddaughter and handed her off to the wife of one of her field hands. Then she told some of those men to bring her son's body to the house. They went to fetch it, but Louvinia refused to let them in. Jonah was laid out in their room. She'd washed and dressed him herself. 'No,' she told Leilah's foreman. 'I'm sorry, but I really can't let you bother him right now.' And she just shut the door in their faces.

"It being summer, something needed to be done. A half-hour later Miss Leilah appeared on Louvinia's doorstep and ordered her to give up Jonah's body. Louvinia refused. So then Leilah had a couple of men force the door. Louvinia crouched by the bed, hissing and clawing like a cat. Until Leilah finally slapped her silly."

Kay winced. "Did that help?"

"Knocked her cold. The men carried the body away, and Leilah took care of the rest. She had a doctor sent round to Louvinia's, who gave her something to calm her nerves. There was a small funeral. No wake, no viewing. I was one of the few invited. It rained the whole time."

"Were the two women speaking to each other by then?"

"Oh, no. Louvinia wasn't speaking at all. She was drugged, leaning on one of the hired men's arms. But her eyes were rolling like a spooked filly's. I was afraid she'd faint, but she didn't. I tried to speak to Leilah, but . . . "

May Olive paused for a moment, and shivered.

Bonnie leaned forward. "But what, Mama?"

"All she said to me was, 'Blessed is the corpse the rain falls upon.' And then she smiled. Oh, it was a terrible smile." The glass in May Olive's hand trembled.

Kay shivered too, in spite of the day's heat.

"Louvinia and Leilah went back to their respective houses. Then, later that day, all of a sudden Leilah gave little Abby back to Louvinia. Even though the woman was in no condition to look after herself, much less a child. Of course it was a terrible mistake."

Perdita stood up. "Please excuse me. I've got to get those things in the kitchen and finish up here. So I can pick up Perle." She gathered up the remains of their dessert. "I'll bring you more tea," she called back over one shoulder.

Bonnie sighed. "Well, go on, Mama."

"It was a terrible mistake," May Olive repeated, "because that night little Abby disappeared."

"Oh my God. You don't mean that Louvinia—" Kay whispered, recalling the smallest grave marker in the family plot now.

"Lord no! She'd never have hurt that child for the world. Not on purpose. But the little thing had been asking for her daddy over and over. No grown-up explanation satisfied her. People said later that Abigail must've gotten up in the middle of the night, wandered outside looking for Jonah, and got lost. Louvinia, in her condition . . . well, she never would've heard her leave."

"The local men all went out to search round the woods and swamp, but never found so much as a footprint. But then it'd rained so heavy the day before. Finally they had to think about the river. Swollen with all that rain. Always been a danger to children. Still is. They dragged it to no avail for days. Finally, somebody said to do what they did in the old days when they couldn't find a drowned body.

"They floated a loaf of bread, hollowed and weighted with quicksilver, from upstream. The idea being the loaf will travel towards, and then stop over, a drowned body. Just an old wives' tale, of course. But this time it worked. When they dove where that loaf had stopped, there was poor Abby, caught on a sunken log, down at the bottom of that black river."

"That's awful," said Kay. "She wandered off, and fell in and drowned."

"Well, I guess. It'd been days by then, and what with the fish and gators—"

"And who was it who told them to use the bread?"

"Why, it was Mattie Swann, Perdita's old aunt," said May Olive. "Folks used to call her Auntie Swann."

TWENTY-THREE

Perle Woodberry flipped quickly through the last few pages of *Cosmopolitan*. Then sighed and slipped it back under her mattress where her mother wouldn't see the forbidden magazine. She wandered into the living room. Her mother had promised to be back at four, and it was ten after now. If she didn't get home soon, the stores would close, and Perle wouldn't be able to get the brushes and acrylics she needed.

It sucked, the way adults were allowed to rule the world. Perle jammed her hands deep into the pockets of her skinny jeans and slumped onto the couch. She had to sit here like a child and wait for her mother to come pick her up and drive her to town. Like . . . like one of those babies she baby sat for . . .

She jumped up and paced the living room, rubber soles squeaking on the shining hardwood floor. Stupid, stupid. Downtown was only two miles away. And only about a mile or so, if you used the shortcut through the state park.

She glanced at the clock for the tenth time. Fifteen after four. Obviously her mother had forgotten all about her promise to be home early. Suddenly it was the most important thing in the world that Perle make it to Minnie Buford's arts and crafts store in Abaton before it closed at five.

She tried her cell phone, but it went right to voice mail. She must still be over to the Abbott's. Never could get any reception there. Perle punched the END button without leaving a message.

Mama just forgot. She promised, but she must've gotten too busy at work and just forgot. That meant she'd probably be home at the usual time, a little after five-thirty. But by then it would be too late to go to town. And she'd probably be too tired to drive all the way into Marianna to the Wal-Mart.

Perle stopped short, jingling some coins in her pocket. The solution was easy. She could go by herself. In an hour, she'd get there and back, no problem. That is, if she ran part of the way. And return home before her mother, who couldn't get mad and yell that something might happen to Perle on the way, because obviously it hadn't and she was already there and back!

After all, Mama's always telling me how important it is to work hard and be serious about your goals. Especially for an artist. It's, like, the most important thing in the world.

She counted her cash quickly, then snatched up her wallet and rushed out. Halfway across the front yard, she stopped, ran back and locked the door. Then walked quickly up the street, but not too quickly. One of the old neighborhood busybodies might see her running and tell her mother.

Sure enough, there was Mrs. Kennedy, out watering flowers. Perle knew the old woman had seen her. She was about a thousand years old, but had eyes like a chicken hawk.

"Hey there, Miz Kennedy," she called politely.

"Child, where you goin' in this heat?" the old woman called back in a sandpapery voice.

Perle gaped at her. She hadn't thought about needing an alibi, at least not yet. "Where? Oh, well . . . I got to pick some, uh, wildflowers. For school. Summer school, I mean." Damn, what a dumb thing to say. Now she'd done it. Lied to the old lady, who gossiped like a mockingbird.

"Girl, please! I got bunches of nice flowers. What you want with them nasty old weeds?"

Perle groped for a plausible story. "Oh, you know. They're for a science class. Got to be indig . . . indij . . . native plants."

"Un-uh." The old woman shook her head slowly, jowls quivering, clucking like a disapproving hen. "They din' teach such trash when I was a girl. Pullin' weeds for homework? Lord have mercy." Mrs. Kennedy turned her back and resumed gardening, still muttering and shaking her head.

Perle sighed, and walked on. As soon as she rounded the bend in the road, she took off. She ran and leaped the curb, then dashed in beneath the pines. The shimmering heat of the asphalt road vanished. Perle grinned at the welcome relief from the heat. Why, she could run through these nice cool woods, dwarfed by giant pines and grandfather oaks, forever. She zig-zagged down the leaf-cushioned trail, dodging stray roots and chuckholes. No problem. She knew the way.

***

Slocum Blunt was in a good mood. A damn shame that he had nobody to waste it on. The realty office was a tomb. Bonnie was off somewhere with her dried-up, sharp-tongued old mama. He hadn't seen a client since nine A.M. What the hell, he decided. Close up early and take a walk downtown.

But there wasn't much going on there, either, considering it was Monday afternoon. Across the street from Jobie's package store Sandy Dink and Bubba Curtis were conferring over the exposed engine of Bubba's

169

metallic blue mustang. They were good old boys, Slocum thought fondly. Just out of high school. Bubba, at least, had no daddy at home. Probably could use some advice from a man.

Slocum put on his best car-expert expression and sauntered over. "Hey there, Bubba. Sandy."

"Hey Mr. Blunt," they chorused.

"What's the problem, Bubba?" Slocum kicked one front tire. "This bitch givin' you some heartache?" It was good to talk to real men, even if they weren't full grown. People who didn't get squeamish and hysterical about what-all you said, and what you did. Not like his wife. Or his sorry pansy of a brother-in-law.

"Nah." Bubba reached up and grasped the Ford's hood to close it. "Just a busted hose. We got it under control."

"Oh," said Slocum, disappointed. "Busted hose, huh? Fucking shame."

"Yeah, well." Sandy wiped his hands on a greasy rag, not looking Slocum in the eye. "Coulda been worse. That's . . . let's see . . . ten bucks, Bubba."

Sandy's father owned the station, but spent most days in a booth at the Landmark Diner, drinking endless cups of coffee and flirting with the aging waitress. He preferred to let his more energetic son keep an eye on business.

Bubba paid with a crumpled bill. All three moved to the glassed-in office of the filling station, where Slocum yanked a cola, a Yoo-hoo, and a peach soda from the humming guts of the stand-up vending machine.

"I'll take the Choke," said Sandy, reaching for the sweating can. "Thanks, Mr. Blunt."

Then they sat, Sandy behind the scarred desk, Slocum and Bubba on old dinette chairs with cracked red plastic seats. Talk had to be loud to be heard over the window fan that roared like a B-52 bomber, sucking in hot air and gas fumes.

Bubba and Sandy began a lazy argument over what to do later on. They complained about the lack of diversions in town, and the high cost of entertaining young women these days. It all made Slocum feel nostalgic.

"Hell's Bells," he said dreamily. "What we used to do was find us some entertainment that didn't cost nothing."

"Shit," said Bubba, draining his Yoo-hoo. "Maybe in the old days, Mr. Blunt. But there ain't nothin' free now."

"That's a fact," Sandy agreed, tilting his chair back until the legs creaked dangerously. "Jesus God, Bubba. How can you drink that fake chocolate shit? Powdered cockroaches, sugar, and water."

Bubba grinned, exposing the gap between his front teeth. He belched modestly. "I'm a man, that's how."

Slocum swigged peach soda. "You boys just need a little imagination. Let me tell you, there's nothing beats some good old don't-cost-a-cent nigger-knocking."

Sandy's chair clunked back down to earth. His eyes were round as the hubcaps displayed in the station storefront. "Say what?"

Slocum smiled and closed his eyes. "It's almost better'n pussy. Back in my younger days, used to be four-five 'a us would meet behind the Baptist church after Sunday night service. We'd grab us some rocks, or maybe borrow a few clay pots from old man Simmons' plant nursery.

"Then we'd go out to niggertown and heave 'em. At men, girls, whatever. Or sometimes we'd fill up balloons with piss or India ink, find some black mama walking down the road in a white Sunday go-to-church dress and— pow! 'Course, you could always slap 'em from out the car window with an old antenna . . . "

He trailed off.

Sandy was frowning at him, eyes narrowed. Bubba was red to the roots of his dishwater hair, and gazing over at the door of the gas station office. A thirty-something black man in a beige linen suit, crisp white shirt, and blue silk tie

171

stood tapping his chin with a credit card. His face was blank, but his eyes said he'd heard it all. Out at the premium unleaded pump, a gray BMW idled.

Sandy jumped up. "How do, Mr. Woodberry." His voice too loud and strained. "Here, lemme get that for you." Sandy lunged for the plastic card like a drowning sailor for a lifeline. Then the two of them walked outside to the pumps, Sandy talking fast and gesturing faster.

"Jesus," said Bubba, the red just beginning to drain from his face. "You shouldn't oughta said them things, Mr. Blunt. He's one of Sandy's best customers. Nice dude, too."

Slocum snorted. "Dude may have a fancy car, and an eye-talian suit, and a pee-h-dee, but underneath it all is just another trash-talkin', jay walkin' n-i-g-g-e-r."

The younger man only shook his head, eyes averted. As if Slocum was something to be embarrassed about, not the fawning cowardice of his friend.

When Sandy returned, things weren't the same. Neither boy even cracked a smile at his best jokes. When Slocum finally realized he was doing all the talking, he got up and left.

It was, he thought sourly, a bad end to what could've been a good day. He crossed the street, slouched over to his car and frowned at it. Sure was a mess. Maybe he should run it over to the big car wash in Marianna, and then get oysters at the little bar where the shucker had such big tits and never wore a bra. Yeah, sure. That sounded good.

He backed out onto Main Street, then turned on River Road. About half a mile later, ahead on the right, he saw a slim black girl walking along the shoulder. She wore faded blue jeans and a tee shirt. Her hair was pulled back into a loose curly ponytail that swung as she walked. A white paper sack bumped against one thigh. Those slender cinnamon arms against peach-colored cotton reminded him for a moment of his failure back at the filling station.

As he neared, he recognized her. Perdita Woodberry's brat. Her name was . . . Penny? No. Peggy? No, no. Perle, that was it. Little Perle. But not so little these days. As he passed he took in the curve of slim denim-clad hips, the adolescent breasts that bounced just a little under her thin cotton shirt.

Bonnie had tits like that, he thought. Once upon a time.

Slocum braked and pressed the button by his thigh. The window whirred down on the Mercedes' passenger side. He leaned across and looked out. The girl was just drawing level with the car.

"Hey, Perle."

Her head snapped around, eyes wide, mouth open. "Who—? Oh, Mr. Blunt. You scared the daylights outta me." She smiled.

"Where you headed, girl?"

"Oh, you know." She waved an arm vaguely. "Just home."

"Your mama know you're out here on this road all alone?"

Perle dropped her gaze to her tennis shoes. "Well, uh . . . yes sir."

He feigned astonishment. "Why, I just can't believe that. Don't she know it's dangerous for a young lady like you to be out all alone? You cain't trust people these days."

***

"No sir," Perle agreed politely, nodding at Mr. Blunt, trying to catch a furtive glimpse of the oversized Fossil watch on her wrist, which her mother had given her last Christmas. Five after five. Damn, she'd be late for sure.

" . . . like we did when I was young, sneakin' out, I mean." The man kept rambling on, smiling at her. "Not that I approve, exactly. You understand."

173

What was he going on about now? Perle was suddenly alarmed. "Oh, but—you won't tell my mama?"

"Oh, 'course not. Tell you what. I'm going to offer you a ride home, 'cause if I don't and something did ever happen to you . . . why, I'd never forgive myself."

"Oh." Perle froze, thinking frantically. She knew better than to get in a car with a stranger. Not ever, duh. But this was Mr. Blunt. Mama worked for him. Well, for his wife. Perle had always admired Mrs. Blunt's nice clothes. And he wasn't a stranger. And if he drove her home, she'd definitely get there before her mother returned from work.

"Well. I don't know. Guess it would be okay."

"Course it's okay. You just toss that in back and climb on in. We'll have you home in no time."

She settled back into the soft leather seat. Slocum leaned over her, smelling strong of some cologne. He shut the door, then locked it.

"Don't want you fallin' out, now, do we? Fasten that seatbelt, honey."

She complied, mentally grimacing. Her mother always said the exact same thing.

**

Slocum shifted gears and drove on, watching Perle from the corner of his eye as she took in the luxurious interior. "This sure is a nice car, Mr. Blunt."

The girl stroked the mahogany dash, ran a hand along the leather armrest soft as a baby's cheek.

"Special order," he said smoothly. "Cost a pretty penny, too."

"Seats sure are cushiony." She bounced a little. "I'd like to get me a car like this when I get a job. Think I'll be able to afford one, Mr. Blunt?"

"Sure, honey." He grinned at himself in the rearview. He could smell her now: damp cotton, soap, clean, warm young skin.

He glanced up at the rearview again. The road behind them was empty.

"And you call me Slocum."

TWENTY-FOUR

But one thing I don't understand," said Kay. "If Jonah died then, how could he be Jack's father?"

"Goodness, aren't you impatient." May Olive set her empty glass on the table with a thump. "I was getting to that part."

"Then let's get on with it, Mama," said Bonnie, rattling the ice in her glass. She removed a cube with her fingers, rubbed it on her neck for a moment, then popped it in her mouth.

"Louvinia must've gotten pregnant right before he died," said May Olive. "Because nine months and one day after the funeral she delivered a big, healthy baby boy, the very spit and image of Jonah Abbott."

"That might be some consolation," said Kay. "It's an awful tragedy to lose a husband and a child at the same time. But at least she still had a son. Not just memories."

"Oh, yes. He was a living memento." The older woman shook her head sadly. "Looked exactly like his daddy, practically from birth. It drove poor Louvinia crazy as a fruit fly."

"Oh no."

"Oh yes. It was clear to anybody who cared to look that the poor woman was miles around the bend. One night, two fishermen found her down on the riverbank, with the new baby in her arms. Barefoot, in her nightclothes, screaming into the wind. They thought she was fixing to toss the poor little mite into the river, so they bundled her up and dragged her back to Miss Leilah's house."

"Then surely since Leilah and Louvinia had only each other, and the baby, they could try to get along," Kay suggested. "To, you know—comfort each other."

"Comfort." May Olive snorted. "Jonah's death left Leilah Abbott hollow as a dried gourd squash. If you'd shook her, she'd have rattled. When the two men brought Louvinia to the door, muddy and half-naked, Leilah said to her, 'Isn't it enough you and your brat killed my only son? I won't let you kill this boy too.'

"Then she snatched the baby up and carried him away. Next day she had her daughter-in-law committed to the state hospital over the way. It must've been fairly easy, since her tosspot mama was always soused and her daddy had died the year before. Her only brother had taken off for parts unknown. Leilah was her closest relative. Nobody around here objected, when you could see plain enough the poor girl was crazy as a loon. When the doctor come to examine her, she told him Jonah had risen from the grave, come to her bed, and fathered her son."

Kay shuddered, imagining that scene. "So that's why Leilah raised Jack. Her grandson replaced the son she'd lost."

"That's right. At first she was all cold and practical. Still grieving. But before long the baby boy had won her over. Soon her sun rose and set with little Jacob Parker Abbott. Though nobody mentioned the name 'Parker' around Leilah after that, unless they wanted to be cut dead on the sidewalk.

"It was her precious Jonah all over again. She loved Jacob, I mean Jack, the same way. I believe he loved her too, but the poor fellow sure looked relieved when he finally left for college. Lucky for him the bottom fell out of the tobacco market, else she'd have kept him here for sure.

"Then he graduated, and took a job down south, in Orlando or thereabouts. Didn't visit a whole lot after that. Not that I blame him. Leilah was never the easiest person to be around, and she got worse as she got older. Whenever he did visit, she followed him everywhere, eating him alive with those hungry eyes.

"When he told her he was moving down to Miami, for good . . . I think that was what finally did her in."

"Excuse me for interrupting." Perdita hurried into the room, one arm buried to the elbow in a straw shoulder bag. She pulled out a ring of keys that might've been the property of a medieval jailer. "I've got to run. Promised Perle I'd be home early, but I'm running late. See you Thursday, Kay. Goodbye May Olive, Mrs. Blunt."

A moment later her Volkswagen's engine whirred and chugged, tires crunching away over the gravel drive.

"Well, now." May Olive looked around. "Where was I?"

Kay held up a hand. "Wait. When Louvinia got out of the hospital, did she and Leilah patch up their differences?" Then something else occurred to her. "I don't remember seeing a headstone in the family plot for Louvinia. Does that mean Leilah wouldn't even let her share the same hallowed ground?"

"I don't know whether she would have let her in or not," said May Olive thoughtfully. "Never got to find out, since Louvinia never did get out of that hospital."

Kay saw for a moment a pale mad face, bar-framed, nail-lacerated, at a window. Aging, growing old. Growing at last still. She shook her head slowly, in pity. "You mean the poor woman died there, all alone. That's just . . . so sad."

May Olive's face hung like a surprised moon, gaping at Kay. After a moment she said, "Oh, my. I thought you knew. She's still there, just as crazy as ever."

TWENTY-FIVE

The blue Mercedes' expensive shock absorbers smoothed out the narrow wooded trail's jolts and potholes. But Perle still felt a queasy bounce in her stomach. "Mr. Blunt?"

"Call me Slocum, honey."

"Mr. Blunt, why we going this way? This heads down to the river."

"Shortcut. What's the matter, think old Slocum's lost?"

"Well . . . no sir. But—"

He glanced over and winked. "Think I'm tryin' to kidnap you?"

Perle didn't answer. She'd just realized the funny feeling was fear.

"Truth is, I do have a little confession to make. I wanted to stop out here for a minute to discuss something with you."

"With me?" she whispered.

"Yes ma'am. With you." He cut the engine and let the car roll to a stop. They were deep in the dusk-dark pines, nearly at the bluff. A trickle of sweat slithered down Perle's side despite the lingering, frigid air from the vents.

"Discuss . . . what?" Her gaze was nailed to the narrow clay path ahead. She couldn't bear to turn her head and look at Mr. Blunt's awful grin. But she heard his heavy breathing, louder than the splash and murmur of the nearby river.

His hand slid from the silver gearshift knob to the edge of Perle's seat. His fingertips brushed her denim-clad thigh. "I s'pose you got a mess of boyfriends," he said hoarsely. "Big, horny black boys who like to do it all night long."

"Do what?" she whispered fearfully. Talking at all was hard, because her teeth clicked together and her throat felt swollen. "I don't know what you mean."

"Fuck. That's what," he hissed. The hand slid up to grasp her thigh, thick fingers digging into the tense muscles. She shrieked and lunged for the door handle, throwing all her weight against the door. It didn't move. She yanked again at the handle, but it snapped back uselessly. It dug into her back as she pressed herself as far away from Slocum as possible.

He smiled and tapped a button on the driver's side of the console. "Automatic locks. Don't want you to fall out and get hurt."

He leaned toward her, eyes half-closed. She cringed back at a gust of hot, meaty breath on her cheek. One hand slid to her left breast and squeezed.

"Stop it!" Perle screamed.

"Now don't give me that trash. We both know y'all start doin' it right after you learn to walk. I'll make it worth your while."

He hesitated. "On second thought, scream all you want. Ain't nobody here but us and I kinda like it."

Breathing in ragged gasps, she worked her left arm up behind her back. Desperate fingers plucked at the lock button. Her right hand jerked the handle again. The door opened suddenly, spilling her out onto rutted clay.

Slocum hung above her, across the passenger seat, halfway out, swearing. But Perle was already up and running. Panicked, confused, she headed toward the bluff that dropped away to the river, instead of the highway.

Behind her she heard Blunt yank his door open and lumber out, after her.

My heart will burst from fear, she thought, as she ran with those heavy footsteps pounding behind her. He sounded so close, she had to look back. Instantly, a cypress knee caught her foot and threw her to the ground.

The last sound Perle heard, before darkness descended, was the snap of one wrist as that hand hit the ground and doubled back under her.

***

Slocum staggered up, panting. He stopped and braced one arm against a pine trunk. "Now," he said, wiping his face on one sweaty shirt sleeve. "We gonna have some fun, honey. So you might as well—"

He broke off, squinting down at the still form tangled in ferns and vines.

"Hey! You gonna play dead now?"

No response from the girl.

He sneered. "Gonna act like my wife, huh? Over her dead body. Get it?" He chuckled. "Well, I can fix that."

He reached down and grabbed Perle's left arm. With a jerk he turned her over to face him.

"Shit." Slocum stepped back. The stupid bitch's eyes were rolled up in her head, only a thin crescent of white showing beneath half-shut lids. Pine needles and oak leaves stuck to her face, glued with the blood that seeped sluggishly from a gash on her forehead.

"Jesus. Jesus!" He bent and put one hand on her chest. The small young breasts didn't excite him now. All he wanted to feel was breathing. But . . . he picked up one arm and let go like he'd seen folks do in the movies. It merely dropped, a dead rubbery weight.

He gagged. "OhJesusChristGodshit," he babbled, falling to his knees. He looked wildly around, then turned back and began throwing dead leaves and pine needles over her, like a frenzied hound burying a bone. When she was covered, he turned and staggered back to the car.

Inside, he jammed the key, then finally managed to turn the ignition. "Accident," he mumbled. "Had a little accident."

When the engine caught he backed in crazy jerks down the narrow path toward the highway.

***

The sound of the retreating car came through the trees, but the mound of last year's leaves didn't stir.

A small dark figure crept from its hiding place in some rhododendrons and knelt for a closer look. It brushed dry leaves away to reveal Perle's battered face.

"Hurt you?" its high voice inquired.

Perle didn't answer.

"Bad blue man." Lala raised her head. Her dark eyes narrowed, staring after the dwindling headlights of the rapidly-departing Mercedes.

TWENTY-SIX

The phone rang early that evening, just as Kay was applying silver tips to Baby Bunting's rabbit-fur suit with an ultra-fine sable brush.

"Hello, Kay." Her agent, calling from New York.

Kay grimaced. Why hadn't she looked at the caller I.D.? "Hello, Maeve."

Maeve Reilly was flame-haired and green-eyed, of Boston Irish descent. At just under six feet, she was noticed and remembered everywhere she went. She attributed only a little of her success as an agent to this. She specialized in famous children's book authors and illustrators, so Kay felt lucky to be on her list. But a phone call from Maeve meant trouble. She usually communicated by I.M. or media mail.

"I had to get your new number from that lawyer friend of yours. One would think you're in hiding."

One would be right, Kay thought. "No, just working hard. And it's . . . it's going better."

"Better? Yes, well, better is good. But I haven't seen anything yet. When will you be sending me the first set of jpegs?"

"Soon, Maeve. I'm halfway through now. And I have roughs of the rest."

"Good. Because I talked to Freddy at Dutton yesterday—"

"Uh oh. Well, I—"

"—and he's not happy. *I See The Moon* is a nostalgia piece, and they expect that stuff to be big next Christmas. But at the rate you're going they'll really have to push Production. And those people hate to be pushed."

"I know how they feel. But I think—"

"Don't think, darling. We don't make money when you think. Just draw. There's no direct connection from the hand to the brain. I don't care what the scientists say. And when you think, we miss deadlines."

This annoyed Kay to silence, because it was sort of true. But the agent's voice droned on, over-killing the subject, just as Maeve always did. "Do you think Sendak or DiPaolo got where they did by sitting on their adorable rumps in their little studios and thinking?" Maeve snorted like a scornful bull. "Do you suppose they tell their agents, 'I think it's going better'?" Her voice rose to a mousy squeak. "No. They don't get contracts for thinking."

"Maeve—"

"I can't sell your thoughts, darling, lovely though they may be. I can't sell anything until it's done. And you can't live on that insurance money forever, you know."

"Damn it, I said I was—"

The connection dropped. "Damn," Kay muttered. Was the whole freaking Florida Panhandle dependent on a single cell tower? Then again, it *had* gotten rid of Maeve.

The phone rang again.

This time the number didn't have a Manhattan area code. When she pressed the screen to answer, a new voice said in a rush, "Kay? Hello, Kay!"

She drew a blank for a second, then recognized the low tone. "Perdita?"

"Yes. Sorry to interrupt your—your evening. But you see, it's Perle—"

"What's wrong?"

"She's . . . I can't find her." The quaver in Perdita's normally calm, assured voice was more frightening than the words themselves. She took a deep breath, then explained that Perle hadn't been there when she'd arrived home from Kay's earlier. So she'd looked everywhere. Then called Perle's friends and their neighbors. By eight o'clock she'd been frightened enough to call the county sheriff. A deputy had informed her that since her daughter was a teenager, and had only been gone for a few hours, she wasn't actually a missing person. "Probably shacked up somewheres," he'd suggested. "You know how they are at that age." She'd hung up on him then.

Her neighbors gathered to help. Based on Mrs. Kennedy's tale of Perle going off to gather wildflowers ("Now I tol' that child she didn't need no trashy weeds") they'd fanned out in small groups to search with camping lanterns and flashlights, calling back and forth through the trees.

But the park's immense, tangled expanse of pines, yews, oaks, magnolias, and rhododendrons, bisected by the wide, swift-flowing river, did not yield up her daughter.

Some of the men were still out looking, but a few female neighbors had insisted on taking Perdita home to eat and rest.

"As if I could do either. My neighbor's oldest son has my car out, looking. And there're a dozen old ladies over here fussing like yard hens." Her voice dropped to a whisper. "I've got to get out of here, to go back and look. But not with them. Could you come get me? Please."

"Of course! Right away. Let me just—oh, Chloe fell asleep upstairs watching a movie. Never mind, I'll put her in the back seat."

She dashed upstairs, pulled on a pair of jeans and some old running shoes.

Rousing her daughter was another story. Kay shook one of her shoulders, patted her cheek, but received only sleepy mumbles in reply.

"Chloe, honey. Wake up, we've got to go somewhere. You can sleep on the back seat, but let's get some clothes on . . . oh, great."

Chloe simply turned over, clutching a pillow in a death-grip.

"I give up." Kay scooped up the sleeping girl, pillow and all. Then staggered under sixty-five pounds of unconscious child, as a fiery bolt of pain shot up from her wounded ankle. They lost the pillow on the first step, but she made it down with gritted teeth, then out the front door, limping awkwardly.

"Mom?" Chloe muttered sleepily.

"Never mind, it's OK, go back to sleep."

She maneuvered her onto the back seat, buckled the belt around her middle, then went back for keys and wallet. As she passed the dining table, she hastily drew a clean sheet of paper over the half-gilded Baby Bunting. Gus liked to sleep and bathe on any artwork left out overnight. Just before she covered it up, the ending of the verse caught her eye.

Sleep, baby, sleep
Down where the woodbines creep.
Care is heavy, therefore sleep you;
You are care and care must keep you.

She shivered, then turned away and ran for the car.

A few minutes later, she pulled into the Woodberry driveway behind two other cars, uncertain whether to get out, honk the horn, or just wait. Suddenly a figure dashed around the side of the house, followed by a wailing chorus of elderly female voices.

Perdita jumped in. "Go, hurry!"

186

Kay backed up, tires spitting dirt and gravel. "Which way?" she cried, feeling like a driver in a bank holdup.

"Down to the old River Road. Then turn left. I'll direct you from there." Perdita slumped back and closed tired, red-rimmed eyes.

"Are we going back to look with the others?"

"No. They did their best, and mean well. But they won't find her. We've got to have help."

"You mean the police? But I thought—"

"No, no." Perdita shook her head impatiently. "I mean real help. I mean my Aunt Mattie."

***

The Volvo bounced over a narrow, rutted clay trail. Branches scraped the roof like cat claws on window glass. The sound set Kay's teeth on edge.

"All right. Go left here." Perdita leaned forward. "There—see? Just pull up in front."

In the clearing sat a small, white-washed cabin. It looked ancient. An added room of mismatched lumber leaned like a crutch to one side. Tacked to the front was a long, narrow porch of unpainted wood. Along its rail rusted coffee cans sprouted red and yellow begonias. All over the sparse lawn, luminous in the headlights, stood a pale, rigid menagerie: one gray concrete lion, an ear broken off. A brown plaster deer with chipped antlers. A variety of painted chickens, ducks, and molting pink flamingoes. Even one five-foot seahorse.

"What—"

Kay had no time to stare, though. Perdita was already out and up on the rustic front porch. Kay hung back to check on Chloe. Her even breathing was reassuring. So she locked the doors, leaving the windows open an inch, and then followed Perdita, skirting the creepy, frozen zoo.

When she reached the steps, a sudden recollection chilled her. A vagrant breeze was pushing the warped rocker on the porch, whose floor boards creaked a mild complaint under its weight.

Yes, it was all there, like in her dream: the rickety porch, the rocker, lush jungle-colored flowers in rusted cans. Only the figure in the rocker was missing. As in the dream, Kay froze. But this time she was awake.

"Kay!" Perdita's voice called from inside.

"I—yes, I'm coming," she said reluctantly, and climbed the creaking steps.

TWENTY-SEVEN

P ast the open door, inside the patchwork little house, the light was dim. Perdita stood near a small brick fireplace with a diminutive older woman. The heat it put out was stifling; Kay was already perspiring beneath her cotton shirt.

"Kay, this is my Aunt Mattie Swann. Mattie, my . . . my friend, Kay."

Without looking up, the old woman ignored Kay's outstretched hand. She scowled darkly up at Perdita. "What you bring this strange woman to my house for?"

Kay felt as if she'd been slapped.

Perdita's voice was low but tight with anger. "She's helping me. That's why."

The woman looked up and regarded Kay for a moment in silence. "Pleased to know you," she finally said in a high voice that sounded stiff from disuse.

"Glad to meet you, too. I've heard a little—"

A brief, harsh cackle. "Now why don't that surprise me."

Kay looked uncertainly back to Perdita, who avoided her glance. "Aunt Mattie knows about Perle. She's going to find her. Sit here with us."

Kay hesitated.

"Unless you'd rather wait outside?"

"Oh, no. It's just that Chloe's out in the car, and—"

"No danger out there," said Mattie Swann, to no one in particular.

"I suppose not." Kay spotted a precarious-looking wooden folding chair and scooted it up closer to the rustic pine table in the center of the room. In the far corner a carved box, set with several candles, a sort of…altar? Draped over it an old belt. Or—no. Kay shuddered. It was a long and wide, curling at the edges, with a dull diamond pattern. A desiccated snakeskin.

Perdita was writing a list on a piece of paper. Kay looked closer. It was a name:

Perle
Perle
Perle
Perle
Perle
Perle

A white enamel bowl with a blue rim sat in the center. Perdita dropped the scrap of paper into the murky liquid that half-filled it.

Mattie sat too, across from Kay, and slid the bowl close. She fumbled in one pocket for a moment, then drew out a tiny dark bundle tied with green thread, perhaps a lock of hair. She dropped it into the bowl, to float on the surface. "Didn't drown. Praise be," she muttered.

Kay glanced at the other two in amazement. What were they doing here, playing at telling fortunes? "Perdita. Don't you think maybe we ought to call the police again, or—"

They both looked up at her coldly, frowning. She shut her mouth abruptly.

Perdita smiled a little. "Kay, even if what we do may seem strange, please don't interrupt. Aunt Mattie has done this . . . well, sort of thing . . . before. Wait and see before you judge."

"But I think—"

"Hush your mouth," the old woman hissed. "No one at this table give a damn for what you think." She closed creased eyelids and, rocking back and forth in the rickety chair, mumbled, "Saw a bird today, flew in and out the house. Never did stop nor rest. The bees, they didn't swarm. No lost souls. No lost souls. Born at midnight on a Sunday, feet first."

She paused, head tilted to one side, as if waiting for an answer only she could hear. Then, eyes still closed, she took a pinch of white powder and dropped it into the bowl, and began to croon again. "Sign me, Lord, a sign. Give back what's mine."

The rocking stopped. The only sound in the room now was Kay's own breathing, much too loud.

When the old woman's eyes snapped open, Kay flinched, nearly upsetting her chair.

"Beside the river. But not in it," Mattie chanted tonelessly. The yellowed sclera of her eyes glowed in the weak firelight. "In the boat place. Buried in treetops. Not dead yet. Not dead." And at the last, a shrill, mournful cry. "Not dead."

Kay looked over at Perdita with alarm when she heard her crying. Tears were streaming down the other woman's cheeks, but she was smiling. "Not dead," she whispered. "Thank God. Not dead."

Aunt Mattie opened her eyes and blinked. "I know where she at."

***

191

In the back seat of the Volvo, Chloe stirred. She grumbled, rubbed at one cheek, and drifted back to sleep, moonlight silvering her upturned face.

A small dark figure darted out from the wild azaleas bordering the house, and wove through the concrete sentinels in the yard. In a dark flurry, a flash of white, it reached the driver's side door. A small brown hand grasped the handle and pulled. The lock clicked uselessly.

Small fingers scrabbled, testing each of the remaining doors, *clickclickclick*. All locked.

The little intruder rose on tiptoes, trying hard to peer over the doors, to look through the windows. Yet no breath fogged their glass. At last, with a supreme effort it hoisted up on the edge, feet dangling, arm muscles straining, one eye peering just over the side into the dark interior.

After a moment bare feet dropped back to earth with a faint thud.

"No blue man," said a child's high, disappointed voice. The visitor wandered away, up the path toward the highway. A giggle like the metallic jingle of pocket change floated back across the yard. "I find you. Hide 'n seek. Bad blue man!"

TWENTY-EIGHT

Slocum crumpled the empty Budweiser can and tossed it out the window with his left hand, popping the last of the six-pack with his right. Both hands still shook despite the calming influence of several hours of beer. Each time he leaned back against the Mercedes' padded leather headrest and closed his eyes he saw the girl's still body half-concealed beneath last year's leaves. The whites of her rolled-back eyes seemed to mock him: *Hey big guy! Want a little bit of this before it gets cold?* So now he kept his lids blasted wide open.

He took another swig, belched, and shuddered. What a fucking mess. And it was all that little bitch's fault. Running like a damn fool, tripping over tree roots. As if he was gonna hurt her! Stupid. Just plain stupid, like all jungle bunnies.

He gulped the dregs of the last Bud. The empty clanked on the others in the ditch beside the car.

Without warning his stomach lurched. In the rearview, moonlight through the tinted windshield turned his face the color of old mushrooms. He considered the effort it would take to lean out and puke into the stagnant green water at the bottom of the ditch.

He poked his head out the open car window and rested his chin on cold steel. Then paused, barely breathing. "What's that?" he mumbled.

Footsteps? He listened intently. Nothing. Spooked again. Nobody would be out in this godforsaken neck of the woods. But the outside air seemed cooler. Made him feel a little better. In fact, almost well enough to go home to that miserable bitch of a w—

There it was again. Slocum froze in his seat. That had been footsteps, all right. Crunching on dead leaves, back behind the car.

He wanted to turn his head and look. No, he wanted to jam his key into the ignition and gun it. To get the hell out of there and be anywhere else in the county. Even home with Bonnie. God, that suddenly sounded good.

Only he was too drunk to move. Much less drive.

He finally forced himself to peer into in the side mirror, expecting to see (Who, big guy, little Perle?) someone coming at him from around the rear fender, her eyes showing white half-moons beneath bruised lids. Crushed leaves dribbling from slack dead lips . . .

Something moved in the mirror just then. Slocum flinched. A high girlish scream burst from his throat. One hand jerked convulsively at the dashboard knobs.

The wipers flicked back and forth. The heater fan roared. And then the running lights outlined the figure of a girl. Not Perle—too small.

"Who the hell?" Slocum demanded, sweat sliding into his eyes. "Who's that?"

A high giggle answered. "Blue man. That you?"

Slocum twisted his head around and stared.

A child in a ragged FSU Seminoles tee-shirt and white cotton panties, not much bigger than a toddler, stood bathed in the bloody glow of taillights.

"Jumpin' Jesus, you scared me. What're you doin' out here so late, little girl? Come on over so I can see you." He opened his door. "Come on now. I don't bite."

The child skipped lightly up to the open door and then stood there on one leg, birdlike, a finger in her mouth. Smiling.

"Well now. Ain't you a cute little booger. What's your name, sugar?"

"Lala," she lisped around the finger.

"La-La? Huh. Weird. Like a song. What you doin' out here all alone. You lost?" His eyes shifted to the woods beyond, narrowing to glare suspiciously at the dark line of trees. "Or maybe you're not alone?"

"Lost," the girl agreed, removing the finger from her mouth. "All 'lone."

"Well, shoot." He fell silent for a moment, as his beer-soaked brain cells puzzled the situation out. "Uh, tell you what, La-La. Uncle Slocum'll take you home. You like that? In the big blue car." What the hell, one good deed at the end of a piss-poor day. Maybe someday he'd need a good deed on the books. "Whereabouts you live, honey?"

"Home."

Slocum sighed. Seemed like nothing wasn't gonna change the color of this day one bit. "Well, get in. We'll figger it out, I reckon."

With a delighted giggle, the girl scrambled up and onto his lap. Her little sandal-shod feet slipped and stomped, struggling for a secure perch. She smelled of baby talc, and wood smoke, and something else he couldn't place. A faint, unpleasant scent.

"Hey! We can't drive like this, kid. Jesus, watch the family jewels, okay?"

"Jewels," she parroted, giggling. "Blue jewels."

"Just like a friggin' parrot," he grumbled, reaching for the key. The girl settled into his lap, her tiny fingers suddenly busy.

"Hey! Uh, what you doin' there, kid?" He gasped as one little hand fumbled at his belt. "Now look here—"

Holy shit, he thought. Is this a kid or a thirty-year-old midget? Despite an earlier pledge—no more women under 21—Slocum felt himself getting hard.

But hell, this was a five year old, for Chrissake. No. No way. That would be just . . . sick. "Hey kid. Cut that out. Don't you wanna go home?"

Instead of answering, the girl stood up on his lap and pulled at his shirt. Two buttons popped off and rolled under the passenger seat. Slocum knew he ought to grab her and shove her away, into the passenger seat. Buckle her in and drive like hell to . . . somewhere. Somewhere safe to leave her. Yet the shame he felt was unbelievably exciting too. The child pushed his head back against the seat, exposing his bare neck. Her breath made cool gusts on a pulsing vein.

She paused then and looked up into his face. "Blue man go home now?"

What the hell. One little kiss. "Shit, not now, kid." He groaned in anticipation. "Go ahead," he whispered. "I don't bite."

But Lala did.

TWENTY-NINE

The county ambulance wailed away, red lights strobing through the pines. Perdita and Mattie Swann rode in back with Perle. They'd found her right where the old woman led them, an abandoned boat launch near the river bluff. Unconscious, completely covered with fallen leaves, pine needles, and twigs. A purpling bruise and a deep cut marred her forehead, and she had a badly swollen wrist—but no other visible injuries. There'd been blood dried on her face, and splashed across on the dead brown leaves.

Kay slid back into the Volvo. Chloe sat up in the back seat, rubbing her eyes. "What's going on?" she muttered sleepily.

Kay reached back and stroked Chloe's tumbled hair away from her face. "We had to, um, come pick up Perle, honey. I'll explain tomorrow. We're going home to bed now."

As she turned the key Chloe tumbled over the passenger seat like a monkey and buckled herself into the passenger seat. And for the first time that hectic night, a disturbing thought occurred to Kay. Where was the little girl, the one called Lala? She hadn't seen or heard a child while they were at Mattie Swann's, where Lala supposedly lived. A narrow cot in the front room had been rumpled but empty.

Had they all just run out, leaving the girl all alone? Strange behavior, since the old woman supposedly doted on the youngster. It would be frightening for a child wake alone, to an empty house, in the middle of the night. Poor thing would be terrified. She too might wander out into the woods.

She remembered May Olive's stories, and shuddered. She sat a moment, letting the engine idle, wondering if she should go back to the Swann house herself. Wondering, indeed, if she could even find it again.

***

Sandy Dink drove the Dink's Service Station tow truck slowly, frowning in concentration. Listening. The front end had given him trouble before, and just a second ago he thought he'd felt—yep, there it was again—a damned shimmy.

"Son of a whore." Now he'd have to take the mother apart all over again, and—

"Jesus!" He slammed his heavy work boot down on the bare metal brake pedal. Screaming rear tires left the stink of burning rubber, laying black exclamation points on the asphalt.

Sandy climbed back down off the wheel, eyes wide. His front bumper had stopped about two inches from a man standing smack in the middle of River Road. The guy's back was turned to the truck.

With an explosive sigh, Sandy leaned out and yelled, "Christ almighty, buddy! You okay? What's your damn problem, anyway, standing out in the middle of the Goddamn—"

The man pivoted slowly, jerkily, and Sandy trailed off into silence.

What the hell. It was Mister Blunt. Must be drunk, just standing there like a freaking statue. Sure looked funny.

Eyes all weird, dressed in a funky shirt with big tie-dye splotches. Huh. Some cool dude. Sandy rolled his eyes.

"Um, Mr. Blunt . . . Slocum . . . where's your car, man?"

Slocum only blinked at him, as if reluctant to leave his spot in the headlights.

Jeez, sucker must really be wasted, thought Sandy. "Well, uh, get in. I'll, let's see—take you home. I guess." He waited, kind of hoping some other solution would present itself.

After a few silent moments, Slocum spun jerkily right and staggered around to the passenger side. Sandy opened the door, but the guy still had difficulty climbing in. After a couple of false starts, though, he made it.

"So. Had a few, my man?" Sandy grinned, thinking, What a tool. He put the truck in gear and started toward town again.

Slocum stared ahead, silent.

"So. You been up to Marianna? Car break down?"

Slocum blinked, but made no answer.

Sandy cleared his throat. "Whatever." He shifted into third, gripping the steering wheel tighter than necessary. Something was giving him the creeps. Maybe it was the hideous shirt. Or that Godawful white face hanging over it. The guy looked like he'd been puking for days. Drinking always made Sandy happy and talkative. But Mr. Blunt acted like . . . well, like a fucking corpse.

What the hey, Sandy thought. I can jolly anybody up. Even him. Get some life back into the dude. Do that pretty wife of his a favor.

He glanced over at the man jouncing beside him on the trucks' vinyl bench seat. Damn, the shocks must be going too, he thought. Gotta look into that. He didn't much like the boneless way Slocum Blunt jiggled there in his seat. Like an egg custard. Sandy had always hated egg custard.

"Hey. What's wrong, Slokey my man? You meet up with an angel, and died and gone to heaven?"

Sandy slapped one knee and snorted, impressed with his own sophisticated wit.

Slocum's head swiveled as if it rested on a rusted ball bearing in his neck. He grinned back with yellow teeth.

For the first time, in the green glow of the dash, Sandy noticed the gaping hole in the man's exposed throat. His eyes widened. Slocum's soft belly jiggled even more, as if he was greatly amused. His lips twitched.

Suddenly Sandy knew that if Slocum Blunt laughed, he wouldn't be able to stand the sound of it.

But instead of a laugh, or even a dry chuckle, only a high thin whistle issued from the ragged wound.

Sandy gagged. "Jesus, man. We gotta get you to a—whoops!" He wrestled the truck back off the shoulder. "—to a hospital or something!"

A damp meaty hand clamped down on Sandy's thigh. He felt the cold clamminess of it even through his heavy work jeans.

Slocum leaned toward Sandy, still grinning. "Little kiss?" he hissed, air leaking from the wound in his throat. Sandy could swear the man's lips never moved, but that the ragged flaps of that horrible wound—

"God! Get it off—get offa me!" Sandy clawed at the dead weight of the terrible hand so hard he swerved off the road. He jumped out of the cab before the truck came to a complete stop, and then ran faster than he ever had managed for the Crane County High School 880 relay. He pounded straight down the middle of the blacktop, breath sobbing in his throat. Away from the thing in the truck, toward town.

He looked back only once. The Ford 250's glowing headlights were jammed like oversized Christmas tree bulbs into the festive red brambles of a thorny pyracantha bush. One wheel hung over the ditch, spinning on air. Slocum was visible through the side window, sitting patiently, head still turned toward the empty driver's seat.

Sandy kept on jogging down the road, leg muscles screaming, gasping for air. He had a wicked stitch in his side, but it wasn't bad enough—not nearly bad enough—to make him stop. He didn't quit running until he reached the edge of Abaton. And even then, he still walked very fast.

THIRTY

In search of the narrow trail that would lead her back to Mattie Swann's house, Kay drove up and down River Road several times. Turned into one narrow, unpaved track after another and met only rutted, brushy dead ends. Once she nearly drove right off a bluff into the river. She'd stopped just short, gasping as the rolling blackness swallowed her canted headlights.

After awhile, Chloe began to whine. "I'm tired. I'm hungry. I want to go home."

"All right!" Kay snapped. She didn't blame Perdita, who was understandably distracted. But she felt like cursing her aunt for leaving a near-baby like Lala to fend for herself. "All right," she said to Chloe, tone apologetic. "I'm sorry. We're going back now."

She spun the wheels backing out of the last dead end, branches scraping the Volvo's fenders. She drove home fast, taking the corners like a Little Havana taxi driver.

Her daughter was pale and silent by the time they pulled into the semicircle drive. She slipped out of the car. "I don't feel so good."

Slightly green, Chloe climbed the stairs to bed. Kay followed close behind, feeling guilty. She'd taken out her frustrations on a child. Her own child. What a bitch . . . but God, how her ankle was throbbing. She limped into her own room, pulled off only shoes and jeans, collapsed across her bed like a tired drunk. And fell asleep almost at once. Dreaming.

Kay knew it was a dream, because Jack was standing in the darkened room. He wasn't really, of course. Still, she wished him there beside her.

So he sat on the edge of the bed, and the mattress sagged under his weight. Amazing how real it seemed. Not like a dream at all. He lay down beside her, a little awkwardly. A cool hand slid under her shirt, down her bare stomach. It stopped at the band of her bikini underwear. She squirmed impatiently. His fingers dipped under the elastic and went unerringly to the right spot.

It was her dream, after all.

She arched her back in approval as those familiar hands stroked her. Good . . . and yet something was not quite right. His hand different than she remembered. Heavier? Colder? But she didn't want to think about it right now.

Her head turned on the pillow, her breath came faster. Only a dream, and it was time to carry it to the logical conclusion. She pulled at his arm, wanting to feel his weight on top of her. That was when she smelled him. Absolutely rank. In dire need of a shower. But still she didn't care.

***

In her room, Chloe groaned and turned over in her sleep. "Daddy?" she whispered.

***

Jack didn't make any further move, and Kay couldn't wait any longer. She sat up and straddled the dark, motionless figure on the bed. In her dream she tugged roughly at his belt buckle, heard the cold metal clank, felt the worn soft leather, and slid her hands up to caress his chest and stomach.

Then she froze, breath stopped in her throat

***

Chloe thrashed beneath her sheet, tangling it around her. "No," she muttered. "It's not him. Daddy!"

***

Kay hurled herself off the body beneath her. "What—who—" she gasped.

Jack's chest and stomach had been firm, muscular. This body was soft and flabby, with a big gut oozing over the belt. She wanted and did not want to see more than the dark outline visible in the dim light. "Jack?" she whispered.

A breathy whistle was the only reply.

***

Chloe sat straight up in bed, body rigid. Thin cords of her neck stretched taut as wires. "Mamamamamama!" she screamed.

***

"Who is it, my God, who is that!" Kay shrieked, scrambling away from the thing lying so heavy and still on the bed.

It rose stiffly and lurched toward the hall, blocking out the faint glow of a nightlight there.

"Out! Get Out!" Kay pressed a fist to her mouth, gagging. The other was still clenched on the sweaty sheet.

She trembled so violently she bit her tongue and tasted blood. She had no gun . . . no weapon at all. The intruder was outlined in the faint glow from the hall. Bigger, bulkier than Jack. What if he didn't leave? What if . . . what if Chloe . . .

She screamed then. Heavy footsteps lumbered down the hall, down the stairs, pounded across the kitchen. The back door banged in its frame.

***

"Mom!" Chloe scrambled from bed, the sheets magically untangled. Crying, confused in the dark, she groped toward the faint lines of dawn rising outside the window. Stumbling, she struck her head against the cool glass pane. She rubbed her bruised temple, whimpering. Outside, down in the moonlit backyard, a small, familiar figure waited beneath the big crape myrtle.

"Lala." Chloe pressed both hands against the glass. As she watched, a larger, darker figure shambled away from the house, toward the little girl below the trees.

Chloe's skin prickled. "Lala, watch out!" She banged a fist against the glass and one pane cracked in a starburst.

When the big man reached Lala, she only smiled up. Then, taking one of his large paws in her own small hand, she led him like a tame bear into the woods.

"Chloe!" Her mother was at the door, then beside her. "Are you all right?"

Chloe thought of what she'd just seen. If she told her mother, it would upset her. There would be trouble. For her. For Lala, out so late at night. And the man . . . it was the kind of thing you didn't really tell an adult. They were so easily frightened.

"I'm fine." She patted her mother's arm. "You're crying. Did you have a bad dream?"

***

"Feeling okay, Mom?"

Kay was slumped at the kitchen table, head on one hand, third cup of strong coffee in the other. "What? Oh, sure, sweetheart." She reached out to pat Chloe's cheek absently. "Just a little tired, is all."

Chloe frowned and looked down at her cereal again. "You didn't hear anything . . . funny last night, did you?"

Kay set her cup down so abruptly coffee sloshed onto the scrubbed pine table. After leaving Chloe's room she'd crept slowly down the stairs, cursing herself for a coward all the way. In the kitchen, the back door was closed and locked. She wheeled and ran down the hall to the front door. Also closed and locked. So it had all been a dream, albeit a particularly nasty one.

"No. Not really. Why?"

"No. Just the wind, and . . . Gus meowing. Stuff like that."

"Oh. Just that." Kay tried not to seem too relieved. "On a windy night, it's more—" She stopped, unsure of what she'd been about to say.

***

Chloe felt incredibly relieved. She didn't want Lala to get in trouble, to be told she couldn't see her any more. Bad enough her mother would see the cracked window in her bedroom. That would be hard to explain. She'd carefully pulled the shade all the way down this morning, but it was only a matter of time before she noticed the damage, and wanted to know how it had gotten broken.

"Well," she said with an exaggerated yawn. "Guess I'm going out."

"Oh yeah?" Her mother smiled. "Got a date?"

"Yeah. Sort of." She grinned. "Out back." She made sure not to let the screen door bang behind her. To not make her mother jump. Not this morning.

Lala was waiting at the edge of the lawn, half hidden by dappled shade. Chloe looked back over her shoulder at the house, then skimmed across the lawn.

"Boy," she panted when she reached the smaller girl. "You were outside late last night. Bet your gramma didn't know."

Lala shook her head. "My gramma knows. Go see her?"

Chloe took a step back. "What, all the way to your house? No. I'm in trouble already. Broke a window. Anyhow, I'm not s'posed to leave the yard, so—" She paused, thinking it over. Of course, if she'd be in trouble soon anyway . . .

"Well, maybe. Mom's working this morning, she might not notice. But we have to be back before lunch."

She let her friend draw her a little way into the trees.

"Wait a minute." She pulled back. "Who was that man with you last night?"

Lala looked back silently, eyebrows raised like tiny question marks.

"Well, who was it? Your . . . your babysitter or something?"

"No!" Lala stamped one bare foot with miniature scorn. "He the bad blue man."

"He didn't look blue to me. I bet he was your sitter, baby!"

Lala shrieked in mock outrage. Chloe bolted, laughing, and let the smaller girl chase her all the way up the path to the woods.

***

Kay was at work on a new pastel sketch for the book's next rhyme, an old British poem that was sweet and unsettling.

Golden slumbers kiss your eyes,
Smiles awake you when you rise . . .

When the phone rang she snatched it up gratefully. It was Perdita. "How's Perle? What did the doctor say?"

"Dr. Williams thinks she'll be fine. A mild concussion from that enormous bump, and they had to stitch the cut over her eye. A hairline fracture. Looks like she lost a boxing match. But she's awake now, already complaining about the hospital food."

"She must be okay, then. Did you find out . . . I mean, did she say anything about—"

"She wasn't molested," Perdita said flatly. "But she doesn't recall what did happen. All she remembers is going into town, buying some things, and starting back. After that, zip."

"Well . . . the main thing is, she's going to be all right."

"Yes, except it means there's some person out there, maybe someone we know, who might try this on some other girl."

"Maybe it'll come back to her."

"I hope so. Well, just wanted to let you know how she's doing. And to thank you for helping us last night."

"After all you've done for me, it seems like little enough. Oh, and I wanted to ask you, is . . . is Lala all right? Tried to find my way back to your aunt's last night to check, but I never made it."

"The road can be hard to find. It's so overgrown. But yes, she's fine. When Aunt Mattie came home, she said she was sleeping like a baby. Never even knew we were gone."

"Oh, well—good. And one other thing. Since I found out Jack's mother is still living in that institution, I'd like to see her. She won't know me; we've never met before. And I understand she's . . . not in great shape. But it seems like the least I can do."

"That's simple enough. My cousin Pat can find out where she is. He'd know when would be the best time to come for a visit."

"This is the guy you were going to bring to dinner?"

"Yes. He works in the forensic unit. You know, with the criminally insane—not geriatrics. But he can find out that much for you."

"Great." Nervousness began to replace the enthusiasm she'd felt. What did you say to a patient who'd spent three decades in a mental institution? A mother-in-law you'd always assumed was dead.

"I'll call right now," Perdita said. "Put him to work."

"Sure it's not too much trouble? He's probably busy."

"Sure. But not too busy to help a young, pretty taxpayer. If he balks, all I have to do is describe you. I can have quite a way with words, when I feel like it."

Kay laughed. "I'm looking for a lost relative. Not a date."

"I hear you. 'Bye." As Perdita hung up, Kay was sure she heard her laughing.

THIRTY-ONE

O h. It's you." Bonnie turned coldly from the open front door. "I thought maybe this time you weren't coming back."

She carried a steaming mug of tea back through the French doors to the study, and sat in a tapestry-covered armchair. An e-reader lay on the footstool in front of it. She picked up the Nook and began reading the historical romance she'd just downloaded, again, with exaggerated interest. If the bastard thought she gave a damn what he did anymore, well. . . .

A shadow fell across her.

"What do you want, Slocum?" She lowered the e-reader to her lap and sighed, squinting up with nearsighted irritation. Her contact lenses were in the upstairs bathroom. She could read the large print on the screen fine without them, but couldn't see much detail on anything else. "God. You look like a hog's breakfast. What's that on your shirt, lipstick? What an awful color—like dried blood. Must've picked a real beauty this time at the truck stop. Can't you at least find one who doesn't make up like *The Walking Dead*?"

Her husband only stood there, silent. Simply hulking.

She drummed her fingers on the arm of the chair nervously. "Well, if you don't have anything to say." She sniffed tentatively, and her nostrils flared. "Lord God, but you need a shower. Bad enough I have to look at you after these binges. Why should I have to smell—hey!"

He grabbed her Nook reader and flung it at the brick fireplace. It shattered, the pieces flying all over the Iranian rug at her feet.

"Jesus. Fine! Stay in here and tear up whatever you like. I'll go to the office. Somebody ought to be there to run the business."

She rose and faced Slocum. He did look absolutely awful. Even without contacts, she could see that. Her eyes filled with tears and she took a step toward him. "I don't even know why you do these things. Why are you trying to . . . to . . . "

Her voice failed her. Because up close now she could see his face clearly. Sickly white with livid blue blotches. His eyes strangely milky, as if filmed over with dust. He didn't blink, not once. And, oh god – the smell! Her throat closed on it, and she retched. It reminded her of the time her little dog Charlie—God, twenty-five years ago—had stepped in a trap and gotten gangrene in his back legs. They'd had to put Charlie to sleep. She peered again at Slocum. And then she noticed his throat.

He was taller, so the huge, ragged hole in it was right at eye level. Why, she could see clear into his . . . his. . . .

Bonnie began to tremble. Surely it would be impossible to live with such a wound.

She whispered, "Your neck."

He reached out and grabbed her upper arms. As she stared, unable to look away, an iridescent green beetle climbed over an exposed muscle and disappeared into the recesses of his esophagus.

"Oh no," she moaned. "Oh my God." She lost her tea and Sara Lee croissant all down the front of Slocum's horrible shirt. He didn't seem to care. Instead, he lifted her right off the floor, until her eyes were level with his. She squirmed and kicked, but couldn't break his grip on her.

And then those dry, scaly lips peeled back from his teeth. He was finally going to say something, and Bonnie was sure she didn't want to hear it. She clenched her eyes shut so tightly stars burst inside the lids.

"Kiss . . . me," her husband's voice hissed, like an old 78 rpm record. But the sound seemed to come from below his mouth, down around the hole in his neck. "Dar . . . ling."

A whole, awful ten seconds passed before she could gather her wits and remember to scream.

THIRTY-TWO

From her seat in Mattie Swann's kitchen, Chloe listened to the rush of the river. She leaned on both elbows at the battered pine table, watching the old woman stuff small white muslin bags with dried leaves and flowers, and something like powdered egg yolk she pinched out of a chipped teacup.

"Is that a sack—a sach—stuff to make your clothes smell good?" She'd seen her mother tuck little pouches of lavender buds into drawers and closets at home.

"Smell good!" Lala's grandmother laughed. "No ma'am. Here, sniff." She thrust the bag under Chloe's nose.

"Eew! That's nasty." She rubbed her nose hard to get rid of the lingering rotten-egg stink.

"Has to have a smell, do it keep away dreams."

"Dreams?" Chloe leaned forward. "What kind of dreams?"

"The bad ones, child. Kind what give a body night sweats and keep you staring in the dark. Little thing like you got no call to dream like that, though."

"But my mom . . . " Chloe hesitated, pretty sure her mother wouldn't like being discussed with almost-strangers.

"What about your mama?"

She thought for a moment of the dark circles under her mother's eyes. Her vacant stare at breakfast. She thought she knew the cause.

"She has lots of bad dreams. Almost every night."

Mattie Swann looked up at her, eyes narrowed. "This true, missy?"

"Yeah. I mean, yes ma'am."

"What she dream about?"

Chloe was stumped for a moment. "Uh . . . well . . . monsters, I guess. Scary stuff, you know. She's had lots of nightmares since Da—since my father died. They got better for awhile, but . . . "

"An' now you all are here, they comin' back?"

Chloe nodded. "I think so. She doesn't tell me about them, though."

The old woman sucked her teeth, then pulled the drawstring tight on a bag and set it aside. "A person got to sleep, sooner or later."

The screen door flew open. Lala ran in, tiny fists full of drooping wildflowers. She jumped up on Chloe's lap, making the chair rock, nearly knocking both of them out of it. "For you, for you!" she shouted, scattering flowers in Chloe's hair and clothes. When Chloe giggled and brushed petals from her face, the littler girl shrieked with laughter. She hugged her fiercely. "My frien', Gamma! Clo is my frien'!"

The old woman smiled, the corners of her eyes creasing like old linen. "A good friend a fine thing to have, baby doll."

Lala nodded and kissed Chloe's cheek with a loud smacking sound.

Chloe blushed and rubbed at the damp spot. "You're so silly," she said, but felt pleased. "Um, Mrs. Swann?"

"Call me Aunt Mattie, sugar."

"Okay, Mrs . . . Aunt Mattie. Do you know what time it is? I have to get home before my mother—I mean, before one."

From one deep pocket the old lady pulled a gold wristwatch with a broken band. She studied the scratched, clouded crystal. "Almost twenty to, now."

"Oops, got to go. Or Mom will kill me." She struggled up from her chair, out of Lala's tight embrace.

"No. Not go yet. Not go!"

"Got to," Chloe said firmly. Then, remembering her manners, she turned back. "Thank you for the lemonade, Aunt Mattie." At the door she turned back again. "I'll come again soon," she promised Lala, who swung her legs on the chair, pretending to pout.

"Wait," said her grandmother.

Chloe let go of the doorknob and turned around a third time.

"Come here to me, missy."

She walked back to the scarred table where the tiny white pouches were piled up like sacks of miniature pirate treasure.

"Here, child. Take this dream-charm poke. For your mama. Just tuck it 'neath her pillow."

Chloe stared at the plump little bag lying on her outstretched palm. Beneath it, the skin on her hand tingled. "Under her pillow," she repeated obediently, then closed her hand tightly around her prize. "Thanks. 'Bye!"

This time she slipped quickly out the screen door, careful not to let it bang, and ran down the pine straw-cushioned path.

***

Lala sulked a few moments longer, kicking at one wobbly table leg. Then she got down and walked to Mattie, twisting handfuls of the old woman's skirt to hoist herself up. She settled down in her lap. "Gamma?"

"What, baby?" She was stuffing another bag, humming 'Shall We Gather at the River.'

"Like Chloe."

"Yes, child. I do like your little friend."

"No, no." The little girl fidgeted. "I like. She my friend."

"A good friend is a fine thing," Mattie repeated, drawing the strings on the bag tighter, as if to bind and imprison something small and desperate within.

Her granddaughter nodded, pigtails bouncing. "My frien'. For always, Gamma." She turned and reached up to stroke the old woman's weathered face with both hands. "Gamma?"

Wrinkled, calloused hands paused in their work. "What you want, baby doll?"

"My friend. For always."

Mattie frowned. "Always be a long, long time for little girls."

Lala scowled. "Keep her for always."

Mattie gazed over her adopted granddaughter's head. "You been lonesome. I know. Though not now, since you found a little friend. But she grow up one day. Go away."

"No!" Lala screamed. "Stay with me!" Her tiny hard fists lashed out. One struck and cut the old woman's lip. A drop of blood trickled from the corner of the pursed, wrinkled mouth.

"Hush now, hush," Mattie crooned, rocking the little girl back and forth. "Gramma take care of you, baby. Gramma always take care. Won't let you be sad. No sir. Gramma see to that."

THIRTY-THREE

So there's no reason why she can't have visitors," Patrick Woodberry told Kay. His voice sounded deep and reassuring on the phone. "Although the unit's social worker said none of the staff could remember anyone ever coming to see her."

"That's terrible. If only Jack had told me."

She shifted the phone to the other ear. Why had he never even mentioned his mother, left all alone in a state hospital? That wasn't the Jack she'd known.

"Well, that's certainly not your fault. But even if it were, it wouldn't exactly be unusual. We get them all—homeless misfits, old folks with no money, crazy criminals. All sent here and left here for the same reason. No one knows what to do with 'em. People the world would rather forget."

"Not anymore. I'm coming out this afternoon." Anyhow, if she didn't get going immediately, she might chicken out. "Now, please tell me—slowly—how to get there."

She wrote down the directions, thanked him, and promised a dinner invitation soon. This one, she vowed privately, would not be a social fiasco. She'd choose her guests more carefully, for their tolerance. The rest could go to hell.

217

The impending good-will mission inspired her; she painted and sketched for two hours and was actually pleased with the results. Around one she went to the back door and called Chloe in for lunch. Her daughter, flushed, dirty, and breathless, dashed out of the trees on the edge of the lawn. Suddenly Kay thought of Perle, lying still as a buried treasure under all those fallen leaves.

"Chloe, where on earth have you been—not to the river?" she called sharply.

"N-no, Mom. Lala and I were . . . playing. In the woods. Not too far, just a little down the path."

She fixed Chloe with "the X-ray eye," as Jack used to call it. But her daughter met her gaze.

"Well, all right. Get washed up to eat now. I've got to go into town for some errands. You're going to stay with May Olive."

"Why can't I go too?"

"Because. I have lots to do, and—you just can't this time. I'm the mother, I don't have to explain." She tugged on a lock of Chloe's hair. "Now, to the wash bucket, young lady."

***

When Kay pulled up in the Reeds' driveway, May Olive was out in the side yard, bent over the garden that filled most of it. Chloe got out with a load of dolls and coloring books.

"Thanks for taking her on such short notice."

"I love to do it," May Olive protested. "I always imagined I'd have grandbabies spilling out of every door. But I guess it wasn't meant to be."

She saw regret flicker in the pale blue eyes that were an older, faded version of Bonnie's, and felt bad for May Olive. "Oh my—your flowers are amazing, even in this heat. What's that you're cutting? Smells wonderful."

"Oh, that? Just sage." She crushed a pale, pebbled leaf and held it up to Kay's nose.

The sharp green scent made her think of Thanksgiving dinners. "Smells different than the stuff at the supermarket. Makes me hungry, and we just had lunch. What are those other ones, over there?"

"Tansy, basil, dill weed, thyme. Oh, and that's rosemary, and French marjoram in the pot. It's too delicate to stay out all the time."

"And that one there, with the pretty white flowers?"

May Olive laughed. "That there's a weed. And poisonous to boot. I've got to get busy and pull them up, or they'll crowd out all the good ones."

"Sounds like more manual labor than I'm used to. Afraid I wasn't cut out to garden. I have a black thumb. Even my weeds die."

May Olive shrugged. "It's not all that hard. Just got to keep an eye on things. And know what to look for. There's always a poison waiting to creep in and take over. You just have to be there when it appears, and know how to fight it."

As they walked to the car she told May Olive that Perle was better. "I just wonder who it was that attacked her."

May Olive nodded, looking troubled. "Yes. What if it was a local, someone we see every day, and even speak to? Makes me shudder to think of it."

"Surely it had to be a stranger," said Kay. "This is such a small place. You know everyone."

As she put the car in gear and waved goodbye to Chloe, May Olive suddenly asked, "You haven't seen Bonnie today, have you?"

"No. Why, is she looking for me?"

"Don't think so. She told me she'd be home all day. But I've called three or four times and there's no answer."

"She didn't call me. Maybe she went in to the office after all."

"I called there too. They got that darned answer-thing on. I refuse to talk to a machine. Gives me the heebie-jeebies. I suppose she and Slocum both might've had to go out to show a house, or such as that. Don't know why I'm even wondering. She went off to the mall in Tallahassee, most like. Girl should've been born with a charge card."

Kay laughed, and the older woman smiled, but the worry-creases around her eyes remained.

"She'll turn up soon, May Olive. Loaded down with packages."

"Don't I know it. But once a mama, always a mama." She waved and turned back to the house, and Chloe, and Kay drove off.

***

Kay's first stop was the craft shop, to pick up thread for Chloe and a new brush she'd specially ordered. Minnie greeted her as though it had been years, instead of days, since she'd last stopped in. "I swanee! Come in, honey. Don't you look fine today. Got a date?"

"Heavens, no." Kay smiled. "Just running errands."

Minnie opened her mouth to say something else, but was interrupted by shouts from outside. Through the front window, framed by hand looms, easels, and quilt hoops, a huge black object was rolling down the sidewalk on the other side of the street. Old folks, dogs, and children scattered in all directions as the thing—which looked like a giant black doughnut—jumped the curb and rolled across the street, heading straight toward the shop.

"My God," said Kay. "What's that?"

Minnie stamped a foot. "Oh, bother that boy."

"I don't see any boy," Kay said nervously. "Just a big black rubber thing. Looks like a giant inner tube."

"A course! It's that Luther again."

220

The giant tractor tire tube was followed by a stocky young man in cut-off overalls. Greasy black hair flopped limply in his eyes as he shoved the giant inner tube with both hands, bellowing, "Pardon us. 'S'cuse me. Look away below!"

"He's coming right this way," said Kay. "So . . . you know him?"

A moments later, there came an earsplitting SNAP. They both jumped. Luther's flushed, sweating face popped in through the open door. He held a piece of old rubber in both hands. Before Kay's heart had stopped hammering, he snapped it again.

"Hey there, Miz Minnie," he bellowed.

"Luther, I'll wear out your trouser seat if you don't get that rubber mess out of here!" She stomped over to the door, an irate gnat belaboring a horse. "You better just—"

"Got any old inner tubes?" he shouted in Minnie's face.

"You know good and well I don't. Now you get. Go on!"

He grinned and glanced over at Kay. "Hey lady. Got any old basketball covers?"

Kay shook her head. "No, I—"

"Luther, get out of here!"

He beamed at Kay, exposing gaps in his teeth, then hitched up his sagging overalls and reached for the inflated tube leaning against the shop door. "Luther's got to be going now," he said firmly, as though she and Minnie would insist he stay. And then he and the tube rolled away. Kay wandered over and stuck her head out the door just in time to see a frail, elderly lady leap out of his path like a long jumper.

"I declare. That boy really should be put away." Minnie sighed, shaking her head. "He's a menace on the streets, especially to the elderly."

"He did seem sort of, um, dangerous," Kay agreed.

"He was once a sweet little child. Maybe it would've been best if he'd drowned in the river the time he fell in. Sometimes folks is gone too long, and shouldn't be brought back, no matter what kind of fancy equipment a hospital's got. They say he's harmless, but Miz Hepple broke a hip once trying to get out of his way. He like to scares half the town to death every time he rolls through."

She tsk-tsked as she wrapped and rung up Kay's purchases. "The world is full of crazy people," she complained. "Never know when you're going to come across one, do you? Well, have a nice time, wherever you're going, honey."

***

The damp vinyl couch stuck with Tupperware-like tenacity to Kay's sweating thighs. She shifted uncomfortably, feeling as if soon she'd be fused to the hard seat. Equally damp was her hand, cramped from holding the bunch of flowers she'd bought to give Louvinia Abbott.

She was waiting in the area a white-smocked aide had called the 'day room'. He'd settled her there on the couch and then disappeared down a pale green corridor.

She had looked around curiously at first, since she'd never been inside a mental institution, or whatever they were called these days, before. The place seemed clean and looked freshly painted, though the walls were a strange pale sea-green, several shades lighter than the turquoise couch. In Miami, the curved Danish Modern pieces scattered around would've fetched a high price for their genuine Fifties' kitsch. Here they just looked like old furniture.

She banged her knee on a low, boomerang-shaped blond coffee table. It was heaped with back issues of Modern Maturity, large-print editions of Reader's Digest, and a single lonely issue of Seventeen. An enormous color television throbbed in one corner like a tell-tale heart. One elderly pajama-clad man was playing cards with an aide, but the idiot box held everyone else's attention, though the actors whining and crying in the soap opera onscreen had lime-green skin.

Out of sight down the hallway, came a clank of metal, the wet slap of a string mop. Imitation pine scent wafted down the hall.

When a hand lightly touched Kay's shoulder, she jumped.

"Here we are, Miz Abbott," A young female aide drawled. She shoved the coffee table aside with one foot and pushed a brightly-chromed wheelchair around, parking it squarely in front of Kay. A gray-haired woman, painfully thin, sat in it, gazing straight ahead.

"There. Miz Abbott, meet Miz Abbott." The aide chuckled as if pleased with her own wit. She leaned down close and patted one papery cheek. "Now don't you go talking this poor young lady's ear off, old miss." She turned away and lumbered off toward the glassed-in office, hips rolling.

Pushing down sudden panic, Kay forced a smile. This is Louvinia Abbott, she told herself. My mother-in-law. Chloe's grandmother. She tried to see Jack in the worn features, but couldn't summon his healthy, good-humored visage from the long, sparse white hair, the sunken cheeks, those faded, indifferent gray eyes. As a whole, it made up a face remarkably unmemorable. Indistinct, as if rubbed over with an eraser. Louvinia seemed unaware of the scrutiny directed at her.

"I'm so glad to meet you at last," Kay said warmly, and then fell silent. What else could they talk about? Sorry I took so long to get here, I thought you were dead. Wow, glad to see you're still barely alive. She was suddenly furious at Jack for leaving her alone to face an abandonment in which she'd played no part.

She tried again. "Mrs. Abbott—Louvinia—may I call you that?"

No response.

"If I'd known you were here, I would've come much sooner. I'm sorry it took so long. But glad I finally found you." She laid the bouquet gently in her mother-in-law's lap. "I brought you these. Mixed, since I don't know your favorite flower."

The woman's hands remained folded and still beneath the heat-wilted bouquet. She continued to gaze indifferently over Kay's left shoulder. She hadn't even blinked yet.

"I-I'm Kay. Your son Jack's wife. He isn't here, of course, because—" She hesitated, unsure whether Louvinia actually knew of his death. She decided to avoid that topic for now. "And Chloe, our daughter—your granddaughter— is nine now. Smart as a whip."

The old woman's gaze suddenly shifted to Kay's face. She leaned forward slightly. "You've seen the little girl?" Her whisper was dry and thin as the crackle of dead leaves underfoot.

"Chloe?" Kay frowned. "Well, yes, of course. Every day."

Louvinia's vacant expression fell suddenly, disconcertingly, into sly, crafty lines. "She's mad at me."

"Oh, no. Certainly not. I'll bring her to visit you. Sometime . . . soon."

Louvinia cocked her head like an ancient, puzzled parrot. Then, slowly, she smiled. "See. She's seen her too," she whispered, as if to some unseen companion, nodding with satisfaction.

Well, dementia was to be expected, under the circumstances. And so many years locked way here. "I will bring her. Later, when you're, um, feeling better. Then you can see for yourself."

"They don't believe she exists," the arid voice confided, as Louvinia leaned a little closer. "She comes tapping on

224

my window at night. I call for the nurse every time. Right away. 'Nurse, nurse!' But they always come too late. Too late," she hissed, shuddering as though a cold draft had suddenly chilled her. She began to mutter under her breath, rocking back and forth in the wheelchair.

Kay sat very still, unsure what she ought to do. Patrick Woodberry hadn't warned her how badly Louvinia had deteriorated. She thought her granddaughter, whom she'd never met, was some sort of ghost who haunted her at night. It must be Alzheimer's. She'd read an article on it a while back. Something about famous people with the disease. Rita Hayworth, Ronald Reagan, even Lincoln had apparently suffered from it. She wished she could remember more details. "I'm sorry, but—you can't mean Chloe. Perhaps some other little girl visits you here? Another relative, I mean."

The old woman looked away. Her withered lips twisted, her thin, bowed shoulders began to shake. She made a dry, gasping sound.

Now I've done it, Kay thought. Made her upset. She's crying. And not a single aide in sight.

She half-rose to go look for one, but just then her mother-in-law looked up. And Kay saw then she was laughing.

"Are you all right?" she asked, thinking, My God, she's totally crazy. Kay thought suddenly, with alarm, of May Olive's stories about the younger Louvinia. Could this sort of madness be hereditary?

The woman stopped laughing abruptly. "I know what she wants," she said in a flat, dead tone.

"What's that?" Kay prompted, thinking it best to play along until she could catch the eye of someone on the staff.

"She comes to the window," the old woman said slowly, like a school teacher speaking to a slow-witted pupil. "And taps and taps. On the glass. She's wearing her nightgown, the white one with little yellow ducks. But I can't see the ducks anymore."

"Why not?" Kay asked, feeling foolishly relieved that Chloe owned no such nightgown.

Louvinia looked at her with something like . . . pity? "Because of the blood," she said calmly. "All the blood. It's everywhere. Little red fingerprints on my window. She draws pictures with blood on the glass. But then she always wipes them off. The pictures are gone in the morning. You can't see then, but they were there!"

Oh boy. This is too much for me, Kay thought. Time to find an aide. She stood up and looked around.

"I had to do it," Louvinia shouted. "For Jonah. It was a fair trade!"

One patient looked up from gazing at the green-tinted soap opera, then away, back to the screen.

"I know what she wants." Those thin, trembling hands rose from her lap like agitated birds. One continued up jerkily, higher than the other, and came to rest, fluttering at the base of Louvinia's throat. The flowers fell and lay scattered around the base of the wheelchair. "She wants . . . she wants . . . to kill me." She paused, drew a deep, shuddering breath. "For what I did. She wants to take me with her!" Her eyes stared wildly at some invisible horror; a demon formed in the shape of a little girl. "But I won't. Won't go!"

This time all heads swiveled to look, suddenly more interested in this real-life drama than in The Young and the Restless.

"Help here, please," Kay called out, but the same aide was already pounding across the gray linoleum. She pushed herself between Kay and the wheelchair, grabbing for Louvinia's hands. Only then did Kay realize with horror that the old woman had been clawing at her own throat. A thin trickle of blood wound down the folds and creases, soaking the neck of her cotton hospital shift.

The female aide grabbed Louvinia's hands but was clearly having difficulty restraining her. A male aide rushed from the office to help. Kay edged carefully out of the way just as her tiny, withered mother-in-law flung them both away, to the floor. A third staff member joined the fray. Finally the three of them, breathing hard, managed to subdue the old woman and hustle her away down the hall.

Kay stood dazed by the couch. What she'd just seen . . . it was impossible. She glanced down at the overturned wheelchair, the crushed flowers. Shrill screams still echoed down the corridor. Louvinia was shrieking, "No, no, no." Or wait—no, she was screaming a name—"Jonah"—over and over again.

A uniformed security guard came in the door and walked up to Kay. "Sorry, ma'am, but you might as well give up on your visit today." He shook his head, smiling kindly.

"I-I guess so," she agreed. "I never . . . I mean, have you ever seen her . . . act like that before?"

"Nope, can't say that I have. 'Course, I only been here six years. You'd be surprised how much damage these older ones can do, though. What'd you say to get her so riled up, anyhow?"

Or was he looking at her with suspicion now?

"I didn't—nothing, really. She just suddenly got very upset about . . . something in the past."

He nodded thoughtfully, but continued to stare at her. She felt hot and a little dizzy. If she didn't get out of this place that smelled so strongly of disinfected death she might throw up on the shiny, clean gray linoleum.

"E-excuse me." She grabbed up her purse and brushed past the guard, almost running by the time she reached the big glass doors and exited the geriatrics building.

Outside, she walked quickly past the huge stately oaks and well-tended flower beds she'd so admired on the way in. Her ankle began to throb, forcing her to limp. Young men in blue denim were digging a new garden bed. Perdita had mentioned that men from the prison across the road were used to keep the hospital grounds looking like a garden-club showplace. As she hurried past, a couple of them looked up, eyeing her with sullen, silent lust. A low whistle. Muffled laughter. She fought the urge to actually run the rest of the way to the car, forcing herself to walk more slowly.

Next she passed a low white building next to the visitors' parking lot. This, she knew, was the library, because she'd stopped in there earlier, to ask directions to Geriatrics. The librarian, a pretty young blonde, had set her work aside to give her guidance. Had even walked outside to be sure she went in the right direction. The same woman was now coming out the front door of the library pushing a book cart. "Hello again," she said. "Had a good visit, I hope?"

"Well, it was . . . certainly interesting."

"Good. Well, got to get these—" She paused, looking down, frowning. "Oh, my! You've hurt yourself."

Kay followed her gaze. A red smear ran over her ankle and disappeared into her shoe.

"Let me get you something to put on that."

"Oh no. No, really." Kay backed away. "It's nothing. An old . . . cut. I have a, um, first-aid kit in the car. Don't bother, please."

She did run now, fumbling for her keys, straight to the Volvo. Once in the driver's seat she pulled her ankle up to look. Then sat staring at it. At the healing oval wound which for some reason now welled anew with fresh blood. "What the hell?" She blotted it roughly with a tissue, then slammed the car into gear, leaving rubber on the asphalt. In the rearview she saw the librarian was lingering on the sidewalk, on her face the carefully-reserved look Kay imagined she saved for only the most unstable of the hospital's patients.

THIRTY-FOUR

Then the aides carried her away. I could hear her screaming all the way down the hall. It was terrible. I had no idea what to do." Kay winced as May Olive dabbed more hydrogen peroxide on her ankle. "Shit, that hurts."

"Nasty." May Olive may have been referring to the hospital visit, the ankle, or Kay's language. She decided she didn't care. All of them fit.

"And this . . .this child. A little girl she claims to see. It can't be real. All that blood." She shivered, even as sweat trickled down her back.

"She's talking about Abby, most like. Her little girl."

"But she's—"

"Long dead. That's right," May Olive put the cap back on the medicine bottle and set it aside. She leaned back and started to speak, then caught herself and looked around.

"Chloe's outside, pestering Brothercat," said Kay. "She won't hear you."

"I was going to say, it sounds like Louvinia still feels guilty about Abby, after all these years. Mind you, I'm not saying she has reason to be. But some in town did, at the time. Suggesting maybe she was more responsible for Abby's death than it seemed."

"You mean they thought she killed her own daughter, after her husband died. But why?"

"Oh, it was just talk. Some busy-bodies haven't got a blessed thing to do but speculate on other folks' business. That sort were of the mind that maybe Louvinia had tried to—now I never believed any of it, mind you—that maybe she had tried, well, to get Jonah back."

"But he was dead. I don't understand."

"'Course he was. But forty years ago people still held some strange notions. Still do today, if the truth be told and you could get 'em to admit it. Back then, wasn't no doctor in the county. You had to go clear to Tallahassee, almost. Well, there was one for a while, but he got sent off to the war, never did come back. A lot of people used herb doctors, and the midwife, of course. Nothing unusual about that. But a few would also visit the conjure woman."

"Conjure. You mean . . . magic? But that's just—"

"Superstition? Foolishness? Maybe so. But fools got money, too. Folks credited some strange powers to Hoodoo practitioners in those days. Would swear by it, said they could heal sickness, cast spells to help or hurt you. Some would even swear, but not too loud, that under the right conditions a conjure man or woman could raise the dead."

Kay snorted. "Like, 'If the moon be right, and the river high'? Sure, May Olive. Nobody believes stuff like that anymore."

"Afraid some do. Didn't you see that special on TV, 'bout those poor zombie critters on the voodoo island—what's it called?"

Kay stared at her. "You mean . . . Haiti? But that's a developing country. The people are poor, have less access to education. They can't help believing such stuff. Anyhow, who around here would be a conjure woman, or pretend to raise the dead?"

May Olive actually smirked. "Well, there was one. Perdita's aunt—Mattie Swann."

Kay laughed. "You must be joking. Oh, I know she grows herbs and dries flowers and . . . and things like that. But who'd ever believe . . . of course she wouldn't pretend to . . . "

"I didn't say she could. Just that there were some who believed she could. Wasn't so easy for a colored woman to make a living in those days, if she didn't want to scrub floors or do laundry. But Mattie Swann, she did all right, even living out there in the swampy nowhere. Never came into town much—still don't."

"But what's all that got to do with Louvinia?"

"There were rumors she'd gone to see Auntie Swann— that's what folks called her, back in the old, not-politically-correct days—directly after Jonah was killed. To make a bargain."

Kay held up a hand. "Wait a minute. When you talked about Leilah Abbott before, you said she had Louvinia practically under house arrest. How'd she slip out to make a deal with the devil without Leilah knowing?"

"Because . . . " May Olive bit her lip and looked away. "Leilah Abbott was my friend. So I didn't believe any of the stories."

"What stories?"

"That Louvinia tried to get her husband back through conjure. That she'd sacrificed her baby girl so Jonah could live again. And that the idea had been planted in her head by Leilah Abbott. They even said," May Olive continued, reddening under Kay's steady, astonished gaze, "that Leilah would have done anything. Sacrificed Abby, Louvinia, and her own daddy, were he still alive, to get her precious Jonah back."

"May Olive, that's outrageous. Anyhow, what would be in it for Mattie Swann?" Kay scoffed. "Did anyone ever see this Abaton Lazarus after he was supposedly raised from the dead?"

"Pftt. Of course not. I said it was a story. The Abbotts weren't well liked, you know. Those who have it all usually aren't popular with those who don't. And no, no one ever saw Jonah Abbott again because he was stone cold dead. Gone. All the crazy talk in the world couldn't have brought him back." She folded her arms as if done with the subject.

"Of course not. What a ridiculous idea."

"Mom?"

Kay flinched. "Chloe, you startled me. Did you just now come in?"

"Yeah. Brothercat went up a tree after a bird. And I'm hungry. Could we have cheeseburgers for dinner, like you promised?"

Kay laughed. "Someday I'll learn not to make wild promises. Sure, all right, help your mother up."

She let Chloe pretend to haul her from the couch. "Thanks for the tea, May Olive. Speaking of zombies, better get this little ghoul home before she starts gnawing the furniture."

"I'm not a ghoul." Chloe scowled.

"Then count your blessings, child." May Olive smiled at Kay over Chloe's reddish curls. "There's plenty of them to go around. I'll see you folks to the door. Then I'm going to phone Bonnie again. Surely that girl must've cleaned out all the stores by now."

THIRTY-FIVE

The next morning Kay opened the back door, calling, "Gus! Come on, kitty kitty kitty."

No answer. She stepped out into the still-cool, dew-speckled say, and her foot slipped. She grabbed the metal railing just in time to avoid a fall down the steps. She looked down.

"Oh, Jesus." There was the carcass of a brown-furred baby rabbit, split from chin to tail, its guts spilling across the step. She was standing in a congealed puddle of blood.

"Shit! That damned cat." She hauled out a plastic trash bag, the dustpan, and then, wincing, scooped the mess up. After three squirrels, two rats, and a mole, she no longer wasted time gagging. Curse Gus and his new-found bloodlust.

In the midst of her clean-up, the cat appeared. He stopped in the middle of the back yard, and sat watching. Surely after being out all night, and since he never ate these kills, he ought to be hungry. But he came no closer.

Well, fine. "That's right, Ratbreath," she flung at him. "Keep your distance."

She was about to hose down the steps when she noticed a small pink object and leaned down to look closer. A plastic barrette shaped like a butterfly. That was Lala's, she was pretty sure. She started to reach for it, but hesitated. It was so caked with gore she decided to simply hose it off into the flower bed on a pink-tinged flood.

Inside, she had two cups of strong coffee to fortify herself. Then turned to the next rhyme in the series, and began sketching. This one made her smile for its astute summary of the eternal maternal struggle.

Mother, may I go out to swim?
Yes, my darling daughter.
Hang your clothes on a hickory limb,
And don't go near the water.

But by eleven it was too hot to concentrate. She was actually dripping sweat onto the watercolor paper. So she put away her paints, though more reluctantly this time, and rinsed out the brushes. The dining room felt steamy as a sauna; the lazy breeze from the ceiling fans wasn't enough to relieve this brain-basting heat. Maybe she ought to drive to Tallahassee and invest in a couple window AC units, after all.

Chloe was upstairs in her room, with two fans blasting, listening to her iPod. She was laboring over a secret project that Kay suspected would be her birthday present in October.

As she rinsed brushes, the bright colors washed down the sides of the old porcelain sink, creating new shades as they ran. She'd used a lot of red today, and the bloody rivulets were an unwelcome reminder of Louvinia's little ghost—and her own wounded ankle. She shifted her weight at a renewed throbbing pain. During her hasty retreat from the geriatric ward she must've banged it against something.

The kitchen phone rang, and she dropped a brush in the sink. Wow, I'm jumpy, she thought, drying her hands on a dish cloth, reaching for the cell phone.

"Hello?"

"Kay. That you? You sound far away."

"Oh—Myrna? Haven't seen you in awhile. How are you?"

"Me, I'm fine. Just thought I'd call and see how y'all are doing. How's that little angel?"

Kay rolled her eyes. "If you mean Chloe, she's fine. Having fun, enjoying the summer, I think."

"Thank the Lord. Guess you been keeping her close to home these days, since our latest tragedy."

"Our latest—you mean Perle's, um, accident?"

"Heavens, child. Don't you get the news on that side of town?   Everybody's talking about it. Another child disappeared yesterday."

"Oh no. Anyone I would know?"

"Well, you know Lester Monk, over to the grocery?"

"Yes. I mean, not well, but—one of his grandchildren?"

"No, no. It was that little Eddie Kellam."

Kay frowned. "I'm sorry, who?"

Myrna sighed. "The little colored boy. The one follows Lester around. Always bringing in soda bottles. They ain't worth spit, of course, but Lester always gives him something . . . "

Then Kay did recall. The child, narrow back bent with the weight of an armload of bottles, trudging past when she'd driven out to shop at the grocery, the day after she'd arrived in town. How his thin shoulder blades had stuck out like little wings. How he'd tugged on Monk's pant leg, smiling up at him. "Oh . . . but how?"

"Well, the Monks was having a purlow—a big family dinner, you know—over to the river park. Little Eddie was invited. He was there one minute, Lester turned his back, then turned around again and—no Eddie. He's real broken up about it. Swears there's no way the child could've got past him and down to the river. But that has to be it. He disappeared like a fruit-picker's paycheck."

"Maybe he wandered off into the woods. He might still turn up. I mean, we found Perle."

"Yes, but she's not six years old. Besides, woods have been just crawling with Monks. They all would've found him already. Sheriff Swinson thinks they might have to drag the river."

"God, that's horrible." She shuddered, thinking of drowned Abby, and a loaf of bread caught in the current, freighted with quicksilver.

"Yep, sure is." Now Myrna sounded almost cheerful, as if unburdening herself of the news had been good therapy. "Happens almost every year. We lose at least one. My old mama used to say, 'The river takes its due.' Just a fact of life."

"I don't know." Kay looked up at the ceiling as though she could see into Chloe's room. "I wouldn't want to live with a fact like that."

"But we do, honey. We do. Anyhow, I heard Perdita Woodberry's little girl is doing better. Hear tell she's home already."

"I know, Perdita told me. But now this river thing—"

"Look on the bright side, honey. It was only the river this time."

"Why on earth is that a good thing?"

"Why, because if it ain't the river, then we'd have to start thinking there's a prevert loose out there."

Kay began to pace. "Myrna, I wish you wouldn't say that. You're scaring me now."

"Well, a body's got to be careful, especially where children are concerned. Now the Judge, he's always saying that to me. 'Myrna, a body's got to be careful. The world's full of preverts.' He oughta know, put plenty away in his time. Wan't enough, though, I guess. Seems like there's still a gracious plenty to go around."

236

"Yes, I guess so." Kay sighed and shifted her weight without thinking, and the ankle sent a pain shooting up her calf. "Ouch, damn it."

"What's wrong?"

"Nothing. Just have this, um, cut on my ankle. Thought it was healing, but I don't know."

"What you doing for it? Got to be careful with such as that. Could get infected. I hear tell there's this flesh-eating bacteria now that—"

"Myrna, please!"

"Well, you ought to go see old Mattie Swann. She'll fix you a catnip poultice, have it healed in no time."

Kay suppressed a snort. "Yes, I'm sure." So May Olive's theory about the old days dying hard wasn't far-fetched after all.

"Like I told—oh dear," Myrna fretted. "Got to go. Looks like guests pulling up out front. You take care now, hear? And kiss that sweet angel for me. Bye now!"

Kay was happy to click END. Myrna's conversational stamina could qualify her for the Verizon Olympics. But as soon as she set the cell down it rang again. She'd jumped the gun on congratulating herself. She glanced at the screen. It was a local number, looked familiar, but she wasn't sure why. Finally she picked up.

It was Patrick Woodberry.

"Oh—didn't expect to hear from you so soon. That anxious for a free meal?"

A pause, then a sigh. "Wish that was what I'm calling about."

"No?" She turned around nervously, to lean against the counter. "Then . . . what?"

"It's Louvinia Abbott. I wanted to call before you got the official news. Thought maybe to, uh, soften the blow."

"What blow? What's happened?"

"Now first let me say, none of this was your fault."

237

"What the hell . . . please just cut to the chase. You're scaring me."

"Sorry." Another sigh. "She's dead."

"Not—Louvinia? But I just saw her, and she was strong as a professional wrestler. Knocked two aides to the floor."

"I heard she got crazy after your visit. That's why I thought I'd better call. Again, not your fault," he added hastily. "She's always been unstable. They had her on a one-to-one special—that's close observation—because the shift supervisor thought she might hurt herself. She got worse, so he called the unit psychiatrist. Finally had to put her in restraints and up her meds."

"You mean they drugged and tied her to the bed or something? I thought you didn't do stuff like that anymore."

"No, not very often. But sometimes we have to resort to drastic measures when a patient gets real violent, so they won't hurt themselves or someone else. Self-mutilation is popular with some folks here. For instance, we have two eye-pluckers."

"Jesus."

"Sorry, I only mention it to illustrate why it's necessary to use chemical or physical restraints sometimes."

"All right, I'm convinced. How did she die? Heart attack, stroke?"

"No." He cleared his throat. "It seems to have been self-inflicted."

"You mean suicide? But you just told me she was tied to a bed! How the hell, sorry, but . . . how did she manage it?"

"The way I heard it, since Mrs. Abbott was in restraints, they felt she didn't need to be specialed anymore. She was left alone for less than five minutes, while breakfast was being served off the ward. She'd seemed a little calmer, so one of the aides went to get her a tray of food, too. When he came back to feed her, she was already gone. It happened that quickly."

"But how—" She had a terrible suspicion she already knew.

"Christ. You don't really want the details."

"No, but I'm her only living relative, as far as I know, so . . . tell me."

"All right. It was strange. And believe me, I've seen a lot of strange before. The shift supervisor said she was able to tear one arm loose from the leather restraint. It would've taken an incredible effort for anyone, much less an elderly woman, to do that."

Kay closed her eyes and gripped the phone tighter so it didn't slip from her sweating hand. "Go on."

"All right. Then she clawed a hole in her neck. Hit the carotid, unfortunately. It was over fast, no question. Aide who found her, they had to send him home. A bloody mess."

Blood everywhere. Even on the windows. Kay squeezed her eyes shut so tightly white flowers bloomed in the dark behind her lids.

"Hey. You still there? I didn't want to tell all that. Just to call before they notified you officially. Sometimes the office lacks the human touch. Not that I did such a great job myself."

"No. No, it's all right. I appreciate the call. When should I expect to hear from the hospital?"

"Later this morning, I guess. Do me a favor? Don't mention that I called first, if you don't mind."

"Of course. And thanks." She hung up, leaned back against the counter, and closed her eyes again. Sweat slicked her sides, trickled between her breasts.

Blood on the windows. Bloody pictures on the glass.

She closed her eyes, but it was no use. Even in the dark, a red tide rolled and surged. She leaned over the sink just in time.

THIRTY-SIX

Chloe lay on top of the sheets hoping for a breeze. It had to be close to morning, by the faint pink glow in the sky. She'd been awake for forever, it felt like, and couldn't go back to sleep. Partly because it was so hot, and partly because she was worried. Her mother had been upset, pale and quiet at dinner. She'd only eaten a couple bites of chicken. Chloe'd had to finish it. After dinner, her mom had gone upstairs. "To lie down for a while," she'd said. But she never went to bed so early. Chloe figured it must have something to do with missing Dad.

She sighed and hugged her pillow, then flung it away. Too hot. What could she do to make her mother happy again? Dad was gone. They couldn't see him until they got to heaven, her friend Monica Ramirez had said.

But what if she didn't get to go to heaven? Chloe brooded over that for a few minutes. Then another unwelcome thought crept in as slow as Gus sneaking up on a bird. What if something also happened to her mother? She might have already stopped eating, like Jenny Schwartz's big sister did once. Who'd had something bad called annarexia. You had to eat, or else . . . no, she wouldn't even think that. She pressed her hands over her ears hard, to ward off the thought. No. Mom would be okay. She'd feed her like a baby if she had to. The same way her mother had once taken care of her. She had an image of her mother sitting in an oversized highchair, wearing a giant bib, while Chloe fed her with a big spoon, and giggled into her pillow.

Still not sleepy. But the TV would wake her mom and she'd forgotten to charge her Dad's old iPod. Without a flashlight, she couldn't read under the sheets.

She sat up. Through the open window, over the usual singing and sawing of frogs and crickets, she'd heard something else.

There it was again: A high-pitched giggle.

"Can't be," Chloe whispered to herself.

She climbed slowly out of bed, avoiding the creaky board in the center of the room. Eased the window sash up and peered out into the yard. Yes. There, on the edge of the trees, half hidden by the pale, papery trunk of a crape myrtle, was Lala.

"I don't believe it. Hey, Lala!" she whispered through the screen. "What're you doing out there?"

"Go walk," her little friend shouted up shrilly.

"Shh!" Chloe glanced nervously back over one shoulder at the open door of her room. "Not so loud. You'll wake up my mom."

"She asleep."

Maybe so. Chloe had finally managed to slip the white cloth pouch under her mother's bed pillow that afternoon. She hadn't even tried to just give the magic charm to her, feeling sure she'd disapprove. "Oh, yeah. That's right." She nodded as if she'd known all along.

"Come down. Come down!" Lala jumped and skipped in the moonlit grass.

"Well, maybe. Okay. Just wait a second."

The other girl shrieked and laughed, and ran out into the center of the lawn. "Hurry!"

"All right, all right," Chloe grumbled, trying to pull a pair of shorts on over her pajama bottoms. She grabbed a pair of Sketchers and tiptoed into the hall. The only sound from her mother's room was soft, even breathing. On the bottom step, she sat to put the shoes on, not bothering to tie the laces. Then ran to the kitchen door and fumbled with the lock. The bolt stuck, then shot back with a loud clunk.

She hung onto the doorknob breathlessly, expecting any second to hear "Chloe! What are you doing up?"

All that came to her was the sound of her own anxious breathing. She pulled the door open and slipped out, closing it softly behind her.

Lala stood waiting under the trees, one hand behind her back. "What's that you're hiding?" asked Chloe curiously. "Something for me?"

***

Kay turned over, sliding one arm beneath the pillow, hugging it to her chest. A small white bag fell out, balanced for a moment on the edge of the mattress, and then fell to the floor.

Her eyelids fluttered open. Outside her window the sky glowed pink, gray, and orange. Almost dawn. She sighed and buried her face in the pillow. Too early to get up, but she was awake now. Yawning, she kicked the sheets away. Hot already, too. Well, it might be good to get up early and do some work. She couldn't remember the last time she'd actually seen the sun rise.

"Okay, okay," she mumbled sleepily, convinced. She swung her feet to the floor and willed the rest of her body to stand.

The sun had begun its climb above the pines, bathing everything below in warm orange and pink.

If I could go downstairs and get that down in watercolors, she thought, I might be the next Caldecott medal winner. Then Maeve wouldn't bark at me on the phone. In fact she could go suck eggs.

Kay smiled. Maurice Sendak, better watch your adorable rump.

She reached for the denim shorts dropped on the floor last night. As she turned to put them on, a slight movement at the edge of the lawn caught her eye. She stepped over and leaned on the sill to look. Someone was moving through the pines edging the back yard.

She drew back a little, crossing her arms over her chest, hoping she was out of sight. It might be a hunter, but he shouldn't be this close to the house. Anyhow, what was in season in August, in Florida?

Just then the figure stepped out from between two trees to stand in a patch of rosy morning light. Kay's hand flew up to her mouth and she gasped, backing away from the window.

It was Jack.

He stood staring up at the house, dressed in dark pants and a white shirt. Not a hunter's outfit, but the clothes he'd been buried in. Even at this distance, his gaze seemed wistful. Hesitant. Bewildered.

No, she must be mistaken.

Just then he ran his hand through his hair in a familiar gesture.

"No," she whispered, shaking her head. "Oh, no."

But it was impossible, of course. Jack was dead. And I've buried him, she thought, not once but twice.

Such rational thoughts. Yet a man who looked exactly like her dead husband was standing out in the yard at dawn.

All right then, she decided. I must be dreaming again. In a minute I'll wake up, and he'll be gone.

The pinch test was simple enough. She gave the skin on her inner elbow a vicious tweak that brought tears to her eyes, let go, and stared at the rising red welt. Then looked out the window again.

He was still there.

So if it wasn't a dream, that left insanity, or . . . or . . .

Or else it was Jack.

"No," she said again. "Not possible."

Kay ran out into the hall, taking the stairs down two at a time. She grabbed the kitchen doorknob and reached to unfasten the bolt. It was already unlocked. She hesitated only a moment, wondering why, then slammed it open and dashed out.

She stood in the middle of the damp lawn in only a sleeveless undershirt and panties, all alone. The man, whoever he was, was gone. She scanned the trees, but nothing human broke the solid ranks of pine trunks lined up like obedient brown soldiers.

Well, she certainly wasn't going in there. She crossed her arms, feeling suddenly too aware of her near-nakedness. Turning away, she took a couple steps back toward the house, then stopped. Someone was watching. She felt the probe of a gaze on her back. Playing some sick game.

She turned back, more angry than frightened now. "Whoever you are, what the hell do you think you're doing?"

Her only answer was the faint echo of her voice through the trees. The pine boughs sighing as if in sympathy. But no one came out and showed himself.

A drop of water hit her chest, then another. Was it raining? She lifted a hand to her face and realized she was crying.

"Damn it, Jack!" She turned away and ran back to the house, locking the kitchen door behind her. Back upstairs, in the bathroom, she splashed cold water on her face, soaking her shirt. She rubbed it dry roughly with a towel, and then thought: Chloe.

She dropped the towel and ran down the hall.

The door to her daughter's room was open. One window shade was up, revealing a single pane cracked in a crazy starburst pattern.

"Chloe?" she whispered, tiptoeing inside. "Are you all—
"

Her daughter's bed was empty.

THIRTY-SEVEN

And the sheriff's office doesn't see a connection between Chloe, Perle, and the Monk child. They say not to worry, as if she ran off to get married or something. She's only nine!"

Perdita sat on the edge of the bed beside Kay, nodding sympathetically. She pulled another tissue from the box on her lap. Kay snatched it, wiped her face, and flung it on the pile around her feet.

She jumped up and stood trembling beside the tall bedroom windows. "Well. I don't care what they say. I'm not going to just sit and wait. They said twenty-four hours until she could be considered a missing person. Can you believe it? A helpless child! There must be a lunatic out there. First your daughter, then Monk's grandson, and now—" She grabbed the last tissue from her friend's outstretched hand. "But they just say, 'No ma'am, we have no reason to believe those cases are in any way related.'" She laughed bitterly. "Yet any fool could see it. Any fool but them!"

The other woman gazed thoughtfully at the floor. "Sometimes the police—their hands are tied. Can't always go to the right places or do the things needed to find people. It's not always their fault."

Kay stared at her. "Why are you defending them?"

"Be still a minute, and listen. Remember how we found Perle? I don't know if it would work this time. Aunt Mattie doesn't know Chloe. But we could try."

Kay stopped wringing her hands, suddenly hopeful. "Of course! Even the police use psychics sometimes. What're we waiting for? Let's go." She bent to grope for her shoes, under the bed, lost her balance and nearly fell over.

"When did you last eat?" said Perdita. She helped her up and eased her gently down onto the bed. "Lie there for a minute."

"God, I'm so dizzy. Wish I could handle things as well as you. I feel so incompetent. A screw-up. Can't even keep track of my own daughter."

"You're not to blame. Don't forget that. You better stay here while I—"

"No! I'm going with you. Just let me—"

"Rest a minute. I've got to go talk to Aunt Mattie first—alone. I'm sure she'll agree to help. But it would be better if I went there first, by myself."

"Perdita, please. I have to go. I've got to get out of here, to do something about—"

"No. Listen to me. Stay here, just for a little while. Calm down, eat something, and get your strength back. Crying and blaming yourself won't bring Chloe home. It might be hard to find her, might take some time. Make up your mind to be ready to do anything I say, when I get back." She looked hard at Kay. "Anything at all."

"A-all right." Kay tried to control the quiver in her voice. "But promise me . . . " She paused, gathering determination. "Promise you'll be back soon. And that you'll tell me exactly what your Aunt Mattie says. Even if . . . even if it's not good."

Perdita nodded. "All right. I promise."

Kay sank back against the pillows, shaking her head. "Who'd have thought I'd ever need to believe in this stuff.

If I hadn't seen how your aunt found Perle . . . but now I'm willing to do anything."

"That's good. You may have to." Perdita smiled and brushed a damp stray curl from Kay's forehead. "Of course you must believe. Nothing will work unless you do. I won't be gone long. You stay here, eat a little something, and wait for me. Promise you will."

Kay tried to smile, but her quivering chin prevented it. "I swear I'll be right h-here."

"Good." Perdita stood. "I don't know if Mattie's even at home right now, so it could take a little while. But don't panic, I'll come for you as soon as I can."

"I'll be here," Kay repeated, and her voice didn't break this time. She reached for her cell phone, which lay on the nightstand. "I'm just going to try to call Mike Delgado. To tell him about Chloe."

"Okay. Try not to get all worked up again."

As Kay hit speed dial, she noticed Perdita picking up something from the floor. She slipped it into her jeans pocket.

"What's that?" Kay looked up.

"Nothing, I dropped some change."

"Well, what're you waiting for? Go on, I'll be fine." She withdrew under the covers like a turtle into its shell.

"See you later, then."

***

Perdita went downstairs. When she reached the foyer, she slipped a hand into her pocket and pulled out the thing she'd found on the floor by the bed. She turned the tiny white muslin bag over in her palm, frowning, then raised it to her nose and sniffed. Her hand tightened around the bag, and then shoved it roughly back into her pocket. She left the house then, fists clenched, eyes dark with fury.

248

THIRTY-EIGHT

All the local cops did was put her name on a freaking list, Mike." Kay picked up the empty tissue box, shook it, and then threw across the room. "I don't know what to do now. But I have to do something, or go crazy."

"And you're absolutely sure she didn't run away? Even little kids have been known to, if they get mad enough at their parents. She's never threatened that before?"

"Of course not!"

Or had she? Kay's brain felt drugged, fuzzy, as if it'd been replaced with a huge, worn-out tennis ball.

"It sure doesn't sound like something Chloe would do," he admitted. "Let me think about this."

For a few endless moments she heard only the faint hollow hum of silence, which reminded her that her best friends were over five hundred miles away. It might as well be five thousand. There's nothing he can do from Miami to help me find her, she thought desolately. He's an attorney, not a bloodhound.

"Kay?"

"Yes?"

"Look, I'm not sure exactly what I'll do when I get there, but I—"

"You're coming up here right now? Mike, that's—that's great."

"I'm coming just as soon as I can catch an afternoon flight. I'm supposed to be in court downtown at three. But I can brief one of the associates. If I can't get a flight soon, I'll . . . I'll charter something. If I can't do that, I'll get one of our grossly wealthy clients to loan me a plane. Then find some way to light a fire under your local constable."

"There isn't a local anything right in Abaton. Only a county sheriff. Guy named Swinson."

"Hmm. More Barney Phife than Andy Taylor? Well, I'll call a friend at the state attorney's office, too. And Kay?"

"I'm listening."

"Don't panic. We'll find her. Try not to worry yourself sick. Stay put, and I'll be there soon."

"That's . . . good." She was crying again, but this time it felt more like relief. If Mike was coming, surely everything would be all right. He knew how to fix anything. Jack had always said so. "Tell Annelise hello, and that I miss her."

"Tell her yourself. Think she'd let me rush off up there all alone?"

She imagined him wearing that familiar, crooked smile.

"But be warned. After this I'm sure she'll drag you both back to Miami with us. Now let's get off the phone so I can put this plan in motion."

***

Perdita slammed the Ghia's door and stalked past her aunt's concrete menagerie. She took the porch steps two at a time, and knocked once on the rough, faded front door. Listened a moment, then raised her hand and knocked again, so hard flecks of old paint ground into her knuckles. "Aunt Mattie! It's Perdita."

The only answer was the whisper of pine boughs, the faint liquid monologue of the river. But the door was unlocked, as always. The rusty iron knob complained but still turned, though reluctantly. She walked into the dimly-lit front room.

A fire flickered in the shallow fireplace, despite the July heat. On the rough pine table near the kitchen sat jumbled piles of leaves, flowers, and grasses. Perdita frowned down, contemplating these a moment, and then walked over to the sleeping alcove where Mattie's old white-painted iron bedstead and Lala's tiny cot stood side by side. A faded quilt with a wedding-ring pattern covered the old woman's bed. A new spread printed with Disney princesses was tucked neatly around the little girl's.

She turned away impatiently and went out front again. No sign of her aunt or of Lala. She circled the house. No sign of anyone at all.

Perdita faced the woods and cupped both hands around her mouth. "Aunt Mattie! I know you're here. It's Perdita. I must talk to you, now!"

She waited. The prolonged silence felt much like the mocking gaze of a clever old woman.

"Damn it." She shoved her hands into her jeans' pockets. A quick stab of pain in the right made her jerk it back out. A short, fat splinter from the front door was imbedded in one knuckle. Swearing, she used her nails to pull it out. A ruby bead of blood welled up.

"Mattie, I have to talk to you. Right now!" She sucked on the wounded joint, fuming.

A twig snapped like dry bones behind her, and she whirled to look.

"Child, please." Aunt Mattie set a split white-oak basket on the ground by her feet. "Why are you hollerin', raisin' Cain in front of my house?"

"You know why."

"I don't know nothing 'cept my own business." Mattie faced Perdita's glare calmly. "S'posing you tell me what you think I know, missy."

251

"Where's Lala?"

The older woman's expression softened like creased, worn flannel. "She out and about. Flittin' around like a wild bird. Four walls don't hold her."

"No, I suppose they wouldn't. Well, I need to see her too. Chloe—Kay Abbott's daughter—is missing. But you already knew that, didn't you?"

Now the soft lines hardened. Her aunt turned her head and spit on the ground. "Think I keep track of other folks' children, like an old black nursemaid? How I know where some white woman's whelp at? Can't she mind even one little one?"

Perdita stepped closer. "The Mother of the Year couldn't keep her child safe if you put your mind and these . . . " She nudged the greens-filled basket with the toe of one shoe, "to see different."

Mattie chuckled hoarsely. "You really believe your old aunt and her root medicines gone and kidnapped a child? Girl, please. You never used to listen to white folks' gossip."

"I don't listen to gossip because I don't need to. I already know how much talk is true and how much isn't. And I know what you're capable of, if you want something bad enough."

The old woman snorted. "Fine college talk that is. Why you think you know so much about my business?"

"Because I believe I know what Lala is," she said coldly, watching her aunt's face carefully. Had the dark, weathered skin gone a shade paler?

"And what might that be, missy?"

Perdita hesitated. She actually only had suspicions, not proof. But her aunt's reaction to her words made her certain she was right. "How old is Lala, Aunt Mattie?"

The old woman looked momentarily confused. "How old? Why . . . don't rightly know. Never kept track of

252

numbers, just birthdays. Child, I don't even remember how old I am, myself! But she's just a baby."

Perdita pressed her advantage. "She's no baby. It was five years ago this summer that she fell in the river and you nearly lost her. Lala was five then. That would make her ten now. A little older than Chloe. And yet look at the difference between them."

Mattie shrugged as if bored with subject. "If it matter any. She just small for her age."

"Oh, it matters. She still looks, talks, and acts like a five-year-old. She's not an inch taller, far as I can tell, than when she was five. Late bloomer, I used to think. So tiny, petite. But that's not it at all. Is it?"

"Still a sassy heifer, aren't you? Going to have your say. Well then, go on and say it."

"All right. When you pulled Lala from the river five years ago, she had drowned. She was already dead."

"People drown all the time and they bring 'em back to life, pretty as you please. Happen every day, I'd bet."

"Not all of them. Not if they were gone too long. It was Perle who found her, submerged just off the bank, her clothes caught on a tree root. Perle couldn't reach her. She had to run and get you. I was at work, and you were—"

"I remember," said the old woman sharply.

"I know you revived her. How you did it, Perle told me a little. What she saw. She said Lala was dead. Cold as a river rock. Like her little kitten that'd been hit by a car. Like Mrs. Satterfield, two houses down from us, who died of a stroke in her back yard. Perle had seen the ambulance come. She said Lala was the same gray-blue color old Mrs. Satterfield had been."

Mattie stared at her niece, but seemed to be seeing something else beyond her.

"Then, when you got her up to the house, Perle said you put the body . . . that you put her on the bed. You told Perle to stay there. She was scared to do it. But I've always told her to mind you."

A lone tear oozed from one of Mattie's eyes and trickled down that wrinkled cheek.

Perdita was astonished. She'd never in her whole life seen her aunt cry. "She said you came back a while later, with something she called 'red water' in a jar. Then you sent her outside, but she went and stood on a crate, and looked in the window. She saw you leaning over the bed, doing something to her little cousin, but your back was to the window so she couldn't see just what. You moved away from the bed, and Lala sat up. And then you let Perle come back inside. You told her Lala had to stay in bed the whole day. To rest. She said the little girl looked all right, except—"

"Except what?" Mattie asked, her back stiff, her face rigid.

"She claimed that Lala was different. I was afraid that the time she lacked oxygen might've damaged her brain, but Perle didn't mean that. She said that all afternoon Lala still felt cold and damp. And that whenever she talked . . . " She hesitated, horrified in retrospect at a thing she'd brushed aside, in her relief at Lala's survival. " . . . that water kept running out of her mouth. 'Lots of water, Mama,' she told me. And I didn't really believe her. 'You imagined that,' I said. But she didn't imagine any of it. Did she?"

She looked hard at her aunt. For the first time in her life, Perdita didn't see Mattie as a strong, wise old woman. Despite the heat, she felt terribly cold.

"So you brought her back, somehow. But not all the way. A doctor wouldn't have done it. Couldn't have, because she was already too far gone. But you did. That's why she still looks and acts like a five-year-old. Because that's what she is. A little girl who died five years ago. She'll never get older, will she? I think I suspected before.

But I didn't really want to know. I still don't. I-I know you loved her, but—"

"Love her," Mattie corrected sharply, eyes glittering like onyx. "She's still my little girl. Always will be. She's just been so lonely for a friend. And she found one. She deserves that much, at least. Oh, but you," she growled. "You want to take even that away. She done no harm to any . . . any *good* people. And you aim to spoil everything now."

"I just came to get my friend's little girl back. Before anything happens to her."

"I don't hold nothing that belong to that woman." She picked up the oak basket and turned away to hobble toward the house. Over one shoulder she called back, "What she owns will soon come back to her."

"If you've harmed Chloe in any way, I'll make sure you regret it," Perdita answered.

Mattie paused, half-turned. "High time for you to go. You don't belong here. Much too educated for us poor home folks. You got no place here now. A business woman! Might get your hands dirty, meddlin' around in what don't concern you."

Then she disappeared inside, slamming the door behind her.

Perdita remained in the yard, biting her lip. She'd remembered something else. Another child had disappeared that day five years ago, presumably into the river. Had the body ever been found? She couldn't remember. A jar of red water . . . she glanced at the house, then turned her back and walked slowly to her car.

***

Perdita's Volkswagen roared to life, and turned out of the yard. One dark hand lifted the yellowed muslin curtain at the front window. Mattie Swann watched her niece drive away, the car a flash of blood-red between the dark trunks of pines.

THIRTY-NINE

A crash from downstairs woke Kay. The room was dark, except for a thin stream of moonlight pooled on the polished pine floor. Beside the bed shards of broken glass gleamed. She must've knocked her cup of water off the nightstand while she slept.

Better clean that up before Chloe comes in and steps on it, she thought. But why did the thought of Chloe make her heart jump? She frowned, still groggy. And then, remembered.

She sat up just as a cloud shifted away from the moon, bathing the room in light. And saw she was not alone.

A man stood at the foot of the bed.

It looked like Jack. But that was impossible. And yet—

Get up, run like hell, her sensible, wakening brain screamed. Get up, get going, get out. But her betraying body turned toward him, her arms lifted in welcome.

He sat on the bed and she wrapped her arms around him, feeling the width of his broad, familiar back. Through the starched cotton of his shirt, though, it felt wrong. The skin cold, damp, too . . . mobile. As if it might slough off like a molting snake's. When he lowered his face to hers, his eyes were filmed over, white as a dead trout's. He breathed on her neck, and it was like a gust of hot wind over rotting

257

meat, like a hundred road-kills piled on an asphalt highway in August—

"Oh, Jesus!" she screamed, and struck at him, rolling away, lunging for the other side of the bed, heart hammering so hard she could not catch her breath.

And then it wasn't dark after all, but still bright, a sunny afternoon. She sat rubbing her bare arms, shivering in the hot, airless room.

Something moved furtively, on the floor near the bed.

She shrieked and scrambled up onto the center of the bed. A weird moaning rose, followed by a plaintive, questioning cry from beneath the bed.

It was Gus.

Kay collapsed onto the sheets, her terror slowly deflating. She leaned cautiously over to look. The cat was crouched there just underneath, and he growled and hissed once, then meowed pitifully. Maybe he'd been sleeping on her chest, as he often did, until in terror she'd flung him off, while gripped by that awful nightmare.

"Come here, Gus. Sweet kitty, I'm sorry." She slid to the floor and picked him up, hugging his soft, reassuring bulk. He stiffened, then relaxed, apparently forgiving her. She carried him downstairs to the kitchen and poured a double helping of 9 Lives into his red bowl. Then she checked her phone. No new messages.

Back upstairs she yanked off the sweat-soaked shirt and shorts and got into the shower. The thought of Chloe missing made her feel suddenly weak. She leaned against the tiled shower wall, letting the spray batter her skin till it stung. It was almost five, and yet still no one had called with any news.

She toweled dry roughly, and was pulling on a fresh shirt when she heard the unmistakable chug of a Volkswagen engine laboring up the drive.

Kay froze, half-dressed. Had Perdita found out something about Chloe? Or would her daughter's face soon be staring from lost-child flyers at post offices and train stations? Were any of those children, who had disappeared one day like an evil magician's trick, ever found? Or simply gone forever, the way children in Abaton vanished into the river's greedy mouth?

As she rushed to the stairs, her phone shrilled. She pulled it from her pocket and answered on the second ring.

"Kay, is that you?" The connection was faint, but at least she had one.

"Yes, yes." Perdita's car had just stopped out front. "Who's this?"

"May Olive. Sorry to bother you right now, but I—" A pause, a gasp that sounded like a sob. "I just had to tell someone."

"What's wrong, May Olive, what's happened?" she asked, as she watched Perdita get out, alone, and walk beneath the front windows, out of sight.

"It's Bonnie. I found her."

"Sorry, I don't . . . was she missing? Did something happen to her?"

"They say she'll be fine. Physically, I mean. But she's not. Her mind isn't, she can't even—"

Downstairs, the front door opened and then closed with a bang. "May Olive, please just tell me what happened."

"I went on over to her house this morning directly, because I still hadn't caught her by phone. Nor Slocum, either. Not that I expected to raise him."

Kay heard Perdita in the foyer. "Up here," she called.

She wanted to tell May Olive to hang up. Didn't she have enough problems of her own? She could call her back later. But the catch in the other woman's voice stopped her.

"Front door wasn't latched," May Olive was saying. "So I went on in. Calling her name. And there she was. In that little sitting room downstairs."

Perdita came in and looked up the stairs at Kay, who held up a finger and mouthed, *May Olive.*

"And—was she hurt?"

A harsh, choking laugh. "Worse than that. Just . . . sitting there. Sitting and staring. Wouldn't speak. I don't think she even knew me. I bent to look, and her skin . . . covered with bruises all over. Hundreds of 'em. Red and purple blotches on that soft white skin. Well, I called 911, county ambulance came and took us to the hospital."

"Is that where you are now?"

"Yes. Doctor says she'll recover. That the attack didn't do no permanent damage. But I know better; I saw her eyes. There was nothin' left in there. My poor little girl is gone."

"Oh, God. I'm so sorry. Maybe the sheriff's office will take it more seriously now. That Chloe—"

"You mean she isn't home yet? I thought surely by now, honey . . . that this would be like the time when Bonnie was little. She ran away all day, hid in Leilah's pecan grove. Came home with twigs in her hair, fingers stained brown from pecan-shell juice. I meant to whip her for bein' bad and scarin' me so. But somehow I couldn't, I just grabbed her up and hugged her til—oh Kay, I'm so sorry. So wrapped up in my troubles I didn't even ask about Chloe."

"It's all right, but I've got to go. Perdita's here and I'm expecting a call. I'll talk to you later. Find out how Bonnie's doing."

"God bless you, honey. She'll turn up. I'm staying close by my girl. Can't even find her so-called husband. Out gallivanting in the next county, is my guess."

They hung up and Kay came down to Perdita. "Bonnie was hurt, assaulted. They're at the hospital. What if this same monster has Chloe?"

Perdita looked away. "I don't think so."

"But how can you know?"

"I have a feeling . . . about where we might find her."

"Did you see your aunt, then? She must've agreed to help."

"No, not exactly. I have to explain some other things to you first. About Lala. About raising the dead."

***

"What're you waiting for?" Perdita said a few minutes later. "Go ahead and say I'm crazy. That you don't believe me."

"How can I believe?" Kay shook her head. "And yet, I can't say that. Not after what I saw this morning."

"This morning?"

"A man I saw, standing at the edge of the woods out there. Before I realized Chloe was gone. I didn't tell you before. Not you, and not the sheriff's office, because I could see how crazy it would sound. He wasn't a stranger. I recognized him right away."

"Perdita frowned. "Then why not say so? They could go pick him up, ask questions—"

"No, I couldn't tell them. Because it was Jack."

"Jack? But isn't that your—"

"Yes. My dead, twice-buried husband."

Perdita stood abruptly and walked over to the window, as though expecting to see the same thing that Kay had just described. "Then maybe it's already gone too far."

"My daughter's missing, but my dead husband's come home," Kay snapped. "Yes, I'd say things have gone a little too far."

"You don't understand. I think Aunt Mattie means to make a . . . a trade. What to her mind would seem fair."

"What, you mean like a ransom, for Chloe?"

"No. Something worse. Lala gets to keep Chloe as a companion, forever. You get your husband back. Perfectly logical, I suppose, from her point of view. Just like—"

Kay stared at her in horror. "Just like before. With Jonah and Louvinia and Abby, all over again."

Those shocking words, spoken out loud, made the whole idea suddenly seem sickeningly possible. "The past repeats itself."

"No." Perdita turned from the window and came back to grip Kay's arm so hard she flinched. "Not if we don't let it. Come on, get up. We don't have as much time as I thought." She pulled her up from the chair.

"All right, but where—"

"Here, take this." Perdita reached into the white cotton laundry bag she'd carried in, and pulled out a flashlight.

Kay took it, trying to see inside the bag. "What've you got in there?"

"Nothing you need to see yet." Perdita tightened the drawstring. "Get your shoes and let's go." She slung the bag over one shoulder and walked out. "I'll drive."

Outside, she tossed the bag in the back seat of the Karman Ghia and turned the key once, then again. No response. Not even a click from the starter.

Kay frowned. "Dead battery?"

"It's new." Perdita got out and lifted the back hood. "Jesus. All the wires are fused." But she didn't really sound surprised. "All melted together. Fine. We'll just take yours."

"I'll drive."

The Volvo started on the first try; the engine ran smoothly. Kay wiped her damp face on the hem of her shirt. "Where to?"

"The cemetery, first. I need to check something."

***

By the time the car passed beneath the black wrought-iron arch of the cemetery gate, shadows were deepening in an overcast sky. The swollen black clouds looked low enough to snag on the tops of the trees.

"It's going to pour in a few minutes," said Kay. She ran after Perdita, who jumped out before the car had completely stopped. They passed the now-familiar landmarks: a carved marble angel, face so worn it looked blind. A huge granite cross tilted at such a crazy angle it looked like a lost piece from a giant child's set of jacks.

Soon they stood before the Abbott family plot. Its black-painted gates, in the dense air before the storm, held the sharp scent of rust and salt tears. And something metallic, like blood.

Perdita looked around. "See anything different?"

Kay scanned the well-tended plot. "It looks about the same to me." The red gash of clay that marked Jack's grave was sprouting fine blades of new grass.

"Right. Neat, undisturbed. Almost perfect." Perdita's eyes narrowed.

"Surely even your aunt couldn't grow grass overnight." Kay had to ask, though it sickened her to imagine such a scene. "If she had him, to trade . . . she'd have to dig it up, right? The grave. But everything seems in place. So how could I have seen Jack, or whoever it was, if he's still here?"

"I don't know. An illusion. Some kind of trick. She knows we don't have time to get an order to dig up graves to see if they're occupied." Perdita turned and stalked back to the car. Kay hurried after, not wishing to linger alone there for even a moment. Not after what she'd just been told.

As she reached for the handle of the car door, a saber of lightning hacked the sky in half. Suddenly she was standing in a downpour.

She lunged inside the car, rainwater dripping from hair and clothes, and looked over at Perdita. "Please don't tell me she masterminded this too."

Sheets of water ran down the windows, as if they were trapped in a carwash, or parked under a waterfall. Trees, shrubs, stone monuments, iron fences, all vanished behind a curtain of rain.

Perdita smiled wryly. "No. But she'd probably like us to think so. There's a limit to what one old woman can do."

"I hope so."

"Let's go. Drive back out to River Road. I'll show you the way to Mattie's house."

"In this storm? I couldn't even find it in good weather." Kay put the Volvo into reverse, hoping it didn't get stuck in the clay that was rapidly turning to red soup around it.

"Finding it's the easy part. In fact, she's probably expecting us."

Kay shivered, only partly because of the Volvo's air conditioning and her wet clothes. "Why do you say that?"

"Mattie's greatest weakness was always vanity, at least according to my mother. I'm not sure I agree with that anymore. But she does have a taste for drama. She's played village witch for a long time. And she likes an audience. To show out, as Mama used to say. But until we arrive, there's no one to appreciate the show."

FORTY

Chloe sat up, yawned and stretched, still sleepy and confused, but awake enough to know she was really in trouble with her mother this time. Maybe for good. She'd be sent to her room forever, or at least until she grew up.

She remembered sneaking outside the night before, meaning to stay only for a minute. Lala had given her a piece of hard candy the color and scent of mint tea. Brown with green specks.

She'd popped it into her mouth, only then thinking to ask. "What is this, a mint?"

Lala only giggled and shook her head.

"Well, it tastes like mint." The candy was good, at first. But gradually she'd detected another flavor. A bitter green taste not like mint at all. And then she'd begun to feel weird. Like she was floating. In fact, she remembered they'd floated down the path in the woods. It had seemed funny then. They'd both laughed and laughed, even when nettles stung their bare legs and low branches scratched their arms and pulled at their hair.

Her face burned and stung now. In fact, she itched all over. What she really wanted was to go home. Take a bath and go to bed.

But where was she? Lying on an old quilt with a pattern like the one on her bed at home. But this quilt was faded and torn, leaking cotton batting in spots. The only ceiling was a canopy of pine branches so thick she couldn't even see the sky. But she heard the river. It sounded really close.

She scratched at her arms and legs irritably. Mosquito bites pocked them like a bad case of measles.

I should go home, she thought. Mom's gonna kill me anyhow. But somehow she couldn't quite make herself get up off the quilt. She wanted to; even tried to imagine it: standing up, brushing off her clothes, walking home. But the pictures wouldn't come together in her mind to make sense. She looked around and realized she didn't actually know the way home. And then she was afraid.

A scraping sound came from behind her. Chloe snapped her head around to look. Lala was there, squatting under an oak, turned away from Chloe, drawing in the dirt with a stick. Beside her lay a big gray tree rat. So still it must be dead. Yes, she saw now that flies were buzzing drunkenly around its trailing guts.

"Lala," Chloe whispered hoarsely. Her throat hurt, too. "This isn't any fun. I need to go home. Mom will be mad."

"No leave." Lala shook her head. "Stay here now."

"But I can't." Chloe really felt awful. She felt like crying. She wanted her mother. "I-I have to go."

"No leave! Clo my fren'. Stay. No leave me ever." She turned to face Chloe, stabbing the sharp stick into the rodent's stiff body. It stayed upright there, quivering. Lala looked down at it, then she grinned at Chloe. Her teeth were like perfect pearls, as white as last night's moon.

266

FORTY-ONE

ain hit the Volvo's windshield faster than the wipers could sluice it away. Perdita leaned closer to the glass. "There! That narrow clay trail."

Kay couldn't actually see it but she turned anyhow, hoping not to end up in the overflowing ditch that ran along the roadside. The car rocked and skidded, then settled into some twin ruts pretending to be a road. A few seconds later, the downpour stopped as suddenly as it had started.

"God. That's better." Kay switched off the wipers. "Now I can see the road, such as it is."

A fat, wet possum chose that moment to wade slowly across the road, stepping over puddles daintily as a dowager at a tea dance.

She slammed on the brakes without thinking. The car bucked and fishtailed over the red muck, then stalled. The startled possum splashed away into the trees.

Kay rested her forehead on the steering wheel. "You all right?"

Perdita nodded. "Fine. But what about the car, can you start it?"

She turned the key once. Nothing. She gripped the wheel with white knuckles and tried again. The engine whined, caught, and they sighed in unison. She pressed the accelerator and the back wheels spun, throwing up a thick wall of red clay behind them. But the car didn't roll forward. She shifted into reverse, then to drive, rocking it back and forth. Still they went nowhere.

Perdita stepped out and sank halfway to the knees in orange mud. "Great. We're bogged down to the fenders. This car's not going anywhere. Grab that sack. We'll have to walk the rest of the way."

Kay stepped out reluctantly. She carried the white sack around the front of the car, shuddering as gritty red slime oozed into her shoes. Perdita rummaged in the sack impatiently and pulled out a small glass bottle filled with amber liquid. She uncapped it. "Hold out your hands."

Kay cupped her palms obediently to catch the thin trickle of oil Perdita poured into them. Aromatic cedar spiced the air, and suddenly the woods smelled like the walls of Leilah Abbott's fancy linen closet.

"Rub it all over, wherever your skin is exposed." Perdita poured some into her own hands and rubbed her face, neck, and arms.

Kay did the same. "Is this . . . bug repellant?"

Perdita smiled slightly and shook her head. "Might work for that too. But tonight I want to keep away bigger things."

"Such as?"

Perdita looked up, the look in her eyes that of a child about to describe some nightmare horror it knew an adult would never fathom. "Things like . . . witches. Ghosts. Zombies. Hoodoo. Magic."

"You mean like people dancing naked and beating on drums with cow bones?"

Perdita stared at her for a moment. "What kind of bad movies have you been watching?" Then she shook her head and sighed. "Hoodoo is private. It's a religion bound up in secrecy. But no – it's not drum beating and wild dancing, except in some Hollywood director's dreams. I've seen it cure people, and I know it can kill them. Still want to come along?"

Kay's eyes widened, but she felt no desire to laugh. That look, the certainty in Perdita's voice, made her believe. "Well, yeah. I mean, I do," she mumbled, rubbing the remaining oil more vigorously into her shoulders and neck. If smelling like the inside of a blanket chest would bring her closer to finding Chloe, she'd bathe in the stuff. Hell, she'd drink it.

Perdita slung the sack over one shoulder and they began the long walk to Mattie Swann's cabin. Kay pocketed her keys out of habit, though it was clear the Volvo was in no condition to be stolen. She looked back once at the helpless car, mired like a metal dinosaur in a tar pit. It had never failed her before. Pushing back a surge of primitive fear, she told herself she didn't believe in omens.

Their shoes squelched in mud so thick it nearly pulled them off. The midsummer moon had risen early, huge and crudely rounded, a pale saucer from a child's drawing. Kay glimpsed it occasionally through breaks in the pines.

The sun was still out too, though now obscured by ragged dark clouds and flying scraps of mist, shedding only a cold and unreliable light.

As they struggled on, stepping over puddles and through mud wallows, Kay also thought she saw a dark figure keeping pace with them back in the woods. Always on the edge of her vision, but whenever she turned her head to look, she saw only trees and the darkness between them. So she said nothing about it, but still tensed at every snapping twig, each rustling leaf.

Cedar oil and sweat glued her cotton shirt to her skin. She pulled it away but the damp tepid flow of air only made her feel stickier. Her thighs ached with the effort it took to keep pulling her feet from the mud. She ignored her outraged muscles and concentrated instead on how good it would feel to throw her arms around Chloe and hug her tightly.

"Just a quarter-mile more," said Perdita, who didn't even look winded. Now, she looked strong, capable, and most amazing of all, almost dry. Kay felt a sharp twist of something close to dislike. Only for a moment, and then it was gone. If I were more like Perdita, I probably wouldn't sweat either, she thought glumly. And my daughter probably wouldn't be missing. Then she remembered what had happened to Perle and felt ashamed of her selfishness.

The mist seemed to be getting denser. Long wisps coiled around the trunks of trees, weaving in and out like hungry cats. Tendrils snaked through the tall grass and bushes along the path.

"Gets thicker up ahead," Perdita pointed out.

"Could we go . . . around it?" A silly suggestion, but somehow she dreaded walking through, not wanting to feel its cold, clammy touch on her skin.

"Mist and fog is just water in the air. Can't hurt us," said Perdita firmly. "Unless we let ourselves get scared, turned around, too rattled to think straight—and then walk into the river. Keep on, and don't leave the path."

Kay obeyed silently, thinking less about the mist now, but rather of what it might conceal. And then suddenly they were inside it, and it was all around, and she could see nothing ahead or behind them.

As they pushed through the curtain of fog Kay stayed close to Perdita's side, too frightened now to feel ashamed of that fear. The mist not only obscured sight, it seemed to muffle sound as well. The sounds from the woods that had troubled her before were gone, yet their absence was somehow worse, like a held breath before something terrible happened. The sound of her own breathing was harsh in her ears.

Perdita isn't frightened, but I'm not like her, she thought. No, I'm just a spoiled, soft housewife pretending to be an artist.

And then something touched her, and she screamed.

Perdita grabbed her arm. "What happened, are you hurt?"

"No, it . . . something was next to me. It reached out and touched me, my arm. It felt horrible. Cold and rubbery."

"Be still for a minute. Just listen," Perdita whispered.

Kay tried to keep her teeth from chattering. Finally she heard Perdita exhale. Could she be frightened too, holding her breath at every strange sound? Kay hoped not. She pushed the thought away.

"Nothing there. Let's go."

"But there was! I felt it."

"Oh, I believe you. But real or not, it's gone now. Come on."

Gradually the haze thinned until only faint gray rags of mist floated softly past their ankles. With relief Kay heard again the creak of branches, the rustle of leaves, the steady slap of their shoes on the sodden path.

When at last it curved, ahead was the faint warm glow of lantern light in a window.

Perdita's steps slowed. "There's the house. Stop here a minute." She reached again into the sack that swung from her shoulder. This time she drew out two small cloth bags swinging from red cotton cords. "Put one of these on, like a necklace."

Kay tied the cord around her neck. She lifted it to her nose, sniffed, and dropped it again with a cry of disgust. "Ugh! What's inside? Smells awful."

"Let's see . . . garlic, oleander, asafetida, powdered cow bone. John the Conqueror root and some other herbs you never heard of." She smiled. "Why, want the recipe?"

"No thanks," Kay said, a hand still cupped over her nose. "I'll get used to the smell soon, I guess. What's it for?"

"A little extra protection. Kind of like a booster shot."

Kay touched Perdita's arm. "You think your aunt will try to hurt us?"

Perdita looked down, frowning as she busied herself tying on her own aromatic charm. "She'll try first to frighten us away. As she's been doing. When that doesn't work . . . if she feels it's come to a choice between us and . . . " She shrugged. "I'm family, but I was never her favorite. She will do whatever she must, to protect Lala."

Kay rubbed her arms. "I have to admit, I'm frightened. Good thing you're not."

Perdita looked up at her again. "But I am." She shouldered the sack again, turned away, and walked on. Kay stared after her dumbly for a moment, then hurried to catch up.

Ahead, in the clearing, warm golden light spilled from the cabin's two small front windows. The door stood ajar. The place looked rustic, but almost inviting.

"Is she in there?" Kay whispered.

"Don't know. But there's no need to whisper. At least— not yet."

As they moved closer, a multitude of pale figures seemed to jump out of the gloom. Kay nearly screamed before she remembered what the shapes really were: the menagerie of stone and cement garden statues that populated the yard. She laughed nervously. "Whoa. I thought for a minute—"

"I know. Don't blame you. Sometimes . . . " Perdita looked around at the statues. "Sometimes I'm sure they've changed places, or even—well, never mind."

They crossed the yard and began to pick their way through that cold, silent throng. Kay grazed her knee on a peeling pink flamingo that leaned out drunkenly in her path. She winced and veered away, carefully circling a crouching cement spaniel. She was sure there hadn't been this much ugly statuary the last time, or that they'd been set so close together. Perdita seemed to be having less difficulty getting through them; she was already much further ahead. Kay nearly called out, "Wait for me!" But she felt too embarrassed. So she squeezed between two rampant gargoyles, ignoring the hard angles, their cold blank eyes.

She sidled past a whole herd of lawn deer, ducked to avoid the sharp antlers of the stag, and then suddenly stopped. Her path was blocked by a crudely-molded lion, yawning mouth painted a bloody red, as if he'd recently feasted on one of the stone deer. This statue she didn't recall at all. And where had Perdita gone?

Kay swore at her own ineptness. The other woman had been just ahead, she'd gone this way too. Kay turned to go around the lion, but that brought her abruptly up against the mossy front of a hideous, grinning dwarf. She flinched back from its slick greenish skin. Fear tightened the muscles of her throat.

Just a wrong turn, she told herself firmly. Statues don't move, no matter how lifelike they might look. She turned around and came face to jaws with the concrete lion again. He looked ancient, his features blunt, as if sanded by time, or a clumsy hand. All except for the teeth, which looked smooth, sharp, and nearly real. Ideal for catching and eating gazelles. Or girls. Staring at them, she lost her nerve, and shouted, "Perdita, wait. Please!" But over the lion's shoulder, which now seemed taller, as tall as her own, her friend was many yards—a whole world away.

She opened her mouth to shout again, but it closed up tight. No sound came out. Perdita didn't turn to look back. Kay realized then the other woman couldn't hear her. A sudden cold breeze seemed to snatch her words and toss them back in her face. The same wind stirred the pine needles and oak leaves at her feet, swirling them in tiny whirlwinds round her ankles. Sent dry leaves skittering like mummified insects, rustling around the cold legs of the patient, waiting statuary. All of them seemed to be leaning in closer, turning to look in her direction. Their blank, chalky eyes like Jack's eyes in her dream.

They're here to stop me, she thought. To hold me at bay like a pack of trained guard dogs.

Well, some damned yard decorations were not going to keep her from getting to her daughter. "I'm not afraid, you crazy old bitch!" she shouted into the blank face of the lion, so hard her spit gleamed on the rough stone. What would her friends back in Miami say if they saw her raving like a lunatic, shouting at a concrete statue like one of the homeless crazies down on South Beach?

She didn't care. "Back off, you slimy rocks," she muttered and without looking flung herself into a narrow gap between the lion and the stag. The small opening seemed to widen. Or maybe it was the lion, real enough for a moment, whose rough flank gave way. As she passed there came a quick, sharp pain in her shoulder, and the sound of tearing cloth. Then suddenly she was past, free and running, with a clear path before her. She saw now Perdita was only a few feet ahead. She walked faster; the thin trickle of hot blood threading down her left shoulder could be ignored.

She ran right up behind Perdita, who looked back and said, "Are you all right?"

"Yes, I-I'm fine. Why?" She actually felt like grabbing Perdita's shirt and just holding on. She kept moving, but threw one glance back. Behind them the lion had turned to face the house. Kay blinked. A ragged scrap of cotton shirt fluttered in the breeze, impaled on one sharp stone tooth.

FORTY-TWO

Damn it," said Perdita. "She's not even here."

When they entered the cabin, both had flinched at the sight of a shape suspended by a rope, dangling like a hasty suicide from the center beam of the ceiling.

As the figure revolved slowly to face them, they saw it was not Mattie Swann. The frayed cord around its neck hung from a rusted tenpenny nail driven into the beam. Its features were crudely painted on a white rag face in brown-red strokes that suggested dried blood. The misshapen torso, loosely stuffed, perhaps with rags, seemed to ripple and quiver in the flickering kerosene glow. Its head was topped with pine-straw hair.

"It's horrible." Kay shuddered. "Is that supposed to be me?"

"My guess," Perdita said. She reached up. Her slender fingers probed the lumpy body.

"Ugh. What're you looking for?"

"I want to see if this is just a warning to scare us off, or if she's planted some kind of spell."

Kay shifted her weight from her aching ankle. The unhealed wound was gnawing at her again. In fact, since they'd walked inside it had been savagely burning and throbbing. Now that the wound was red and swollen again, the imperfect impression around her ankle bone looked more familiar: the mark of a small child's bite. That was crazy. And yet that was what little kids did – they bit. "But how will you know?" she asked Perdita.

"If I find something of yours, or mine. A piece of clothing, a lock of hair, some jewelry . . . then I'll have to do something about it."

"So your family is . . . what should I call it – witches?"

"You don't need to give it a name," said Perdita. "It's just, well, practical. Around here."

"At this rate we'll never get to Chloe." Kay slumped against the jamb, careful not to brush against the hanging thing.

"That's exactly what she wants you to think. Get discouraged. Give up, go away. Make it easy for her to take what she wants."

"Maybe we should call the sheriff's office. Tell them—"

"Tell them what? All right, let's get them out here. Show them a table full of wildflowers and herbs. A silly hanging dummy. The nice old colored lady who heals people for a living. And don't forget the little orphan she's raising out of unselfish goodness. And we can also file a complaint about how your dead husband's been visiting your house without your permission."

Tears stung Kay's eyes. "It's all true, but they'd laugh. Or have us both committed."

Perdita nodded. "That's my guess. So don't let's give up just yet. Who will help Chloe then? Ah, here it is." She pulled a small wax figure from a rip in the fabric. "How attractive. This one's got my hair. Hand me the sack, please."

From it she pulled a wooden staff, its handle delicately carved with realistic-looking leaves and berries. "Holly-tree wood. This belonged to my mother. She used it as a walking stick, mainly. Holly is sacred. Once upon a time, folks planted holly hedges to keep witches away." She peered at Kay, who only nodded wearily. Perdita frowned. "We'll be testing that theory tonight, so best pay attention. Bring me a big scoop of dirt from the front yard."

Kay went down the porch steps, returning quickly with a double handful of rich, clay-streaked earth.

"Now scatter it along the doorstep."

She spread the dirt carefully in a line there.

Perdita knelt and swirled patterns in it with the end of the staff. She reached again into the sack, pulled out a squat cardboard cylinder, and held it out to Kay.

"But that's just . . . salt?"

"Yes. Strong because it's incorruptible. They used to put it inside the cradles of newborns to protect them until they were baptized. Now, go back into the yard. Walk in a circle around the house, pouring a thin line of salt on the ground as you go. Don't leave any gaps. When Aunt Mattie returns, she won't be able to cross over and come back in here."

Kay gaped at her. "Seriously?"

Perdita smiled wryly. "Well, that's my plan."

Kay took the box. "Wait," said Perdita. "I need a little of that." She poured herself a palm-full of salt. Then turned back to the limp figure twisting slowly in firelight. "Now for this dirty sack of laundry."

She took a deep breath.

"Like child inside mother,
Calf inside stable,
Guard us well and protect,
That no man nor woman . . . ."

She paused for a moment, frowning, then added:

"—Nor child shall injure us.
No witching, no demon's work,
No spells or false words.

Let the dead remain in their place."

Perdita cast the handful of salt she'd saved from the box onto the dirt-covered doorstep.

"I forbid you all this house
and the ground on which it stands.
Deny you entry to every room,
each window and door,
knothole and chimney-crack.
For good grows strong
on the weakness of evil."

Kay went to carry out her part of the spell, then came back up the steps brushing grains of salt from her hands. "Perdita," she said, feeling more and more troubled. "Where'd you learn all this?"

"Wondering if I'm a conjurer too? A witch like my aunt?"

"I—no." She felt her face heat up under Perdita's mild steady gaze. "That's not what I meant. It's just—well, this isn't exactly the kind of thing you learn at a state university. Is it?"

"Actually, as I understand it, you could – in some folklore classes. I found some of it just yesterday, in the university's library, in Tallahassee. In the anthropology section, folklore section, a few other places. But yes, some of it I grew up with. My mother, Mattie's sister, worked with herb cures, too. But she never used them in the ways Mattie sometimes has. They always fought about that. Remember I once mentioned Obeah? Goes way back in the family, before they came here from the islands. Though I never thought to make use of the stuff myself." She shrugged. "I was too smart, too educated, too . . . modern for backwoods hoodoo. And yet here I am. And you, too. A pair of amateur witch hunters."

"It's the amateur part I'm most worried about. Where'd you get all the stuff, the herbs and things?"

Perdita laughed. "Not at Monk's store. I took most from Miss May Olive's garden. I wonder if she knows what-all she's got growing there? I don't think she'll mind me borrowing a bit, though."

"And when does the real witch arrive?"

"Soon, I hope. I've baited the hook by making her home off limits."

"Then why should she come back at all, if she can't walk into her own house, her own yard?"

"Oh, she has to come back. She draws some of her power from this place. Doesn't dare stay away too long. That would weaken her."

"And in the meantime—"

Perdita walked out and sat down on the top step. "We wait. It won't be long now."

Kay suddenly felt both weak and unbearably thirsty. "I could use some water."

"Inside, the pump at the sink. Mattie's well water's the finest in the county."

Kay rushed back into the house, driven by the most intense thirst she'd ever felt. To the right was a small open kitchen area. She rushed to the deep porcelain sink, which had an old-fashioned pump. With near-desperation, she grabbed the stiff handle and began to work it up and down. It moved only a little at first, making a hollow sucking sound—as if it were dry, or badly clogged. Funny, she thought. The sink itself looked dusty, as if it hadn't felt water for years.

A thin stream trickled from the pump nozzle. A few dark drips moistened the sink. She looked at them longingly, and pumped harder.

But wait. Were the drops moving? She bent to look closer. "Oh my God," she moaned. It wasn't water coming out of the faucet, but tiny black insects; spiders and cockroaches. Now, slugs were squeezing out, plopping onto the porcelain sink bottom. She meant to let go, to stop wrenching at the handle of the pump. But her thirst was so great, her hands seemed welded to it. And the denial of something as simple and real as water made her angry. There must be water in there. The best well water in the county. Perdita had said so.

She pulled on it harder, dragging the peeling iron handle down so roughly her shoulder muscles ached. Her hands grew slippery with sweat. Now toads and frogs squeezed out of the nozzle like toothpaste from a tube. Impossibly large for the opening, and yet they emerged, one after another, with a sickening pop. It was like a scene from a grotesque children's book, an evil fairy tale come to life.

"Stop that," she hissed. "Damn you to hell, you perverted old bitch!"

A sudden whoosh and gurgle. Rusty water spurted from the pump faucet, gushing as if from a severed artery. The bugs and frogs and toads vanished, washed away by the red-tinted, metallic-smelling water. Kay gave the handle a few more good jerks to clear the rust from the pipes, to pull up the promised cool well water.

It was then she realized what she had pumped wasn't rusty water, but a basin full of blood. And that wasn't all. Something else was there in it, just breaking the surface. It looked like . . . a finger. A tiny perfect child's finger with a pearly-pink nail. Afloat in a sink of blood, so pure, white, and spotless. Her eyes filled with tears for this cruelly severed part of a child. She reached out gingerly, to fish it from the metallic-reeking sink. But just as her fingertips brushed cool smooth skin, the rest of the hand shot out of the congealing red mass and grabbed her wrist in a viselike grip. And then it began to withdraw, down the drain. Kay's own fingers, her whole hand, and then her wrist disappeared. Then, impossibly, her forearm.

She tried to scream for help, but her throat was so dry, closed up, only a hoarse whisper emerged. Her face was now inches from the blood, its iron stink was choking her—

"She's on her way," Perdita said from the open doorway. "What's wrong, are you sick?"

Kay looked back over her shoulder, then down at the sink again. For god's sake, couldn't she see?

But now only clear water was splashing out of the pump, in a clear shining stream. Otherwise the sink was empty, clean, white and shining.

"No, I'm fine," she mumbled, pushing away from the edge of the sink. Nothing could induce her to drink from that clear, innocent looking stream now, thirst be damned. "How do you know she's coming?"

"Look there." Perdita pointed to the doorway, to the dark wall of pines across the clearing. Thin misty fingers encircled the dark trunks of the trees. "The horror-movie atmosphere again. Just fog, don't let it scare you."

"Of course not." But her hands trembled as she wondered what she'd be forced to hallucinate next. If that was what it had been . . . when the moon was swallowed by clouds, she was actually glad of the dark. It meant she didn't have to know yet just what it concealed.

Tonight everything's dangerous, she thought. Even my own mind. And especially the light. It reveals too much.

The mist closed in, snaking through the statues in the yard. But when it reached the grainy white boundary she'd poured from that generic salt canister, the tendrils seemed to dissipate. A few faint wisps drifted almost to the porch steps, and vanished.

And then the moon emerged from its hiding place in the clouds.

An old woman stood at the edge of the trees, still and silent, in dark imitation of the rigid, pale statues between them.

"There she is, Perdita. Can we do something? Let's ask where Chloe is, at least!"

The other woman shook her head. "Not yet. Let her speak first."

She turned from Perdita to look at Mattie Swann again, but the conjure woman was gone. Kay looked all around the yard and at last saw her, standing near the statues now, closer than before.   That frail-looking old lady had somehow crossed several hundred feet in a couple of seconds.

"Perdita," Kay whispered. "Did you see? She just—"

"Stay calm. Sit here, next to me. She's not coming any closer. See?"

It was true. Mattie had actually stopped just at the line of salt. She glared down at it, then turned the dark hollows of her eyes on Kay. "Believe I got something belongs to you."

Lantern light from the house glittered in Mattie's eyes and reflected back red sparks. Or so it seemed to Kay. "Yes. My daughter. I want her back."

"Sit down, you fool." Perdita's nails dug into her arm as she jerked her back down onto the step. "It's a trick. Don't answer her. Don't say anything."

The elderly voice floated up, now slow and sarcastic. "Now I know how you Abbotts do love your children. Wouldn't want no harm to come to any little one of yours."

"What's she talking about?" Kay whispered anxiously.

"The past, clearly. Maybe Louvinia. Or even Leilah Abbott."

A cicada sang his harsh song in the silence that followed. The metallic buzz scraped at her nerves.

At last Auntie Swann spoke again. "Are all Abbotts sorry fools?"   She spat on the ground. "You fixing to collect your property or not?"

Without waiting for an answer, the old woman turned away, pointing to the woods behind her. A figure stepped out of the trees and walked toward the house.

Kay began to tremble. "Oh my God, it can't be. But it is."

Perdita frowned. "Is what?"

"Jack. It's Jack."

The man stopped a short distance away from the old woman and stood motionlessly, waiting.

Perdita laid a hand on Kay's arm. "Do not get up."

"But it's Jack. Don't you see, he—"

"I don't think so."

The man raised one hand slowly—in greeting, or perhaps a plea. His lips worked for a moment. "Kay," he rasped.

She squeezed her eyes tightly shut, until his image was blotted out by a red haze. When she opened them again, she saw—Jack. But not the amiable, preoccupied man who'd been prone to breezing through the house and then out again, on his infrequent breaks from work.

No, it was a younger Jack she saw. The one who'd rushed home, who stayed up late into the night, talking. Who always came home in time to read their daughter a bedtime story even when she was very small. The one who'd had spent half his first paycheck on long distance calls from Miami when she was still in college. The ideal memory-Jack she would've given anything—except Chloe, never Chloe—to have again. To keep.

"Kay," That lost, familiar voice. "I'm . . . home."

She rested her forehead on the rough denim knees of her jeans, and cried. The last six months now seemed only a dress rehearsal for the loss felt now. Between sobs, she heard Mattie Swann chanting something which sounded like, "What is given now, you must take." Vaguely she wondered what it meant.

"Kay. We can go home. Everything will be fine. But only if we leave now."

She couldn't stand any more. She jumped up and ran across the yard, as Perdita shouted behind her. For this moment she cared only about one thing—reaching the husband, the whole lost life, now miraculously restored to her.

She was only a few feet from his outstretched arms when Perdita's fingertips brushed the back of her shirt. Kay lunged and grabbed Jack's left hand. It felt solid and real. Alive. This was no hallucination. She gripped it tighter and then—

She was tackled from behind and dragged back screaming and kicking across the scuffed salt barrier.

Still she clung stubbornly to his hand. "No, Perdita! Let go. It's Jack. Look!"

But she felt a dreadful tearing then, the sound of heavy wet paper parting as it slowly ripped in two. And she fell back with Perdita, already on the other side.

Kay looked up, dazed. Jack still stood, arms open. But his left hand, the one she'd grasped, looked strange. And she still held something . . . she stared at down at her own hand for a moment, puzzled, which clutched a glove. Then she realized what it was, screamed and flung it away. She'd heard the skin of that . . . *thing's* . . . hand tearing away, coming off like a surgeon's rubber glove.

Gagging, she rubbed her hand clean on pine needles. When she looked up again, Jack's features were quivering, sliding, melting to rearrange themselves into the bloated, splotched countenance of Slocum Blunt. His skinned right hand dripped dark fluid slowly onto the ground. His lips jerked back over yellow teeth like gray earthworms on a hook. His ruined face appeared hungry for something she didn't even want to imagine.

A hiss began somewhere below his throat. She stared with fascinated horror at a gaping hole there, where black crawling things emerged and disappeared again. It was from this awful cavity that a whisper finally emerged from the frayed lips of the wound. "Kisss?"

Past even screaming now, she pulled herself away, flung off Perdita's hands, and ran back to the sanctuary of the porch. Where she hunched, sobbing, rubbing her soiled hand on her jeans.

Perdita got up more slowly. She looked first at the ruin of Slocum Blunt, and then at her aunt several yards away. The old woman returned her niece's gaze impassively. As if none of this had anything to do with her.

Perdita backed up a few steps, then turned and walked to the house again. She sat beside Kay on the steps.

"Did you see that?" Kay whispered. "His hand. His face. His . . . his throat. Who or what could've done that?"

"I don't know," Perdita said. But she didn't meet Kay's gaze.

Now out past the yard, and the woods beyond, a child materialized from the darkness between the trees. Moonlight silvered her pale, smudged face, her copper hair. Kay bolted upright at the heart-stopping sight of her daughter, alive. "Chloe!"

Perdita kept a tight grip on Kay's arm. "Wait. It may be her, or it might be something else. This could be another trick."

"But it *is* Chloe. Just look—"

"That's what you said about the other one," Perdita noted flatly. "We'd better get a closer look. But neither one of us will cross that line again. For any reason. Agreed?"

"Okay. Yes."

They walked down the steps, into the yard.

"All right then," Perdita whispered. "Now call her by name."

Kay opened her mouth to do so, but then hesitated. The child was still walking, almost halfway across the clearing now. But the memory of Slocum's face twisting, melting like a guttering candle . . . the feel of his sloughed skin in her hand . . . she clenched her fists, took a deep breath, and tried to make herself believe that whatever had happened to him couldn't touch her child. "Chloe. Come here, to me!"

"Mom!" Chloe started toward them. But then another small figure shot from the trees, running after her daughter with shrill outraged cries.

"That's Chloe. I'm sure of it." Kay edged up until the toes of her shoes touched the salt line glowing whitely in the dusk.

"We'll know for sure soon. When she tries to cross." Perdita's hand gripped Kay's shoulder. "Remember, whatever happens—"

Kay nodded. "—we stay here."

They could hear the slap of small bare feet on wet grass. Chloe dodged through the garden statues as if playing thread-the-needle. Lala's shorter legs pumped desperately, but she was falling behind, wailing. The sound of small running feet seemed to attract Slocum Blunt's attention. He jerked around, head cocked quizzically, hands clenching and unclenching as if they already encircled a child's throat.

"She's running toward him," Kay gasped. "No, Chloe, don't come that way!"

Perdita pulled her back. "No. Let me take care of this."

Slocum's back was now to them, his attention on the approaching girls. Perdita hurled the holly staff at him. It bit into his congealed flesh like a knife sinking into butter. He pitched to the ground with a hoarse, shrill scream, clutching and tearing up clumps of earth and grass. Despite her earlier vow, Perdita rushed out over the line and leaned hard on the makeshift stake. with a look of profound disgust she pinned him squirming to the ground like a large gray beetle. A bubbling began under his skin. The stench of spoiled meat rose. The insect spasms of his arms and legs slowed until at last he lay still, grinning blindly into the dirt.

The running children were close enough now that Kay could see tears streaking the dirt on her daughter's pale, tired face. Do dead children cry? She could almost smell wild, woodsy child-sweat and earth, even as she tasted fear, bitter and metallic on the back of her tongue. The air crackled with the kind of energy one feels just before a lightning strike.

Kay glanced away from Chloe then, at Lala, and realized the little girl was pursuing her daughter not with childish adoration, but in a murderous fury. And where was Mattie Swann?

The old woman was still in the same spot, squatting, hands busy in the dirt, tracing patterns and singing to herself. A week ago, Kay would've thought: Poor crazy old thing, she's lost her mind. Instead, the sight of that frail elderly shape muttering doggedly at the earth sent animal terror skittering through her mind, uncontrolled trembling through her body.

And like a cornered animal, Kay reacted. She bolted past Perdita, grabbed her daughter, and dragged Chloe back behind the salt boundary. They fell in an awkward tangle of arms and legs, Kay laughing and kissing Chloe's flushed cheeks, her sweaty forehead. She was safe again, at last.

But then, through the russet tangle of Chloe's hair, Kay saw Mattie Swann look up at Lala, and see the danger. The old woman's face crumpled in fear. Slowly, as if in a dream, those thin dark arms flew up, palms outstretched as if to stop time. Her wrinkled lips moved to shout out a soundless warning, or perhaps a protective spell.

Kay stood, hugging Chloe tightly to her, ready to bolt if need be. Lala was almost upon them, pearly little teeth bared in a snarl, face and arms covered with scratches. Where was the giggling girl with soft brown eyes and neat pigtails who'd sat at her kitchen table wearing only a cocky grin and white cotton panties? That child had perhaps only

287

really existed in the twisted mind of a dangerous old woman.

She curled herself over Chloe as Lala stepped over the magically-marked ground. The line of salt flew up in an arc, like a reverse snowfall. Lala was showered with it, outlined in pale green fire.

Kay pressed Chloe's face into her shoulder. "Don't look now, baby," she whispered.

The green flames spread. But she felt no heat from the pale, crackling flame that curved like a welder's arc around the small glowing shape which jerked and wavered as if torn between two planes. Then it shimmered and blew apart in a bright burst, like white phosphorus. A stench of sulfur and singed cotton filled the air. A scrap of lace drifted back to earth, landing inches from Kay's foot.

Hoarse screams pierced her head so sharply it felt as if they came from her own throat. She closed her eyes, but could not block out the terrible sounds of anguish. Kay felt it, too: that final heave, a hideous trembling, and then the slow and tortured giving in to unbearable pain.

Kay carried Chloe over to stand beside Perdita. She could think of nothing to say, so she simply enfolded them in the warm embrace of her arms.

"It's done," said Perdita flatly, as if finished with a distasteful cleaning job.

"You did what you had to. Chloe's not hurt. Just a few scratches."

"Don't let her see this." Perdita wrenched at the holly stake that still pinned Slocum's corpse to the ground. When it came free and the wreck of his body collapsed. Kay looked away, remembering how the realtor had leered and flirted with her as they'd stood in her driveway a few weeks before. Her knees felt spongy, too rubbery to hold her up.

Chloe buried her face deeper into her mother's shirt. "Smells awful here. Can we go home?"

"Soon." Perdita leaned for a moment on the holly cane, as if she too needed some extra support.

She must be tired; Kay felt exhausted. With Chloe safe, and her fear ebbing, she only now noticed the burn of pulled muscles, the mingled sting of briar scratches and insect bites.

"But what about . . . her?" Kay nodded at Mattie Swann.

She was slumped with one hand braced on a stone gargoyle, her face an ebony mask of grief.

"What's to be done with you now, Aunt Mattie?" Perdita's knuckles tightened on the cane. "Will you simply forget all of this? Somehow I think not. You want too badly to be the sorcerer, the one to be respected and feared. But your work had become so evil, you trade in stolen children. Or has it always been like that? Mama once told me that—"

"Your mama was always a fool." The narrowed old eyes glittered like onyx and ivory in the half-light. "Whatever I take I pay well for. Got more feelin' in my little finger than you find in a whole pack of Abbotts. And Abbotts," she paused and spit on the ground. "are always willing to trade. I only raised what I seen fit to, real or not. What difference how real, if they get what they want? It all come to pass in good time, anyhow."

Perdita slammed the holly cane so hard into the ground, the wood quivered as it struck earth. "Talk is nothing, old woman. Worthless words. If you have so much skill, show us a little right now. Raise up that devil-thing you called a child. Make it live again."

The old woman's eyes shone redly. It must just be a reflection, Kay thought nervously, hugging Chloe to her. From the lantern light. Her eyes just caught a glow from the house.

Mattie Swann pulled a small bottle from one deep skirt pocket. She muttered as she poured a trickle of some red liquid on the ground. First only the thin dark arms trembled. But soon Mattie's whole body shook as if with palsy.

"Perdita," Kay whispered, "what're you trying to do? This doesn't seem safe, to provoke—"

"I know. But I have to be sure." There was a fine sheen of sweat on her face as she watched her aunt closely.

Just then Kay felt a tickling on her arm, like an insect crawling over bare skin. Shifting Chloe, she brushed at it, and the wiggling thing stuck to her hand. She looked down, and in the dim light, saw what it was.

A sticky bit of charred cloth and burnt flesh wriggled against her skin like a living maggot. "Oh my God," she cried, and shook it off. Now she saw the ground all around them was boiling with similar bits, writhing and squirming, pieces of an animated puzzle determined to solve itself.

"Perdita, stop her!"

The other woman only stood calmly, gaze locked with her aunt's. To Kay's amazement she yawned, and then smiled. "You can't do it," she said.

The wriggling pieces slowed, then stopped moving altogether. With a sob the old woman hurled the empty bottle away. It hit a tree and burst, striking sparks. Her knotted fists clenched until blood ran between the fingers and dripped on the clay-red ground.

Perdita turned to Kay. "That's why. To see that she's finished, and that this is over. Even she knows it now."

"But what do we do, just . . . leave her here? What if she gets her power, or whatever it is, back again?"

"I think we're safe from her now. For how long? I don't know what might happen later. You can't buy insurance against evil, but. . . ."

"But. . . ?"

"She used to tell me that all things came from the water. And that's where she'd go back, if she had to," Perdita said suddenly. Her voice was cold and toneless.

"You mean, drown herself? But why would she do that? Can't we have her arrested and put away somewhere instead?"

Perdita laughed, a short contemptuous sound without humor. "No."

Chloe twisted in Kay's arms. "Mom, Mrs. Swann is leaving. I mean, she's already gone."

It was true. The old woman no longer stood in the midst of the statue garden. "But where did she—"

"Over there." Chloe pointed to the woods.

A bright patch of skirt was just disappearing between two trees. Then only the swaying branches of wild azalea marked the old woman's passage.

"We'd better stop her," Kay suggested, though she did not feel eager to go in there after her.

"No need. That leads down to the river. She's chosen to end this on her own terms."

Kay gritted her teeth. "If you say 'the river takes its due,' I'll scream."

"Not from us. Not this time," Perdita said. "But I ought to follow and be sure she means to do it. Stay close to me. She can't hurt us now. Hasn't got the power. And once she's gone, we have nothing to fear from her again."

Words meant to reassure, but somehow they had the opposite effect. Kay felt panic. She only wanted to run away, maybe back to Miami. Anywhere else. To get as far from Abaton as modern transportation would permit. How much better to be a child again, like Chloe. Then she wouldn't have to know what she knew, or to deal with it. No one would expect her to. Yes, why not leave now, walk if she had to, then pack up and—

But then guilt took hold. Of course she could go, but this place was Perdita's home. She wouldn't leave, at least not from fear. She was the brave one. The one who'd made it possible to find Chloe.

So Kay set Chloe down to walk. She took her daughter's hand and followed Perdita. Unwilling above all else to be left alone with the grotesque remains of Slocum Blunt for company. She fit her own steps to the sure impressions left in the damp clay by Perdita. Step on a crack, she thought. Watch your step. If only she had something, a sure talisman against evil.

Perdita stopped suddenly, at the slope where the ground fell sharply away to the river.

Kay nearly ran into her, immersed as she was in nursery rhyme magic.

"Be careful here," said the other woman. "This bank is steep and slippery. We'll climb down at that low, flat spot over there. I'll go first. You hand Chloe to me, then come down."

One by one they slipped down the bluff, dislodging clumps of mud and sand and stones that tumbled and splashed into the swirling black water.

Kay slid down last, smeared with red clay and river slime. "Where'd she go?" she shouted above the roar of water rushing downstream. The dark current carried along broken branches, old tires, plastic bottles and lost shoes, like a black conveyor belt to Hell.

Perdita didn't answer her at first, but only stared down at the river. At last she pointed. "There."

A short distance from shore, a billow of dark cloth swelled, ballooned and then receded beneath the tannin-dark water.

"She's gone to the river, like she always said she would. Now I may be willing to believe it's over."

Perdita's tone was cool, neutral, but moonlight illuminated the tears on her cheeks. "And so, now, Chloe, we can go home." She anchored the walking stick firmly in the sloping clay bank. "I'll go up first, then help you two."

Perdita grasped the stick and stated to climb the bank, but after her first step up, a large section of the blood-red clay collapsed and she slid down into the water, immediately submerged to the knees in the swift current.

Kay threw herself back toward dry land, dragging Chloe along, then reached out a hand to Perdita. Her fingertips just brushed the other woman's. She leaned out farther, hand inching closer with agonizing slowness.

Something was moving, just beneath the surface of the river.

She reached again and finally grasped Perdita's wet, slippery wrist. But the sight of gnarled brown hands scuttling like crabs beneath the surface almost sent her tumbling into the current after her friend.

"Mom, come back!" screamed Chloe.

She braced herself, groping with the other hand for a firmer hold on something, anything solid. Her desperate fingers closed around a cypress root projecting from the bank like a hard, cold elbow.

"The stick," Perdita gasped. "Get the holly branch."

Kay looked over one shoulder. The holly staff was still embedded in the hard-packed clay of the slope behind her, out of reach. "But if I let go, you'll be dragged out."

Perdita shook her head. "Just get it."

Kay felt another strong tug as they were pulled a little farther out.

A fold of calico cloth billowed at the surface.

This can't be happening, she thought. Not now. She shouted, "Chloe—bring me the holly stick!"

The sharp command seemed to rouse her daughter from a frightened paralysis. She turned and reached up, yanking at the branch, finally pulling it free. She held it out toward the struggling women in the water.

"I can't reach it." Kay's grip on Perdita's hand was slipping. "A little farther, Chloe!"

Another, stronger pull. Perdita lost her footing and her head submerged for a moment. Kay's arm was nearly jerked from the socket.

But then the other woman struggled back up, coughing. "Best . . . let go. Take Chloe . . . run."

"No. I won't leave you here."

Kay thought frantically. Her daughter stood holding the sharpened stake like a scepter, a bedraggled princess in a macabre fairy tale. Kay glanced down into the water again, and saw a billow of cloth. Thin dark limbs. The pale gleam of an upturned eye. "Dear God," she whispered, and tightened her hold on the cypress root. It seemed a good time to pray, but nothing coherent came to her terrified mind.

"Chloe, listen," she said finally. "Reach that branch farther out, close to my hand. But don't come so near the edge! That's right. Now, when I lean out to grab it, you let go. Understand?"

Her daughter nodded tearfully. "But—"

"You have to let go of me," Perdita gasped.

"No I don't," Kay snapped. "And Chloe? If . . . if we both should go under, climb up the bank. Get my phone from the car. If it doesn't work, run to the house. I know you know the way. Uncle Mike should be there by now. Tell him what happened."

Chloe nodded tearfully. "Okay."

"All right," Kay said. "Now!"

She let go of the cypress root, snatching for the holly branch at the same time. She lost her grip and fell against Perdita. They went down, and the foul brown taste of the river invaded her throat. She opened her eyes under the water, fearing what she'd see. It was only possible to make out the vaguest shapes in the murk. She felt slime-slick river bottom under her feet, long fronds of river grass wrapping her legs. And then, two dark shapes rose before her. One must be Perdita, the other, Mattie Swann. But which was which? She could've screamed with frustration, but had no air to waste.

I must decide, she thought, terrified of making the wrong choice. Soon it would be too late to choose.

She lashed out awkwardly, stabbing at the shape nearest her. The sharp stake seemed to glide through the water with a will of its own, as though the choice had already been made for her. The second figure—Perdita, she hoped—drifted maddeningly out of reach. And then she was out of air.

She broke the surface, swimming hard against the current. From the shore her daughter waved and shouted, but she couldn't hear the words.

Afraid it was useless, Kay still sucked in a deep breath and shouted, "Perdita!"

The current dragged her along until she struck against a submerged oak. It knocked the remaining air from her lungs, but she hung on until she could pull herself up onto the largest branch, above the surface.

Something solid yet yielding bumped her right leg. She wanted to flinch away from it, to just collapse onto the fallen tree. Instead she slid back into the water. Clinging to the branch with one hand, she grabbed at the floating shape and fished it roughly up out of the water.

Perdita's head broke the surface, Kay's fingers entwined in her hair.

Was she alive or dead? Couldn't tell yet, but at least she had her. Getting a grip on Perdita's collar, she pulled her along with her, toward the shore, using the long crooked tree branch as a sort of life-line.

Halfway to the bank, the swollen, grimacing face of Mattie Swann bobbed out of the water, just a few feet away. Kay gasped and nearly let go of Perdita. Then the swirling current lifted the old woman's body to the surface. The holly stake jutted from the center of her chest. A rush of water swirled the corpse's skirts as if she were taking her leave. And then the wild current carried the body on, downstream.

Hand over hand Kay dragged her limp burden to shore. She collapsed onto the clay bank and Chloe rushed over to hover anxiously beside them.

She lay with her cheek pressed to the wet clay, breathing hard, trying to summon the sketchy details of a life-saving course she'd taken one semester back in college. Then she took a deep breath, and went to work on Perdita.

In a few moments she was rewarded with a gagging cough. She turned her friend's face gently to one side, and an impressive amount of water ran out of her mouth.

Perdita's eyelids fluttered open.

"You all right?" Kay asked hopefully.

"God," Perdita rasped. "I always . . . hated . . . river water."

FORTY-THREE

S o long, guys." Mike Delgado said, waving as the county sheriff's car pulled away. He shut the front door and came back to the living room.

"Chloe's some lucky kid," he said. "If those boys had been the only ones looking, she'd still be lost." He dropped into an armchair across from Kay, and Gus jumped up to claim his lap. Mike frowned. "Now why does he always do that? He knows how much I hate tabby cats." He stroked the sleek orange back as the cat purred like a lawnmower. "Yeah." Mike shook his head. "A real lucky kid."

"Aren't we all," Kay agreed.

She wasn't sure where they had found the strength for the long walk from the river back to the car. Or summoned the wits to pull the floor mats out of the Volvo and stuff them under the wheels so Kay could free the car from the mud. She barely remembered the drive home.

Now she was stretched out on Leilah Abbott's good tapestry sofa, muddy shoes and all. "But our luck was really due to Perdita. She was the brave one. She knew where to look. I'd still be upstairs wringing my hands, if not for her."

"When we should be wringing the neck of the pervert who took Chloe," said Annelise, as she came down the stairs. She settled on the arm of Mike's chair. "At least she's safe now. All tucked in. And so tired I didn't have the heart to make her take a bath. I did clean her up a bit, just to be sure it was really Chloe under all that dirt and slime. I'll buy you new sheets tomorrow."

"New sheets aren't high on my list right now. But I could work up some enthusiasm for a new body." Kay touched a blistered heel and winced. Strangely, the wound on her ankle had closed and was now just a pink crescent of scar. "After tonight the only thing that seems really important is that we're all still here."

Mike shifted but the cat hung on with determination. Gus stared up at him adoringly, eyes half closed, paws kneading in ecstasy.

"Watch it, buddy. Hook one more claw in my thigh and you'll be Kitten McNuggets." Mike glanced up and frowned at Kay. "This is the part where I'm supposed to say what a fool you were to go looking for Chloe without the supervision of a tactical genius. Like one of those deputies. Or me. Plus how crazy and irresponsible it was to—"

"Mike—" she groaned.

"However," he said, in his best jury-swaying voice, "considering your astonishing success, I'll keep my stupid opinions to myself. And nominate you both for a time-share position as new sheriff."

Perdita sighed wearily. "No thanks. One rescue every now and then is a gracious plenty."

"But I'm sure a satisfactory schedule could be arranged." Mike grinned at her. "Would you consider out-of-town consultant work? You could be a world-class investigator. It's a damn miracle you found Chloe after she was abducted by that Blunt psycho. She could've ended up like—" He blanched and abruptly fell silent.

"It's all right," Perdita said. "Perle's going to be fine. Except for a bruise on her forehead, she's back to normal. As normal as any teenager can be, that is. And the guy who attacked her will be . . . taken care of. Arrested. So everything turned out fine."

"So it seems. He shouldn't be too hard to find. Owns half the town, doesn't he? Probably won't go away."

"Right," she agreed. "At least, not far."

"No, he'll just get out on bail and hire some slick, headline-grabbing lawyer," Annelise fumed. "Hopefully not anyone we know."

"Well, I'm not available." Mike patted her arm.

Kay studied one broken fingernail with great interest. "So . . . " She shifted in her chair. "Something's poking a hole in my back." She reached behind the cushion and pulled out a shiny silver ballpoint. "This yours, Mike? Looks too expensive to let your friends sit on. Annelise should make you take better care of your things."

He frowned. "Isn't mine. Oh, wait a sec. Must belong to the deputy. The one Gus bit. I'll call the sheriff's office tomorrow."

"All right." Kay yawned. "I'll leave it on the table. Bedtime for me."

Annelise smiled. "Better do a quick sponge-off, at least."

"Can't you just buy me two new sets of sheets?"

"My, how greedy we've gotten since leaving the big city."

"Presents are what friends are for, right? And Perdita, I know Mike said he'll drive you home. But if you'd rather stay here . . . "

"Thanks." The other woman rose slowly from her chair, wincing. "But the most wonderful thing I can imagine right now is to go home and collapse in my own bed."

Kay went over and hugged her quickly, then turned to Mike. "Get her home before one of us passes out."

He saluted. "Done, ladies."

Kay and Annelise followed them out the front door, and waited until the sound of the rental car faded down the long drive. Back inside, Kay told her friend good night. Then she paused at the foot of the stairs. "Guess you're going to wait up for Mike?"

"Yep. I'll just put these dirty glasses in the kitchen. Straighten up a little. God, I'm doing housework. Only for you, my dear. Go on up! You're dead on your feet."

Kay suppressed a shudder and started up the stairs, as Annelise gathered empty glasses and carried them off to the kitchen.

Halfway up, Kay heard a hesitant knock on the front door. She stopped on the landing and called, "Lise, can you get that please?"

The sound of dishes and silverware, the rush of water came from the kitchen, but no answer. Obviously Annelise couldn't hear her.

"Perdita must've forgotten something," Kay muttered, walking slowly back down. "Crap. Should've given Mike a key."

She turned back the deadbolt, and the door swung open on the night. Moths bumbled softly into the porch light, wings whispering. Cicadas were sawing away in the magnolias.

The front porch was empty.

She realized then she hadn't heard the car return. So it wasn't Mike and Perdita. Or even the deputy, back to reclaim his silver pen. She reached behind her for the brass doorknob, feeling a shiver of dread.

Out in the yard, beyond the warm golden halo of porch light, shadows were shifting. Rearranging into a figure she knew.

"No," she whispered, yet was drawn on against her will. She descended the steps slowly, hand slipping down over the railing reluctantly, nails rasping faintly on the varnished wood.

He stood out in the yard, motionless beneath the huge old magnolia, facing the lighted house. The grass, still cool and wet from the earlier storm, felt springy beneath her bare feet. She stopped a few paces away.

Yes, there he was, though not as she remembered him.

Of course she knew that death brought terrible changes to the body. Her roommate in college had been a pre-med student who'd delighted in recounting each grisly assignment, sometimes more than once. "First, there's rigor mortis. Then discoloration. And later, swelling of the face and body. Plus eruptions all over like acne. Eventually the skin comes off in flakes, the veins go all brown and rusty with old blood. Hair loosens and falls out. And the eyes . . . Kay, are you okay? Want me to stop?"

Yes, she had wanted her to stop. Long before the eyes.

The eyes. Dear God, she thought. When is the body really dead? Once I thought I knew.

"Jack? But you're . . . you can't be here, not like—"

So the old bitch had raised him after all, to use as a dreadful, back-up bartering chip. Or simply a last grim, cruel joke. And now we're to be . . . haunted? Perhaps that's not the right word, she thought.

He shuffled a step closer. Raised a withered hand to touch her hair. She flinched back, out of reach.

He stopped and tilted his head, as if puzzled at her reluctance. What do the dead know? What do they see? God, the eyes.

She squeezed her own shut, hard, to summon up a red-streaked darkness. To summon up anything but the remnants of a man standing before her. "Please. No more. I just can't stand any more. You're dead. Go away. Go . . . somewhere. Anywhere. Please. You'll frighten Chloe."

Even more than you frighten me.

But when she looked again, he still stood there, swaying slightly. Terrible in his patience.

"What do you want?" she cried.

His gaze swung, like a compass needle to north, and caught on the faint glow of nightlight from Chloe's second-floor room. He took another step, as if to move past her.

Fear allowed her to move then, to leap forward and shove him roughly. To shout "No!" as if he were a misbehaving dog. She felt something crack in his chest, beneath her hands. His body felt spongy, yet somehow hollow.

He stopped and swung his face back to her, his demeanor mildly reproachful.

"So you can hear me," she said, trying not to meet that vague, filmed gaze. Even so, it seemed to mirror her own misery and throw it back at her. "Can you . . . can you speak?"

His jaw clenched, worked side to side. His mouth stretched in a grimace. A low noise, a groan or a growl, emerged.

Kay swallowed. "And you know Chloe's up there."

His face turned hopefully in the direction of the window again.

"But you can't go up to her. Can't let her see you, not like this. Oh God." She began to cry in great heaving sobs. "Surely you realize that. If . . . if she saw you now, it would kill her."

He looked away from the window, back at Kay. And waited, as if listening again.

"And so," she spat out in a desperate rush, "you have to leave. You can't stay out here. Because in the morning . . . you just have to go. So leave now and go to—" She stopped, confused. Go where? "If you're worried, well, I will always take care of Chloe. She'll never forget you, Jack. But you have to leave us alone now. And go on, on to . . ."

She stopped, again lost for a good answer.

They stood for a moment staring at each other, in a silence broken sporadically by cicadas and pond frogs. And then, the faint distant splash of the river.

Jack turned suddenly away from the house. Toward the woods, in an attitude of listening.

"What is it?" she whispered, forgetting that he couldn't say, fearful something else terrible might be coming this way.

Slowly, awkwardly, he fumbled at the front of his stained white shirt. The rotted fabric ripped as he slid a hand inside. He withdrew something and held it out with trembling shredded fingertips, to her.

She forced herself not to flinch away this time. The object he pressed shakily into her outstretched palm was round and flat, light and brittle. The color of old bones. She closed her fist around it, too tightly, and felt it crack in half. She opened her hand to look. Two halves of a sand dollar lay there. She stared at the broken pieces for a moment, confused. And then remembered: The first funeral in Miami. Chloe's last gifts to her father. A framed family photo and her treasured perfect sand dollar.

Kay curled her fingers around the two pieces, cradling them gently. "I'll give this to her in the morning. But what do you want me to say?"

His hand crept up and came to rest over his heart.

She nodded, looking down quickly. The sand dollar blurred and softened as her eyes filled with tears and she could no longer see the rough edges that divided it.

He turned away and moved off slowly, with a tired, dragging gait, across the driveway and toward the woods. And as he drew farther away she no longer saw the ruined flesh, the stiffened limbs, the bruised, shredding skin. Now she wanted him to come back, just for a minute.

She tried to call his name, but her throat tightened on the sound, and it came out as a whisper. He's leaving us again, for the last time, she thought. And then suddenly it came to her and she remembered what to say.

"I love you, Jack," she called after him. "We both do."

He paused for a moment, without turning around. And then he vanished into the darkness between the trees.

Kay's legs gave way. She sank onto the shell drive, but barely felt the sharp edges slice her knees. Nor the heat of the blood that trickled from the cuts and was soaked up by the dry red clay below.

Inside the house someone was calling her name. But she remained kneeling there, not answering, not moving. Staring at the dark gap in the trees where the narrow curving path led down to the river. She knelt there for what felt like eternity, until she felt a hand come to rest on her shoulder.

"Kay," said Annelise softly. "I went upstairs to ask you something and you weren't there, so I—what're you doing out here? Oh my God, look at your poor knees. Did you fall?"

Kay shook her head. "Not exactly. I was just . . . listening."

"To what, for heaven's sake?"

"The river."

Annelise frowned. "But I don't hear any—"

"Shh." Kay laid her hand over her friend's. "You have to be very quiet. See? There it is."

Annelise nodded hesitantly. "Oh . . . right. I think so."

"Maybe it's not such a bad thing, that river. I mean, nothing is really entirely evil. Or completely good. Right?"

Annelise frowned again, this time her eyes clouded with worry. "Well—no. I suppose not. But come on inside now. You should be in bed. I mean, look at you now—talking crazy, you're so exhausted."

Kay smiled a little at that. "Yes, I guess you're right."

She rose and, arm in arm, they walked back to the house, and disappeared inside.

***

Beyond the house, past the moss-draped trees, the river wound black and powerful, its surface roiled with light and shadows, its cold heart mysterious, carrying all its secrets down to the waiting sea.

THE END

The next Dark Florida novel by Elisabeth Graves is DEVIL'S KEY.

"[this] Florida native breathes life into all her characters -- dead or alive." --*St. Augustine Record*

Lucy Fowler plans to spend winter break on an island off the coast of Florida, to finish writing her thesis. She needs one last interview with an elderly midwife. Lucy almost cancels the trip after she's brutally assaulted on campus. But in the end she goes, hoping work will be therapeutic.

On remote, isolated Ibo Key, Lucy learns midwife Esther Day is now confined to a psychiatric ward. She also learns that there was once a thriving black community, Revelation, on the island. Its residents all vanished one night long ago. Lucy decides to write about the ghost town, but no one will talk about what happened. Eventually, she uncovers the terrible story behind the town's destruction. Esther's rival, Soulange, once owned a mysterious book . . . a centuries old grimoire revealing the arcana of Obeah. An odd little man tells Lucy the island is cursed. That every man, woman, and child on it will soon die. And she begins to see glimpses of the past.

But by then she's stranded, trapped by a killer hurricane. To escape she must face her own connection to both the victims and perpetrators of a long-ago massacre . . . a crime so monstrous it invites the arrival of an evil old as time.

Available in trade paperback or ebook!

About the Author

ELISABETH GRAVES, descendent of an old Florida family, grew up in a small citrus-industry town not far from Disney World, her first employer. A former wardrobe assistant, theme-park waitress, seafood-joint cashier, graphic artist, advertising copywriter, and forensic librarian, she lives on a Central Florida lake that houses many an alligator and poisonous snake. She likes to read the headstone inscriptions in old cemeteries in her spare time.

NORTHAMPTON HOUSE PRESS

Northampton House publishes carefully selected fiction, lifestyle nonfiction, and memoir. Our logo represents the muse Polyhymnia. Our mission is to discover great new writers and give them a chance to springboard into fame. Check the Northampton House list at www.northampton-house.com, or Like us on Facebook – "Northampton House Press" – to discover more innovative works from brilliant new writers.

www.ingramcontent.com/pod-product-compliance
Lightning Source LLC
Chambersburg PA
CBHW030419180626
46812CB00005B/2076